THE CHANGELING'S CHOICE

Book II of the Troutespond Series

Elizabeth Priest

First published by Luna Press Publishing, Edinburgh, 2019

www.lunapresspublishing.com

ISBN-13: 978-1-911143-43-7

Contents

*To the Kingdom of Effpia
and the Crew of the Emancipated Catfish.*

A Quick Fix

You'd think that being privy to all the secrets of the universe would mean some sort of knowledge of the end of times – all that stuff that humanity has been obsessing over since there was a high place to stand and words to shape around, "Dudes, what next?!"

No. I don't get to know anything like that. As far as I know, no one else does either. And I work for some pretty important people.

As far as they're concerned it's all about balance – don't let it get knocked one way or the other and the world will keep on ticking away, same as it always has, same as it always will.

Which leads me to why I was wandering around a dark field, hefting lumps of rock and breaking nails when I should have been inside with a mug of hot chocolate and rather a lot of A Level coursework to be finishing. When powerful forces of nature call you up and say something along the lines of, "Some hooligans kicked over the standing stone in Waitington, be a dear and set the ley lines straight before we're up to our ears in pixies…" you can't really say no.

Fucking pixies.

I shouldn't be prejudiced – one of my newly acquired best friends was currently a sort of pixie. Though she didn't know it, and was a total bitch anyway…

"*Fucking pixies*," I said out loud, in case any were listening. I fumbled the slippery rock I was carrying and squeaked as I jumped out of the way before it could land on my ever-so-crushable toes in their pretty red tennis shoes. They were probably ugly and mud-coloured tennis shoes right now. I couldn't tell, it was that dark.

Being a pagan sucks, guys. Stay Catholic – demons are sexy. Nuns are hot. Spending your days believing in a dude who does all this for you is a hell of a lot easier. I guess I still do, but I certainly don't give him as much credit as I used to, especially when a load of other dudes keep stopping to ask my opinion on stuff.

Top tip: don't ask random pagan deities if they're Jesus either. Even if you have a pretty good argument for symbolism crossing over, they're not going to stop and listen to your dissertation on the subject.

I had a pretty good cairn built up, considering I'd only Googled how the hell to fix a wonky ley line all of forty-five minutes ago and spent ten minutes marvelling at the internet and the knowledge contained therein before grabbing my rock haulin' bag (a woman is prepared for anything) and heading out into the fields behind my house. Now my pile of rocks was about two foot high and reasonably sturdy, and I'd said meaningless incantations every few minutes over it so it was getting powerful.

From the hill I could see all of Troutespond – hard not to really. It was a titchy little town. Over thataways was the church, with a cute floodlit effect so even at night we could see how small and falling-to-pieces it was. Sorry – I shouldn't mock… I know the guy who built it with his own hands back in Ye Middle Ages. It makes all the services we held to our dear old St Troute's departed soul just a little ridiculous when he likes sneaking in from time to time to hear how we're doing with those eternally bequeathed Masses.

Off beyond the church lay a collection of houses that had probably been here in some form or another since the year dot. In their current incarnation they were little two-storey red brick Victorian creations, presumably after the old houses had been purged with fire when history was done with its lice and plagues phase like some unwashed teenage boy. The Bilsworth Historical Society apparently gets rather pissy over how little medieval history is preserved around here, when fifteen miles down the road you have a pristine full-sized model village posing as the town of Ransley. One of the carelessly built houses ruining everything for everyone had our friend Tanya in it – the girl kept around by Ally and Teb to make them feel normal in comparison.

Beyond Tanya's house, away down the high street and onto a wide modern road that connected to the motorway, was the school – dark now and invisible, and therefore not worth thinking about. Yuk. Just a couple more days, in total, of exams, then a few months of boring summer and I'd be off at university, probably doing exactly the same, just a million miles from home. I'd no doubt be near enough fields to haul just as many rocks in further education.

I swept my gaze east as I tried to sweep my hair back just as easily. It was all stuck to my forehead, and didn't go half as willingly. I tried not think about how revolting I currently looked. I could see the village green, a dark triangle between the lines of streetlights. The lights forked after the green.

One line went down into the bright northbound flow of the motorway that walled our town away from the rest of the world. Massive earthworks had raised it up on a bank lined with still-growing trees that had yet to block it from our sight. It was now a huge solid bridge that created a firm barrier to prevent most attempts at wandering off in that direction. With hills hemming us in on the other side, the valley felt narrower here than at any other point between Severstrong Abbey and Waitington. The magical borders came up sharp and surprised against the new embankment, trapping all our local mythology in here to stagnate. Driving along the huge road was a sort of empty sensation after the richly fermenting mythology rammed into every corner of the village and surrounding area — it was a traditionless wasteland patrolled only by lost and drifting souls… I usually go by train to places. Trains are *good*. They have all sorts of magic that cars don't. Tradition and style. Which are about the same as magic.

The other fork of the road was the continuation of the "high street" – a word deceptive to modern teenage ears, which thought "Yay! Shops!" on hearing it. There were shops if you liked cream teas and fourth-hand sofas. The high street disappeared off around the hills to the next tiny nowhere village, but before then it passed a blob of more pale lights – the new housing estate that contained, somewhere on its edges, Ally. She's dotty in a "should be an old lady already" kind of way – all tea and shuffling along in slippers and forgetting where she put her glasses until she remembers she has 20:20 vision and doesn't need them. Lately she had almost accidentally taken a turn for the Gothic. She had joined many heavy metal fans in the eternal struggle for how to stay cool in the blazing heat while wearing a floor-length black coat. She made this look dorky too, somehow. If she had a superpower, it would be creating awkward moments.

My other bestest best friend in all the world (and I guess that sarcasm extends to all of them, because I'd known them about two months now, and only felt so close because there was literally no one else in the whole world any of them ever talked to, odd little shut-ins that they were) was Teb, and I had no idea where she lived. One of those lights – or dark windows – was hers, and not knowing which one made me very conscious of the way she might have been watching, smirking and giggling to see me muddy and hot and sweaty. In a town as small as Troutespond, you did not avoid people.

I suppose it was nice of the Piper to suggest that I do all this heavy lifting in the cool of the night, because the summer sun was worth a whole extra leather coat even to someone wearing just the shorts and t-shirt I was. I'd probably have passed out if I was doing this much work in the middle of the day. Instead I had the feeling that I was more than likely to be arrested or, if I'd judged the field wrong, shot by a farmer for trespassing.

I figured I was almost done. One genuine(ish) pagan setting up a ritual site, bolstered by all the curses I'd thrown at the task, sat ready to catch the loose energy and realign everything a fraction. The site was already attracting slight flickers of power as things on the Other Side sensed my efforts, and drew in.

There were a lot of Other Sides, and all of them were hideously curious about what happened in this world. I dunno – must be crappy daytime TV or some other quality that they lacked. I had learned of their interest the hard way.

Speaking of hideous and curious… Something was giving my cairn a really good nose around now, like a doggy finding something thrilling (old shoe, leaf, bit of gum on the pavement – I've seen them freak out at it all). The trouble with creating doors to the Other places was that something would inevitably want to *use* them.

I wished I had a shovel as I raised the rock that I'd been about to drop on top of the pile. My arms instantly began wobbling like crazy… I needed to do push-ups or something, I thought distractedly. Upper body strength – that was the key to smashing pixies with rocks.

The flare of power built around the cairn in a huge rush. I didn't have much of the Sight – I mean, Ally's Mum made us all look blind in comparison – but I could at least see when things weren't normal. I wish there was a description for what the burst of fairy magic around the stones looked like.

It was sort of like light, but without illuminating anything. If anything the field felt darker than ever, this lonely corner of dry ground under the shelter of a huge oak prickling with fairy power to distract me from seeing the mundaneness of the world. For a moment I was almost blind to everything, as in my head I was forced to imagine the flare, and then light returned – moonlight weakly covering the ground in blue, amber from the streetlights of the cul-de-sac providing a bit more orange. Neither were much – out in the countryside once it's dark, that's pretty much it for seeing stuff. I'd got decent enough night vision for identifying lumps of rock and stacking them – not for fighting a damn pixie who, if it glowed, would only make it *harder* for me to see.

It was somewhere around me – the connection was weak. It wasn't in any solid form. A file that got corrupted in transfer. Unlike the quirky photos of Tanya's holiday to Yorkshire, there was the ability for the file to change its shape – to learn, edit out the massive data errors and find a new shape suited to the hundreds of pictures of dragons idling in her Downloads folder. Okay, shutting up with that simile/metaphor/messily murdered literary device, before I have to fight a fucking dragon.

There was no tradition yet of what the pixie *should* be, no legends attached to the cairn to guide it. It didn't know what shape it could take… Which meant, seeing as it was me and the tree here, I was more than likely going to have to end up bludgeoning a weird horrible clone of myself to death with a rock. I took a step or three back, dragging in a long breath of the cool night air, readying myself for super awesome nightmare fuel.

The wind caught along with my breath – an unnatural pull that sprung up from nowhere and whirled in the tight little area around me. Dry old leaves around the base of the tree swirled upwards as something burst out of them. I threw the rock. It went right through, clattering against the cairn, spilling a few stones. The connection faltered a little, but the pixie was already through, fighting for appearance.

The leaves weren't just being flung around in the wind, I realised with a thump of dread in my stomach. They were forming together into a mass of rustling shapes around a dark, dusty body, not quite animal in shape, too humanoid to be anything other than disturbing.

I backed slowly away as it got its bearings. It was a thing of the elements – air and dirt and leaf, and in the dark it was wild and angry – but slow, too. The wind could take it so far, but it wasn't going to be too smart. Mud and dead leaves. Powerful in their own way, but not a thinking body, nor a combat body.

It might not even be expecting to fight, actually... Probably had been expecting just to nose around a bit, settle itself into a comfy hole and take the time to learn some good tricks. But here I was, and though I kept backing away, I intended to beat it back into the dust it had been.

I finally reached the hedgerow, which had once seemed absurdly close in comparison to that minute-long crawl. The creature was still looking around and seemed to have caught something interesting in the air as it began drifting slowly toward the lights of the village. I sure as hell wasn't going to let it wander loose through the streets of Troutespond. The trouble with our village was that, unlike everywhere else, stuff like this tended not to die. In a big town this idiot creature would have been a swirl of circling leaves in an eddy of the wind, and then no one's problem, concrete and lack of faith breaking its fragile magic.

Pity I believed too damn hard in it, and my fear wasn't helping my case. People believe a lot harder when they're terrified. The Piper had yet to put me through a cheesy movie training montage where I find myself and my inner strength, yadda yadda, so I didn't have the faintest idea how to face an enemy fearlessly.

Heart thudding, I searched through my bag quickly as the leaf monster stopped and finally realised I'd thrown a rock at it. It set its course towards me. It had a lumpy, juddering sort of walk. Now it was moving it realised the body it had crafted was all wrong, and it shuddered, forming anew.

I was suddenly facing down an eight foot tall mud wolf that was totally solid and shedding cascades of dust. It opened its mouth slowly, jagged brown-green teeth that had once been leaves stretching long, dripping drool. It was starting to gain enough substance and power to create more than it was given – attested by the fact there was no hole in the ground to support the sudden huge increase in its bulk.

"Fuck fuck fuck fuck fuck fuck!" I cried, flicking the lighter I'd finally unearthed with shaking hands, like the cold turkey smoker who's finally cracked. Sparks flickered around my smarting thumb, but nothing caught as the wolf took a step towards me, all deadly purpose now. It knew I wanted it gone.

"*Fuck,*" I added, the flame finally appearing and huge jaws snapping at me. I ducked, rolling to the side, and dropped the lighter, because I am not Buffy the Vampire Slayer, or even Alana the Pixie Slayer, just a chubby teenage girl who liked pretending to be occult on the weekends once upon a time. I wasn't the chosen one so much as the picked upon one. Someone out there on the playground of happenings was pulling my hair and stealing my shoes. That bitch

Fate and her friends. Stupid fancy clique.

Yeah, the things you think in the split second when the wolf monster chasing you stops to howl at the quarter moon in a voice that comes from primal fear's darkest nightmares, before turning to you with eyes burning with wild blue lights. It snapped at me, and I fell over on my butt. I could imagine my dear best friend Teb laughing at me, and got up again on shaky legs.

I set off at a jog in a sort of loop around the tree, hoping it'd somehow let me get back to the lighter. The wolf *flowed* after me, and a moment later I was caught up in huge jaws, scrabbling against razor-sharp teeth, squealing in horror. I mean, um, crying brave defiance and cussing at it.

My leg was half rammed down its throat, kicking uselessly, missing tonsils as I flailed wildly. I took a moment to get some better bearings on where I *was*. Turned out to be pretty awesome: half out of its mouth, pushing with one hand against its nose, the other trying to resist the force of its jaws, my other leg hanging out its mouth. I kicked that foot a bit feebly, just so it felt like it was contributing to the situation.

I finally landed a squarer kick in the back of its throat as it made a swallowing motion – for a moment I was sucked wholly into its mouth (you know, I was pretty sure it was longer than eight foot at that point, but I didn't really have time to measure it) and then it heaved and I was thrown up onto the grass, sticky and revolting. I think if Teb *was* watching, she'd be wetting herself about this point.

"Fuck," I added, trying to turn that landing into a more graceful way of rising to my feet. I staggered and landed flat on my face, winding myself on a tree root. The wolf was moving again, and I jumped half up, flinging myself beyond the cairn – and then I heard faint music. The sweetest tunes out of a flute you'll ever hear – and I don't care how many amazing flute players you know, he's better. His magic was there in it all, making it about the most enticing sound in the world. Even coated in fairy drool and scratched, bruised, and aching, I wanted to start dancing. I didn't.

The wolf had stopped and, shrinking down to Great Dane size, padded off towards the tree, tame as anything. I saw my lighter in the grass, grabbed it, and flicked it a couple of times before flame appeared. With the Piper's magic filling the air it was both harder to concentrate, and far, far easier to work the magic – I gathered the flame's magic up inside and focussed it hard, with sort of voodoo-intense fury, at the wolf. A moment later it burst into very satisfying witch fire – white-hot and quickly consuming. I smiled to myself and flicked the lighter closed, pocketing it.

I'm not a smoker.

Real Life Problems

I took my lecture on listening to him and doing what he wanted with bad grace, once the cairn was finished and sealed – no more pixies getting through that sucker any time soon. I knew the Piper must have been around for most of the fight – if not all of it, assuming he'd felt the transgression of one creature passing between worlds the moment it had happened, and rushed to the scene with all the speediness of one to whom time and space mean little. Bastard had watched to see how I handled myself against the pixie – it was only fair that I got to finish it off. Though I wouldn't have said no to watching it eat *him*.

Let's see him fight it one on one, no magic, I thought viciously as I climbed back in through the downstairs bathroom window, high but Alana-sized, conveniently above the recycling bins. I made a very undignified crash-landing in the bathtub.

I lay in the tub for a while feeling sticky and muddy. I was covered head to foot in some sort of unidentified goo and had picked up a field worth of dirt from all the rolling around. My hands had already been black from the hard labour before then. I had one of those travel-sized tubes of hand sanitizer in my bag, but the thought of it had become laughable within a minute of starting the task, let alone the fight.

Now I slowly peeled off my shoes, then my shorts, t-shirt and underwear, dropping them over the side of the bath, filed under "burn until purged" to deal with later. I turned the taps and lay back with a groan as hot water splashed over my feet. I eventually struggled to sit up and sponged myself a little clean to shift the worst of the mud before I dared put the plug in and let the bath fill.

About an hour or so and an incident of nodding off in the tub later, I realised I could not wallow for the rest of the night in increasingly tepid water. I wrapped myself in a big fluffy towel, scooped my filthy clothes into the laundry basket, slid my bag over my wrist and picked my shoes up by the backs of the heels, pinched and held away from me. I carefully pushed open the bathroom door.

It was long past midnight now and the house was dark aside from a dull glow from the upstairs landing outside my room. I listened for a second and then stepped out into the hall.

"Alana."

I shrieked, and span around to see Mom standing in the doorway to the living room. Maybe there was some sort of deep instinctive thing there, that your brain automatically discounted lurking family members as a threat, picking up their scent along with all the little warning signs that someone was hovering a foot away from you and brushing them into the bin with a "Naaah, they're family! Never mind them, there're sabre-toothed tigers out there somewhere…"

In that case my brain was an utter moron and really should have learned by now that the last thing I ever wanted to see was Mom in the middle of the night after I'd been out. I'd have taken the sabre-toothed tiger any day. I could take a wolf already.

"What are you doing up?" I demanded, heart thudding, mind racing through lists of excuses, each more implausible than the last. When the bare truth was already a fanciful story you had to think hard. I only had one hand free, and I scrabbled to make sure my towel was properly affixed, the fold pinned under my arm. She may have known me from my days as a messy pooping baby, but I had to cling to every shred of decency in this particular situation.

Besides, imagine *her* changing a diaper? All smooth blow-dried hair, wearing pearls just to go to the shop… She was just too *clean* and *rich*. She must have hired someone else to handle me, but I didn't remember it. Even now while she wore a large fuzzy dressing gown she still had this sort of impeccable air, like if she suddenly found herself on national television she'd only need a bit of powder on her nose before the cameras could roll.

"I should be asking you that," she responded. "It's one o'clock in the morning… Where have you *been*?"

"In the bath," I said. "I like taking a good hot bubble bath to unwind…You bet I need it right about now."

"Don't get cute with me. I know you weren't in half an hour ago. Where have you been sneaking out to? I know this isn't the first time."

I didn't dare look down at the sneakers still wobbling about in my hand, probably leaving little scuffs of mud on the towel as my arm sagged from the effort of holding them in front of me, weighed down with a bag as well.

"I was literally just out in the fields behind the house, enjoying some air," I said, wishing my voice didn't sound so wounded, so much like I was protesting my innocence in the face of all evidence. "Did you go into my room? How did you know I wasn't just sleeping? Considering how much work I've been doing that is really quite likely."

"Have you finished?"

"Huh?" Her shift between gears had been abrupt enough to cause temporary mental whiplash.

"Your coursework. Is it done?"

"I'm almost very nearly done," I half-lied. "Just the title pages and bibliographies and the like. I just needed a walk and a bath before I dealt with it."

Inwardly I was sighing. She may have seen my shoes, but perhaps that was normal… Even in the dry weather we'd been having, fields under trees, those well-trampled by walkers and farm animals, could have patches of perma-mud which refused to harden or dry out. I could wait for her to go to bed and run a load of laundry to hide the dirt on the rest of my clothes but then I'd have to stay up half the night. If she got to it before me then she'd bark yet more questions at me. Depressingly enough, she'd probably assume the only reason I'd be so happy to roll around in the mud was if I had someone to roll around in it with me, and my gods I would have been happy to have *only* been hiding a secret girlfriend from her.

Fixed grin in place, I sidled past Mom. "Now, if you don't mind, I have to finish my A Levels."

*

My room was a mess, with books and papers piled on every surface. It seemed almost ridiculous that I'd managed to acquire so much in a matter of months, but the school has no respect for the rainforest. I think we'd been given whole photocopied trees worth of paper. And even that hadn't been enough to ward off a dozen trips to the library, emptying it of anything vaguely relevant to the topics I studied. You'd have thought that, in the technology age, everything would be on the internet or they'd be making use of the fact everyone sat with their nose in their phone any time they weren't being called on for direct eye contact.

However messy it was, this room felt like a safe haven from the rest of the house, and as soon as I had a chair wedged under the door handle I felt almost as relaxed as I had in the bath. I pushed a few piles of reused rainforest from my laptop and opened it, plugging my phone in to charge, letting the whole thing load while I went to find some pyjamas.

Our messaging service of choice was buzzing on my phone by the time I sat down again. I opened the chat.

It was Tanya's stupid, smiley-infested screen name bothering me.

-i'm bored. have you been out fighting pixies again? tell all!-

I groaned — she always did this. I took one step towards the paranormal and she jumped on me, somehow *knowing* I'd been having some out-of-the-ordinary experience. Ridiculous pixie-junkie girl that she was… She was the sort of person you were constantly guiding around all the hazards of life because she would determinedly go poke them if left to her own devices. I'd only actually had to rescue her from pixies once… That one trip into fairyland I'd screwed up pretty badly, though. It had been resolved to the Piper's understanding of a fair balance, and almost within the rules of the fairy world, but not to any standard that a rational human being would appreciate.

It wasn't even Tanya who'd screwed up in the deals with the fairies – it had been Teb. Teb had done the whole "take me, not her!" thing which had gone *oh* so badly for her, and we'd ended up with a changeling copy to take home. Not content to leave the scenario so weird as having to deal with a malicious fairy creature pretending to be our best friend, Ally had struck a deal with our history teacher's girlfriend – and top fairy in the Queen of Winter's chain of command.

She had switched Teb's consciousness between bodies, so whatever we had with us, it looked like Teb, acted like Teb and remembered being Teb. Once we'd got home the Piper had wiped her memory of the whole thing, pretty much for the sake of not having her melt down from the hideous realisation she wasn't in her own body anymore. Now we walked a ridiculously tentative line, trying never to reveal the fairy world to her. Thing was, it was uncomfortably easy, in a way that made me feel ethically wobbly. Unlike Tanya and Ally, Teb had no rational reason to ever want to believe in fairies, and had doubted it right up until she clapped eyes on the fairy world herself. If she found out it existed all over again she probably wouldn't sprout antennae and go on a murderous magical rampage. But she'd chosen the mind wipe, so we were being respectful of that. Some people don't want to know.

I'd been beyond a mind wipe when the Piper had found me (as was Tanya after her little trip to fairyland, seeing as she'd believed this crap forever and it had been a pretty slow build-up to her trip by all accounts – Ally he let off because he *likes* her). Since the Tanya incident (which I guess had become rather more the Teb incident by the end), I'd often wondered if I would have taken a clean start had he given me the choice. It was a toss-up between how much I'd learned and matured in that time – my awareness of magic, the love and loss I'd been through, the battles I'd fought and won… And if I wanted to be the same as I'd been before – all boring emo "I am so dark and misunderstood" rich kid angst, the thought of which disgusted me now.

When I wasn't being almost eaten by giant wolves, I didn't regret my decision.

I opened my essay, wanting to do one last proofread before I printed it, accepting that I wasn't going to have time to come up with any more genius ideas for it before the deadline tomorrow morning. It was a bit short but at least I could just make it look like I meant it to be. The messenger buzzed again, and I groaned. I'd forgotten to reply to Tanya.

-*alana?! are you there?*- and a bunch of frowny faces.

Nothing for it but to reply, really.

-*Sorry, can't talk. Fighting off alien invasion. Look to the skies, my friend!*-

I put my phone down with the intent to ignore its screen for at least an hour, and got to work on the essay. Pity real life wasn't solved quite so easily.

Ally came online twenty minutes later and started chatting with me — rather more sanely. Maybe Tanya was asleep now, because she didn't weigh in, so I was left to help. Ally was apparently convinced she'd mislaid every single piece of important helpful paper they'd given her over the two years that she'd been studying this course. I sighed, spending more time reminding her of word counts and the proper way to paragraph, number, frame quotes and the like than working on my own essay. She can be very engaging when she doesn't try.

-Gods, I can't wait for this to be over

it's three am already!-

I blinked at that message in surprise, and slowly dragged aching eyes up to look at the clock in the corner of my screen. Twelve minutes past, actually. But since dark had fallen life hadn't stopped moving for me — I felt like it should be six in the morning already. Three was still an almost acceptable time for students to be getting ready for bed. One more hour would be pushing it. A little.

-Urgh, so it is

I can't believe how long I've been working on this!

Might just print it off and go sleep

I'm sick of coursework.-

As I was typing the group chat buzzed with Teb posting an angry face. At three a.m.? Little Miss Sensible was not the sort of person who'd be online this hour... I at once got the feeling something was bothering her — bad dreams. Pixies. The Green Man. She had them all wildly fighting it out in her head, and it was driving her crazy because she couldn't remember them...

I blinked away the sudden bizarre images of crystalline trees and swirling fairy lights to find that Ally had switched to using the group chat as well, instead of just, you know, talking to her in private without inflicting her on me. Perhaps for the best — if someone triggers sudden visions in me, I should probably be keeping a close eye on them. I can't tell how many of my powers are just me being amazing, and how many are things the Piper put in me so I'd be useful to him. I know how I burn things with my mind was taught to me by someone *very* different.

The towel slid from my hair and landed with a 'flump' behind me, jerking me back to this world. I looked up to find that while I'd been spaced out the conversation had started in earnest. I quickly jumped in, brushing damp hair from my eyes. I never let Teb get too friendly with Ally, because of all of them she was the most foot-in-mouth human I'd ever *met*.

-TEB! You're awake a bit too early to go hand it in, you know?-

-Har har har. I just couldn't sleep and wondered who else was up. I see you defy all probability to add yourself to that number.-

-HEY!

my dad took the parental controls off so I could stay up writing my essays!!-

It was true I wasn't used to talking to her late at night – I still had a dim impression she had to be on the downstairs computer in her cold living room, though I knew she had a laptop and was curled up in bed at that moment, papers sliding constantly off the covers, endangering her laptop as she dived to catch them.

-*Why do you *need* the internet?*- I asked her. -*I've been distracting you for hours, really. If we're going to be honest with ourselves.*-

-*Wikipedia, duh.*

I'm not going to reference it before you yell at me Teb

I just need to have something reassuring me I'm not making it all up.-

I could *hear* Teb's eyeroll. -*You're writing about the Nazi occupation of Guernsey. I think it's fairly safe to say you could make it all up and no one would know.*-

-*That's plan B.*-

I thought someone ought to address the important issues here, while weird feelings still tugged at my mind every time Teb said something. She was hiding something; that much I could tell without even thinking, and if I *did* think on it, there was plenty that I should probably know:

-*So anyway, what IS Teb doing awake instead of being the responsible one?*

she's supposed to do all the sleeping for us so we don't have to.-

Teb and Ally immediately began typing responses but Ally stopped when Teb hit reply, clearly the faster of thumb. -*I know I haven't got my A Level in Biology yet, but I'm pretty sure that's not how it's supposed to work.*-

-*Ah, I can see you're going to get an A.*-

-*I hope so. I just couldn't sleep, and I knew you'd all be awake. Though I thought Ally would be off poking weird guys with dreadlocks in lieu of being online.*-

I froze, my fingers hovering above the keyboard, trying to swallow back alarm before I typed something stupid. The "guy with dreadlocks" she was referring to was the Piper, or, at least, Ally's perception of the Piper… Ally had met him before Teb and Tanya had, and made a rather big fuss about their strange midnight encounter, also insisting that he had an awful hairstyle. I'd have thought the Piper would have removed all memory of himself from Teb's mind, but apparently he'd thought Ally going on about him was perfectly on par for normal Ally behaviour (to be fair, it actually was, if you focussed on the isolated incident before it ballooned into whatever the hell had happened in March).

The fact that Teb sort of knew about the Piper didn't sit well with me though – she must have been almost remembering, and fighting her subconscious over all the details. One of the few things she'd remember with any certainty was Ally's telling of her meeting with the Piper before she understood what she'd seen. That she was still remembering it and dragging it up, scratching at the surface… I was worried.

She *had* to be dreaming it, I decided. That was the only way she'd have access to the images that had just flashed through my mind… I decided to take a risk – she'd presumably talked to Ally about any dreams, if there were any, and bringing it up would score points on my side against Teb, apart from anything else. So, out of friendly concern and the fact Ally hadn't said anything yet, clearly waiting for me, as the agent of the cover-up operation, to do it… I typed a message.

-were you having more of those weird dreams?-

I sat back with a grin, waiting for the response. It didn't take long.

-how the fuck do you know about those?! ALLY-

What did surprise me was the response I got from Ally, who I knew was on my side, but on the other hand, wouldn't have known what I was trying until she'd seen it on her screen too. *-I'm sorry! I was trying to explain why you were cranky the other day.-*

I took that little comment as a tiny extra victory on my side.

-NOT HELPING. Urgh. I need new friends-

-Well, university is only a few months away. You can replace us then.-

-Alana! Teb is not replacing us.

Teb, I was joking

I was trying to get Alana's dream dictionary from her so I could find out what they mean.-

(So *now* she hit on a decent excuse…)

-Tho it's probably, you know, exam stress and your suppressed desire to murder people who litter.-

-And people who don't spell "though" right.

Well, it was nice of you to try and help, but dreams don't mean squat.-

Oh no – she wasn't ducking out of it that easily! Now that I had confirmation that she was dreaming these things, I wasn't going to let it go until I'd worked out all the details – what can I say? I wanted to help her. Let's see – Ally mentioned a dream dictionary and had said "what *they* mean"… More than one dream, but all with one theme? That was pretty easy to guess… Why would she be so uncomfortable about mentioning them? As far as I remembered our trip to the fairy world hadn't exactly been full of adult themes… Except for the Green Man, of course, who was a walking adult theme…

I felt a sudden clench in my stomach – what if they weren't *memories*, but *new* dreams? As I stared at Teb's name floating on the screen rather more unwelcome flashes of green danced through my mind, until I did the cliché action of furiously rubbing my forehead as if that would make them stop. It seems to work when people on TV do it.

-But they've all been almost the same and keeping you awake. And grouchy. You can't blame us for being concerned, even if only because we're fed up of you yelling at us. It's too stressful when we have exams to worry about and all, you know? Besides, Ally said you'd been having sexy dreams too, and I'm curious now. lol.-

-lol is the word of the devil. Begone, creature of the abyss.-

And she suddenly dropped out of the conversation. Just up and quit the group chat. One thing was clear – she didn't want to talk about it.

I swallowed back the weird feelings that rose inside me at her half-joking insult, and focussed back on the screen: Ally was still in the conversation, and typing at me.

-Wow, Alana

Did you get that all from Tanya? Bit low of even you to use that against Teb.-

-No

I didn't really know any of it

What's the deal?-

-Been having "sexy dreams" of the Green Man pretty much non-stop since we got back. I wanted to ask you what it was, but wasn't sure how tactful that would be

she's whining at me on a private chat now. Thinks you're a total cow.

But I guess that's nothing new.

How did you know about them?-

-Guessed.-

I was going to leave it at that, but I thought I owed Ally an explanation that would stop her digging into it on her own. *-I think she's seeing what her changeling's doing. You can't break a bond with your body as easily as Cathy made it look when she did her magic body swap.-*

-You are never ever ever ever allowed to tell her that even though it's not her body anymore.

She'll still think it is.

She's been saving herself for Mr. Right ever since forever. If she knew her body's off having lots of kinky faery sex probably right now, she would probably

I don't even KNOW-

-Stab me, first and foremost.

Wait… just how kinky are we talking?-

-This is TEB

she probably thinks holding hands with a dude is kinky.-

-Really can't see how a girl like that ended up with the embodiment of sex and fertility.-

I frowned suddenly, thinking about the rites that came with the Green Man — May Day, in particular. I remembered the sun beating down on us for the first time this year, as if it had known that we were performing a ritual to draw out its power and spread it between us. The short procession, the hardcore pagans who'd come from far and wide to celebrate, babbling to each other earlier about the proud heritage, the unending traditions, the rarity of a well-celebrated and understood event. Then the building tempo of the music, the intensity of the dancers as they led the leaf-cloaked figure onto the stage in the middle of the village green. Teb's face, earnest and wide-eyed, hands clasped together, flushed and forgetting, perhaps for the first time, to worry what other people thought. Just for a moment she'd given over her whole mind to the ceremony, and as the morris dancers raised their sticks I'd seen her flinch… And when it was over, I caught, out of the corner of my eye, her wiping her face to clear it of tears. Her silent, pensive mood, embarrassed but also still oddly moved, as we sat in the garden at Tanya's house drinking lemonade and vigorously applying after sun to Ally before she completely peeled away to the bone. If I'd had any nails left to break, I'd have probably taken them out now, as my fingers slammed down on the screen.

-OMFG, Ally! MAY DAY WAS LAST WEEK.-

-Um, yeah? We were all there, getting sunburn and watching the morris Dancers?-

-AND WHAT DID THE FREAKING MORRIS DANCERS DO!?!?-

-Um

looked like prats with bells on?-

I was already typing the answer and she just took advantage as I did it all in one chunk. *-THEY FUCKING KILLED THE GREEN MAN We sat there and watched as they beat Teb's lover to death with sticks! That wasn't just something mad people do because they think it's fun. It's symbolically important! THAT ACTUALLY HAPPENED TO HIM SOMEWHERE ELSE AT THE SAME TIME. FUCK. Ask her if the dreams have changed!-*

-Um

Okay

Why? What's happening?-

I took a deep breath and tried to type a bit slower so I wouldn't have to go back and correct a million errors like I'd just done in the last message (it really ruined the apparent urgency I was trying to convey).

-Nothing much, but as far as the fairies are concerned, they have a human girl in their world with no one stopping them playing with her

You remember how pervy the pixies were!

And now the Green Man isn't around to stop them having a turn! I'm sure he was protecting her while he was there, if only because he's a possessive creature, but he's dead now. It's midsummer madness over there until the Lady wakes up at the turn of autumn

and Teb's real body is trapped out there, and Teb clearly knows at least a little of what's happening to it!-

There was a pause, presumably while Ally typed stuff to Teb. I spent that time unable to do anything but chew my lip and shiver, staring intently at the last line of the conversation, waiting for it to tell me Ally was typing again. No way could I concentrate on my essay with *those* kind of thoughts in my head.

Finally Ally replied.

-Well… Crap.

She says they've stopped

And that there's nothing to worry about. And to back off and mind my own business or she'd kill me.

She definitely thinks I told you all about her dreams by the way. Thanks for using your psychic powers to make her annoyed with me.-

-We've got to get her body back, or she's going to be on the fast train to crazy town.

Or her real body will be seriously hurt and we'll have to keep her a pixie forever.-

-Back to the Fairy world?-

-Looks like.
See if your mum has any nice herbal tea things that will make her sleep better
She could do with forgetting a few nights here and there.
We'll have a chat with Tanya
she knows that place better than I do
Let's see if we can make a plan in the next few days and sort this all out before Teb knows what's happening.-
-I think Tanya wants to go shopping tomorrow
Let's spring it on Teb
see if that doesn't cheer her up!-
-Good idea
After this coursework, we won't need an excuse to want to go out and have fun-
*-Awesome!!! And thinking of that I'd better print it out and try and get *some* sleep tonight.-*
-Okay. Night. Xxxx-

I stared with horror at the kisses I'd somehow managed to type, willing them to vanish from the screen, destroying all evidence I'd accidentally managed to sound sentimental and cutesy.

*-lol, night Alana. *hugs*-*

She went offline. I dropped my phone on the floor, moved my laptop safely back and applied my forehead to the desk with some force. Yeah — concern for Teb and making plans and shit? That was all professional… Trying not to sound like an utter loser in front of Ally — who didn't care and was an even bigger loser herself when it came down to it, but I just *couldn't stop feeling like an idiot anyway?!* That was me being screwed up.

I hit the print button and closed my eyes with a groan, listening to the whirr and thunk of my printer like it might hold all the answers. It said nothing though, so I slid my essay into my bag. Well, time to lie awake for the remaining half of the night. I had a nice long list of worries to keep me going now. Such as how it felt trying to go to sleep knowing you were in for a night of dreams about being chased by horny goblins. Delightful.

Something Purple, Something... That Rhymes with Purple

I turned up to school the next morning a little early with precisely no sleep to work on. I went straight into the common room to find that absolutely no one else seemed at all worried by the deadlines. I could see one other person from my history class, and they were sleeping on the soft chairs that were set up in messy rings around the large room. Of my friends I was the first one there, and had a feeling I'd continue to be so for a while yet.

I went to the little sixth form office where the hand-in boxes were and dropped my essay off. Then, for want of anything better to do, I hopped up to sit on the table beside the clunky cardboard letterbox, knowing it was the best way to catch my friends as they came in. The office was just off the corridor outside the common room, and there was still a steady flow of ikkle kids hurrying past on the way to their lessons ("ikkle" being anything lower than sixth form – though all the year seven boys and half the girls seemed to be taller than me somehow). The girls all gave me awed sorts of looks to see a woman as fine as me still trapped in school for one more month – the boys I knew would wet themselves if I winked at them. I swung my legs, watching them dodge out of the way. *So* much better than a sixth form college like my mom had tried to convince me to go to.

The secretary looked out of the office window. "Don't sit there, love."

I made a show of sliding off while she retreated into the safety of the office again, then jumped right back up onto the table, ignoring how it also creaked in protest.

It was, rather predictably, Teb who turned up next. Ally is predictably late, and Tanya is just plain unpredictable. And, as a mildly psychic person, I do not say that lightly. I didn't normally like being left alone with Teb, but seeing her wandering up to me looking about as tired as she ever could, and in the worst sort of mood to boot, made me more uncomfortable than I'd ever been in her presence. I didn't want to think about it.

She was at least well-dressed, as always. She and I alone had a sense of style that, well, made sense. She wore a nice, trendy t-shirt that showed off her curvy figure, the pale colour making her dark skin beautiful in contrast. She must have been revising in the garden, the furious glow of the white page in front of her doubling the tan… She had three-quarter-length jeans, with purple flowers embroidered around the pockets – so *expensive* trousers too. I'd noticed, but never dared comment, that she always wore *something* purple, even if it was just a hair tie or something inconspicuous like that. She also had on the most knackered pair of purple ballet flats I'd ever seen. The kind of shoes that, to the owner, feel like an extension of their own body, the scuffs and holes only the marks of love, not imminent unravelling. I wasn't going to comment.

"I was thinking we could go into Bilsworth when everyone's here! Victory shopping or something!" I said brightly.

She gave me an incredibly suspicious look while she dug out a massive set of colour-coded folders from her bag, and took out not *one* essay, but four – apparently the sciences were pretty demanding to study. I would have no idea except for watching Teb slowly break down over all the work her lab reports demanded since I'd met her. All the work and the pixies.

As she fed her essays and projects one at a time into the hand-in box, I saw her ridiculously long name go past several times – I'd made a point of trying to learn it, especially after the events of March, when it had played such a key role in the events that had taken place… Teb Nandi. Not an easy mouthful to swallow.

"I don't know why we have to celebrate everything with shopping," she snapped when she was done. "Surely spending well-earned money makes you feel *worse?*"

"Not when you have kickass new shoes!" I pointed out, swinging my feet in *their* knackered red pumps extra hard, catching some poor lad running by right where my words had said. He squealed and stumbled, turned to see who had assaulted him and looked up at two sixth form girls, Teb loomingly tall and achingly pretty to boot. He legged it after his laughing mates without a word.

"I just prefer saving for university," Teb said. "I hear plenty of horror stories about what it's like, and I don't want to live off Pot Noodle and lentils when the time comes."

"Calm down," I said, rolling my eyes at her obsessive tendencies and mad over-preparedness. "You're free for now, remember?"

"I have, like, fifty exams," she said with a scowl.

"You know, there are only two Literature exams and one for Media?" I checked. Just… seeing how sanely she'd been thinking when she'd picked her A Levels.

She responded by whacking me on the arm with her folders as she crammed them back in her bag. I can't tell whether it was hitting me or getting that load off her back that made her look so happy when she straightened up again. I rubbed my arm and scowled at her.

She might not have remembered what she said to me right before her memory was wiped, but I remembered it and that was what pre-memory-wipe-Teb had wanted. For me to know that she wished we weren't friends. I don't know if that had subconsciously carried over or if I'd just found it next to impossible to reach back out to her as a stranger when we started afresh, but I certainly wasn't disrespecting Teb's final wishes.

Tanya turned up next, before Teb and I could scowl holes in each other. Tanya took the summer weather seriously – though Ally had said that she'd once come to school on a snowy day in a bikini, so perhaps she just liked baring flesh. At the moment she was wearing a long, baggy white t-shirt with "BOO!" on it in pink writing, and not much else as far as I could tell. A pair of sunglasses were perched on top of her head, and her masses of blonde hair were dragged into a ponytail just above her left ear – she normally went for bunches, and with her kiddy wispy fringe and delicate looks she appeared about ten most of the time. Somehow having all her hair in one place, even with the fringe, aged her up ten years. All the leg she'd suddenly produced helped too.

Mind you, I wouldn't have put it past her to have forgotten to put trousers on, and to coolly go along with it and make it look intentional.

"Heya!" she said, grinning at Teb and me in turn with one of her mad wide smiles. "We going shopping when Ally gets here?"

"Where is your coursework?" Teb demanded, looking Tanya up and down with a more practical eye than I'd done – she had nothing but a little purse on a very long string, unless she'd found some very inventive way of concealing a folder somewhere.

"Handed it all in last week," she said innocently, like there was nothing strange in having done so. She might seem airheaded, but she made even Teb look a bit dumb when it came to applying herself to schoolwork – she was just not made for the real world. As far as I could guess, Tanya was going to end up as an eccentric university professor, and probably a mad cat lady spinster. Or else hilariously matched with the most sober, normal man you could find in England. After Ally's Dad, of course.

"But… But…" Teb spluttered, apparently even having known Tanya all her life not enough to prepare for this revelation, "you spent the last week complaining about it!"

"Yeah… I saved up all the complaints so you wouldn't feel behind when you were still working," Tanya said calmly. She had the sort of soft, breathy voice that was perfect for one who was always away with the fairies. She always sounded vaguely defensive… She was not in the habit of offering up information without being asked.

Teb turned to me, almost with tears in her eyes, trying to find some sort of agreement that Tanya was insane – some way to vent the frustration without physically hurting her friend.

I shrugged.

"Hey guys! Sorry I'm late!" Ally panted, appearing through the doors of the common room with all her usual elegance and collectedness – she was leaking papers all over the place, her hair unbrushed and therefore looking like it was an independent entity trying to consume her head. She was wearing a very long, incredibly awesome black-and-white patchwork coat, and was hot and flushed even from the run from her dad's car to the hand in boxes, all of a few dozen feet.

The Piper had probably not intended for her to wear the coat all summer when he'd lent it to her in the chilly spring. A gift from him had done what had seemed impossible though – for the first time in her life, Ally was remembering to wear a coat. Unlike Tanya, who defied all expectations to get there, I'd been wondering how Ally hadn't died of hypothermia from sheer forgetfulness before now. I'd first met her back in a chilly snap in March, and she'd been wandering around in a t-shirt and flip-flops.

"The deadline isn't until three twenty," I reminded her, grinning despite myself, seeing her looking so utterly panicked and bothered, clearly out of bed for ten minutes, her essay unstapled and loose in her arms, mixed in with whatever paperwork she'd carried with her.

"Yeah, but we've got to make the bus," she gasped, dropping the pages on the table and sorting out what was essay and what was not.

"Did you *all* agree to go shopping without me?" Teb said accusingly. Someone was clearly feeling left out.

"Um, you *are* coming with us, big deal we forgot to tell you first," I pointed out, lying through my teeth just a little. To be honest, we hadn't told Tanya either, but she always just sort of *knew* these things.

"I might have had other plans! Or… Or not have finished my Chemistry coursework! It's not due until tomorrow!" Teb protested, a petulant sort of note to her voice. That "not finished yet" excuse was her worst yet.

"Other plans like *what?* We're your only friends," I pointed out, and watched as she flicked to a very satisfying fury. I couldn't do with her crying all over the place. She seemed to resent the implication that we were the best she could do in terms of friends.

"For crying out loud – do you have plastic pockets?!" Teb snapped, rounding on an alarmed Ally, who responded by knocking her carefully-sorted pile of essay papers.

"Oh no! Do we need them?"

"You were just going to give it in all loose like that to be sent off to the exam board?" Teb suggested, slapping the big cardboard box with our futures in it.

I quickly looked through my bag and pulled out a few spare, having bought a large pack in preparation for all these essays. Ally was doing her stupid panic dance – "Oh crud crud crud… where can I… oh! Thanks Alana! You're a lifesaver!"

I dragged my eyes from the spectacle of Ally failing to master the basic technique for cramming essays into plastic pockets to see how Teb was doing – shaking with fury, her eyes brimming over, twisting the straps on her bag until I worried she'd break something.

"Teb?" Tanya said tentatively, gesturing for the safety of the common room beyond.

"Yeah?" she said in a hollow voice.

"Come with me a sec," she said, taking her friend by the arm and leading her away, out of my sight. Leading Teb out of sight of me, it might be better to say.

"Wha'? Where'd Teb go?" Ally asked, looking up from handing in her essay.

"Emergency meeting," I said distractedly. I spent an awful lot of my life since I'd ingratiated my way into this group of friends in a battle with Teb, both of us vying to make the other snap first. I couldn't believe I felt *guilty* for winning. "You know, that's your bibliography there on the floor."

"Oh… *crap*."

*

Our history teacher, Mr Brooke, showed up as we were still jimmying open the hand-in box, Ally with a hand deep inside, me still sitting on the table beside it, laughing nervous giggles, still not quite recovered from the shock of discovering that I maybe cared about what Teb felt. *Maybe.*

"Hi there, girls," he said, making Ally scream a little and scratch her arm on the cardboard as she dragged it free of the slot. "Having some essay trouble?"

I held up Ally's bibliography; the introduction of teacher troubles just made the whole thing eight times as funny, rendering me speechless with laughter.

He took it from me, and gave it a once-over. "Hmm, used Waltham-Bawldryton's *A Brief History*, I see."

"Only as an opposing viewpoint!" Ally said hurriedly. "I explained it all in my essay… Not that it matters, seeing as I've locked it in that box, *sans* bibliography…"

He gave her a smile and a wink. "Well, as you're my favourite student…" he turned from us and got to work ripping open the box in ways we'd dared not. Ally and I exchanged a "Bleh!" look, eyes crossed, tongues stuck out. We agreed on one point that no other girl in the school seemed to – that Mr Brooke really wasn't *all* that… Everyone else seemed utterly charmed by his youthful just-out-of-teacher-school looks and friendly manner, but Ally apparently has really high standards that so far only the Piper had passed, and I, well, don't really like dudes to begin with.

This "favourite student" thing was a new development – he'd treated me with worried horror for the last term, seeing as the first time he'd met me it had been at his exorcism. Ally, however, had turned up on his door and promised him his supermodel-esque fairy girlfriend and, sure as cheese, she'd showed up last week, temporarily free of all bonds of the fairy world during the wild summer, determined to stay with him as long as she possibly could. After his dubious, semi-grateful but mostly-confused treatment of Ally, previously a student he'd ignored in return for her ignoring him… the last week he'd barely been able to stop smiling, and if he was allowed a say in the marking of these essays, Ally would probably be getting a triple A***, whether that mark existed or not.

A moment later Ally was hastily shoving the last page of her essay into the plastic wallet, and Mr Brooke was borrowing some tape from the office, beaming and twinkling and making apologies to the suddenly-softened heart of the receptionist, who was so taken with the youthful history teacher that she didn't even notice me still sitting on the table.

"Oh, by the way, Ally," Mr Brooke said, as he got to work taping the box shut again around her finished and completed and never-more-to-trouble-her essay, "Cathy is coming in today: I think she was hoping to see you. Wait around here a minute? She should be here already, really…" Ah, *that* was why he was in the office – not because he cared to see his essays handed in, but because his girlfriend had to check in through this office as a visitor.

"Sure," Ally said. "We're waiting for Teb and Tanya before we leave anyway."

"Leave?" he frowned.

"Study leave?" she prompted.

I coughed to cover a "Ha!" that burst out of me a bit too quickly.

"Oh, right," he said, scowling, clearly of exactly the same view as I was. "Well, I'll still be in when all your lessons are scheduled – if you want to come in to ask me anything, or for some help with revision…"

"I'm fine," she promised him. Ally wasn't the brightest spark in the school, but she loved learning all the same, and usually got well above average results in things where extra work helped – in Maths and the Sciences, which she'd dropped like goblin poop after GCSE, she'd done rather badly and always been labelled an average student for it. Now without those to complicate things, she might have a hope of coming out on the good side of the A Levels. Teb was overstretching herself and so, even though she was far smarter than Ally when it came to remembering how trigonometry worked, was probably going to get the same sort of results, except in much harder subjects.

I, meanwhile, was plenty intelligent, on top of my sparkling wit, beauty, and all that, but taking three months out of A Levels to be demonically possessed and other such deviant behaviour, getting expelled from school and transferring over with no coursework done to a new school in the last term before the exams, along with continuous distraction from a certain Piper, well… I was only looking at rather forgiving universities. Damned if I wasn't trying to leave in the first place though: I couldn't bear the thought of spending another year living at home while I retook my A Levels.

Cathy chose that moment to show up – smiling and skipping as she came in from the street, wearing all white, in the form of a short frilly skirt that trailed down further than her knees, but showed flesh almost right up her leg, and a tight tank top… She looked stunning, because she was meant to, with knee-length red hair and huge sparkly green eyes.

It was all just a fairy disguise, but she wasn't in the same league as the pixies I fought, or those that made themselves into changelings. She was a handmaiden to the Lady of Winter, and an important one too – it wasn't too hard to imagine that if someone ever managed to bump off the Lady, Cathy would be the fairy to take her place, because things flowed smoothly like that in the fairy world, and her powers would easily grow to accommodate a new role should it be required of her. It was almost too cliché – fairy princess falls in love with mortal man. But whatever. They can do that in their own time.

"Hey Ian!" she said brightly, dancing past the secretary who waved a guest slip at her with a sour expression at Cathy's lack of respect for signing in. The fairy girl wrapped herself around our history teacher, and Ally and I made the "Bleh!" face again while they were occupied.

Cathy eventually let "Ian" go, and turned to us – "Hi Ally! Hi Alana!" she said brightly. As with the internet, when dealing with fairies one should never give away one's real, full name. Fairies have a lot of power over someone once they know, as she proved with Teb. I was hoping that she'd been respectful of the fact that in a school real names were flashed all over the place, and wasn't looking. The thought of what she could do with us if she did know was rather too disturbing.

"Hey," I said dubiously. Ally smiled rather more widely. She had a healthy respect for fairies, but that didn't stop her *liking* them. I'd never understand it. I quit believing in fairies too soon in life, if I ever did, so when I was reintroduced to them they were nothing but something to be suspicious of, only showing up as something to be dealt with in my job.

"What did you want?" Ally asked, sounding utterly guileless… She knew that pixies tended to do dodgy deals, and yet she *trusted* Cathy not to screw us over. I wasn't even sure how much we owed her compared to how much she owed us.

Apparently not much. "I just wanted to say thank you again," Cathy said, her *voice* all sparkly, so cheerful was her manner. "And to let you know, well… You know where Ian lives, if you ever need me…"

"Oh you do, do you?" I asked, surprised. Ally went a little pink.

"Well, he lives in the next house down from me… It's kind of hard not to know he's there…" She shrugged and turned back to Cathy. "Thanks… I'll remember that."

Apparently a fairy's happiness weighed in as more important than a huge life-changing bit of magic, as Cathy had done on Teb. That Cathy seemed to treat it as nothing more than a throwaway favour was scary to put it in perspective.

"Well, I ought to get to class — the year sevens are probably killing each other by now," Mr Brooke said, seeing our business was done.

With excellent timing Tanya and Teb returned. No, wait, Tanya was involved. Having carefully picked the moment to reappear, Tanya led Teb back into the hall.

"Hi Tanya!" Cathy said — that greeting sounded much more sincere, and Tanya grinned and otherwise looked like she was greeting someone she knew as well as Ally or Teb. "And you must be Teb?" Cathy added, looking at our tall, grumpy friend. Teb was a little puffy-eyed, but looked more shocked than anything else at the moment.

"That's Mr Brooke's girlfriend," I clarified, in case she hadn't realised.

"Uhuh," Teb said distantly. Maybe she'd assumed Mr Brooke was gay or something. Or maybe the weird memories that were always fighting in the back of her mind were giving her a powerful kicking of *déjà vu*, as she looked in the eyes of the one who'd saved her from two months of being the Green Man's devoted mistress, at least in mind, though not in body. I wanted to steer them away — get out to the bus, and Teb away from Cathy, but Mr Brooke apparently cared enough about Teb's essay to ask her how it had gone, and she had to make a few anxious replies. He beamed at her, forgetting about his class for another minute, apparently *really* not interested in going to teach it while Cathy was holding his arm, snuggled up to him all comfy and loving.

Apparently thinking the same as I was, Ally said, "Uh, we've got to go get a bus, sir… Sorry."

"Oh! Right, yeah… Bell rang a while ago, huh?" he laughed nervously. "Come on, Cathy — you'll love the year sevens."

"Thanks again, Ally!" Cathy said brightly, and with that they hurried off, I swear actually skipping along holding hands. Urgh, newly-in-loves.

"'Thanks'?" Teb queried with a raised eyebrow. "What does Mr Brooke's supermodel trophy girlfriend have to thank you for, then?"

Ally shrugged. "Family friend. Helped them get together. I think he's actually the trophy boyfriend, though."

Teb thought about that and shrugged, suspicions bleeding away again.

"Well, shall we go for the bus?" I prompted.

Here There Be Goblins

Stepping free of school while everyone else was starting it for the day was very liberating. I'd never got study leave before, but they'd had it for their AS levels, and GCSEs too—very unfair. I cursed my mostly-private education for the millionth time as we set off, feeling the eyes of the school on us with a smug sort of satisfaction.

The bus stop was just a short way down the hill, back toward the village square. We all had bus passes because in a town this small, without a train station since the 60s, there was really no other way to get out that wasn't extremely expensive (learning to drive) or unreliable (a parent's whim of whether they would pick you up or not, no matter how far away you were stranded, storms, blizzards or wild wolves closing in).

I could afford to learn to drive if I wanted – I was one of the "rich kids". But I didn't want to feel obliged to my mom for anything. An already strained relationship had been recently shattered. I wasn't sure what she was more disappointed about – the lesbian thing, or the fact I didn't go to church any more thanks to practising hokey Wicca I'd picked up from the internets. Wouldn't have let her know any of it was going on, but being possessed by demons does tend to make one a little less responsible for one's actions. Since I'd come home, repentant but no longer interested in being a Christian thanks to the things I'd seen, I'd been counting down the days until I finished school and moved out. In the meantime, I had the nasty feeling she might try to buy me back given half the chance.

The good old baking hot exam weather (that would surely disappear the moment the holidays started in earnest) made for pleasant bus waiting, and Tanya relaxed right into it, sitting on a hot brick wall beside the sign, stretching herself out to sun. She was wearing tiny shorts under her t-shirt, I was relieved to see. Ally sweltered a little in her warm coat, making a half-hearted attempt to roll up thick sleeves. She was an awkward, lanky girl, but the Piper was tall as anything and usually quite broad as well. Kinda Idris Elba sort of dude, most of the time. The coat swamped her when draped over her shoulders. Teb stood, arms crossed, sulking and staring into the distance.

I looked around and caught sight of the church a few houses down. There was a sudden rise in the ground, a bump rather than a hill, which gave it a loftiness and presence it shouldn't have otherwise had. Of course, the Piper had seen that it was built on an ancient burial mound, repurposing the land and stopping any more angry spirits emerging from the barrow. Close to us was the pond that gave the town its name. It might not look like much more than a muddy hole in the middle of a graveyard, but it was a powerful, terrible doorway to the fairy world — one way only. Even going through it knowing other ways out — and using them — leaves you permanently tied to the town. "St Troute", or, well, the Piper, had jumped in that pond before to save a girl from the fairies, and been trapped for the spell of a mortal lifetime here in the village. He'd built the church mostly to put the grounds around the pond, to try and give the area some sort of formality, a reason for people not to wander into it.

The bus was both not technically due for five minutes and probably at least ten minutes behind schedule on top of that. Still, part of Troutespond's various army of elderlies slowly appeared, clustering in a safe distance away from the scary teenage girls who reminded them of *their* wasted youths, though I'd wager that they intended to have more of a rowdy time in town than we did. The vicious oldies of this village had a reputation to uphold, after all. Bilsworth would be shivering at the thought of the first busload of them arriving, aimed at its tea shops.

One of the old men ended up sort of distant from them, as if ostracized. He drifted out from them to stand closer to us. His effect on Teb, who stood at the edge of *our* group, off in her huff, was fascinating and also rather funny. She froze, her head flicking towards him and then away again as fast as she'd looked, but her eyes carried on drifting unstoppably back. Her aloof expression melted away to be replaced with the most perfect look of horror I've seen away from Munch's *The Scream*.

I gave the oldie a closer look, wondering what on earth could have made Teb freeze up like that. A *very* quick glance checking for genitalia that should not be showing. A more morbid check for Horrific War Wounds or Horrible Disfiguring Illness. But the man looked about as clean and whole and sane as someone pushing seventy-five could be. Bushy white mad scientist hair, long dark cardigan, slippers on his feet... If I was the sort of person to have or care about family, he'd probably have reminded me of a beloved Grandpa or elderly uncle.

He turned and smiled at Teb and I think she almost fainted. She staggered over and sat down on the wall beside Tanya, shaking, her normally brown skin turned a sickly pale shade of yellow.

"Are you okay?" Ally asked at once, turning to Teb with alarm, only realising something was up long after it had become an issue.

"Have you had *anything* apart from that chocolate bar to eat today?" Tanya added, looking completely unconcerned. She knew what was going on – I could tell that easily, because she got more and more cool as she got into odder situations. But instead of eagerly helping, she continued just sitting back and watching the road. I wanted to catch her eye to see if she'd tell me, but she clearly didn't feel like sharing.

"Yes… Yes, I'm fine!" Teb gasped, sounding anything but. She looked down at her comfort shoes and did some sort of self-control breathing exercise things. I sat next to her, wondering just how far I could push her for information when I was probably high on her shit list for the day already.

"Are you okay? I mean, for going into town… You should go home if you feel ill." Sometimes it was so hard pretending I didn't care – maybe not for Teb, but I felt like there might be some professional interest in it for me on why she'd just acted as she had.

"No! I'm fine!" she protested, swinging right around into angry from her previous freaked out state. I loved how I could do that to her – it reassured me that Teb could never truly fall into despair when I was around for her to hate.

"I'm just saying! I don't want you puking all over me – and the bus – if you do feel rubbish."

She just folded her arms, gave me a murderous look, and then set to work glaring down the bus – or, the corner the bus was going to come around any time sort of soonish.

I sighed. Yeah, I'd get it from Tanya on the bus – much safer for my own health.

*

At last the bus, in all its crappy white-and-green-and-splattered-with-mud-to-the-roof glory, appeared around the corner, rattling and wheezing its way up to the bus stop. Teb jumped up at once, elbowed her way to the front of the queue, flashed her pass and dragged us to the back of the bus before we could argue.

We ended up bullied onto the back row, Tanya taking one window seat. Ally sat as a buffer between me and Teb, who wanted to do some dark staring out of the other window. Ally's two-coloured coat was black side facing me, and it had heated to molten properties in the sun. I figured her right side was maybe a little cooler, that being the white half of the coat. Damn the Piper, I thought vaguely, as I waited for the hundreds of oldies to slowly cram themselves in, fishing for passes in their pockets and bags before hobbling into their seats. Mr Creeper, who'd freaked Teb out so much, sat right at the front. He didn't even glance our way. I wondered if he knew what he'd done to Teb.

Finally the slowly chugging engine revved a few times, the bus's hydraulics hissed and raised it up, and we rumbled on. I turned to Tanya, who smiled at me with a great big stretched grin. Or maybe her real smile used all her teeth. Quite likely.

"Hey Alana," she said, like I hadn't been with her pretty much all morning so far. I glanced over at Ally and Teb, who were having their own conversation. It was suitably trampled under the sounds of the bus as it clunked and screeched its way out of the village, building up speed as it got out onto open road. Trees and the occasional fancy house whizzed past us.

"What was with Teb just now?" I asked, keeping my voice low, just in case talking about her made my voice magically carry over the noise of the bus.

"Goblins," Tanya said disinterestedly.

I nodded, wondering at what stage in my life I'd passed the point where this seemed so normal I realised I should almost have been expecting it. I had another look at our friend up at the front of the bus, and he still looked like an old dude with hairy ears, but now that I was looking for the supernatural explanation (and also kicking myself for *not* thinking of it earlier – this was Troutespond and my job was sorting this crap out) I could tell there was just something not *right* about him. The human appearance felt like a cover pulled over a more awkward shape underneath, like an attempt at subtly wrapping a bike for someone's Christmas present.

"Goblins make up twenty percent of the workforce in this country," Tanya said brightly. I never asked where she got these statistics. For sanity's sake, I was going to pretend that she made that up out of nowhere.

It was true that a lot lived here – like with ghosts, interlopers like Cathy or the pixies, wanderers like the Piper and a miscellany of other magical peeps and beings who I really could *not* be bothered to name if they weren't an immediate concern of ours, goblins sort of just were *here*. They didn't bother us, by and large. Young ones could be a bit wild, though, keeping to themselves in parks and overlooked urban corners. But then who are we to point fingers? Disaffected youth will be disaffected youth, and the Piper's there to have stern words with them when they do the Goblin equivalent of lobbing bricks through windows or vandalising bus shelters. That was why you *heard* of them, because that was all they'd ever done to get on the human's register. That and, if someone did through whatever strange methods become able to see them (I wasn't sure where on the bizarre scale this ability appeared, because Teb had broken through the *roof* of it), they look so fucking weird I was surprised Teb hadn't ended up curled on the floor moaning in fear. She was made of tough stuff.

I heard the conversation between Teb and Ally getting louder – "... And a freaking huge coat you *still* don't have an explanation for!"

"Charity shop," Ally said at once, before I could intervene.

"Really?" It sounded a bit defeated – whatever Teb had been blowing up over, Ally had already punctured her.

"I wanted a black one, but it was all raggedy when I bought it, so Mum confiscated it, bought me the white one, and patched them together."

"Your mum made that coat?" In the months I'd known her, Ally's Mum had produced any number of amazing self-taught skills from under her big floppy straw hat, obsessively making this and that weird hippie trinkets, but apparently she'd never dabbled in sewing before, if the sound of Teb's scepticism was telling me anything. I couldn't help but laugh – the thought of Ally's Mum sewing for all the strange and divine creatures of the universe made a strangely fitting image.

"Why not?" Ally asked defensively, as Teb glared at me, and I lost it completely imagining Ally's Mum now engaged in one of those gadget scenes in spy movies, handing out wickerwork creatures to the suave hero along with convoluted explanations of their use in combat.

"What do you mean, 'why not'?" Teb demanded. "What am I missing here?"

I stopped laughing at once, all the giggles slain by that sharp comment – she knew we had a lot to hide, and she was calling us out on it. Here? Now? At the worst possible time, when she was already cracking under the strain of the shit the world was doing on her? (Okay, fair enough, this was probably the best time for *her* to snap and ask what we were doing behind her back… But we sort of needed her not to know.)

"I didn't mean it that way," Ally said, blushing. I don't know how, but she made it sound like Teb had implied some sort of gross innuendo ended the conversation. The thought occurred to Teb as well and, even with her utter confusion and probably the least comprehension for why it had been embarrassing, she still blushed and looked away out of the window. I resisted the urge to give Ally a high five. She probably hadn't even meant to do it.

New Look

Bilsworth appeared quite quickly – sooner than Troutespond revealed itself on the road, anyway. Our little town was centred mostly on the short high street, but large houses set back from the road, that claimed to be in Troutespond, stretched sporadically some miles along the roads east and west of the town. Bilsworth might have started the same size as our cutesy home, but had filled in all the spaces between those houses, so in an instant we went from fields to rows of identical little houses. One bus stop later we were standing in the high street, gasping in the hot, tar-smelling summer air like it was a chill winter wind.

"Let's go to New Look," Teb said, gesturing to a big building that was so white, smooth and air conditioned inside that I could almost taste the tang of recycled air from the bus stop. The streets weren't crowded at the moment – there were several mums with pushchairs, and the procession of oldies from the bus making their way in pairs or threes towards the more respectable tea rooms or clothes shops. It was still early for professional young people running about to grab sandwiches, far too early for the onslaught of school kids and harassed parents.

"I thought you didn't want to go clothes shopping," I said automatically, though I was already setting off toward the cold air. Didn't want to argue *too* hard with her, or we'd spend five minutes bickering on the hot street.

"Well, I do now," she said, her tone as stiff as the rigid way she was walking.

Tanya wandered alongside her (it didn't matter how purposefully we were heading somewhere, Tanya would turn that action into a wander) and patted Teb on the arm in a comforting sort of way. "If it makes you feel better I think our year seven maths teacher was a goblin too," she said.

"Could have been," Teb said, completely distracted as she looked up at the big

New Look with glassy eyes. We had reached the wide-open doors that spilled cold air out into the world. I was torn between smacking my head repeatedly on the huge display window until I fell through into the sanctum of the shop dummies, or just waiting to see how long it took for Teb to twig what Tanya had said.

She got halfway to the shoes before she walked sideways into a display of sunglasses. Tanya was on her heels, grinning, and allowed herself to be grabbed and hauled behind a barrier of ceiling-high shoes and boots on trendy Day-Glo shelves.

"Well, that was well-handled," I said brightly as Ally fanned herself and breathed in the air conditioning with sweet relief on her face.

"Good grief, this day is turning out weird," she said, then hesitated, and looked at me with a frown. "How weird is it going to get?"

"Far, far too early to tell. I think whatever we think is strange is going to be ten times as bad for dear old Teb, though."

We peered from behind a display of impractically short dresses as Tanya placated Teb – they looked like they were getting on okay. I trusted Tanya, though she might not have the most orthodox methods. They were her friends and she looked after them. I pulled Ally away to try on sunglasses.

"If you're going to wear a long dark coat, you need cool shades to go with it," I explained, forcing a pair on her.

"I don't want to look like I'm from the Matrix!"

"Pretty sure that was what the Piper intended when he made that coat," I said, pushing the glasses onto her face when she refused to put them on, and turned her to look in the mirror.

"I look ridiculous!" she protested with one of the arms of the glasses hanging over her ear.

"You just need a cooler hairstyle, and you'll fit in *fine*."

"I don't want to fit in! People get shot all the time in that movie!"

"Look, if you're going to transition from hippie to Goth, then fine, go ahead, but don't come crying to me if everyone laughs at you wherever you go – I'm only trying to help."

She scowled, putting the sunglasses back. "I'm not a hippie – Mum just irons those flower designs onto all my jeans and I'm too lazy to look up how to get them off again."

"The iron-on transfer is for *life*."

She continued pulling on her puffy fringe in a hopeless sort of way.

"Let's at least get you some lighter clothes," I suggested. "You're baking alive in that coat." I went to the nearest rack, grabbed a whole bundle of light, summery t-shirts, and dumped them on her. "Here, let's find you some shorts to go with those."

She looked down at the armful of consumerism I'd given her, wailed and ran off to Teb for help in a well-trained reaction to danger. I laughed and looked around for something nice I might actually want to buy. There were a lot of awful brightly coloured clothes here, but also a smattering of decent handbags, a few hats that I kind of liked, and to be fair, not all the clothes were *that* bad… Perhaps my former emo self would have rolled her eyes and suggested torching everything in sight, but after a few months of Ally and her friends, I was a little scared and excited to find that the mainstream didn't bring me out in hives like it used to.

I picked up a few things covered in massive sequins, a pair of large sunglasses (because looking like some sort of insect was apparently fashionable), then spotted a beautiful pair of thick purple wedges, the heel a good three inches high. The very shape of the shoe was beauty distilled into fake purple suede, and I knew who would kill to have them.

I put them on top of my pile, wandering over to where Teb was still calming Ally down, assuring her that I wasn't about to drag her off for a makeover. Her eyes flicked towards me, took in the shoes and her eyes went wide, like she'd stumbled on the lost treasures of some forgotten world.

"What the hell do you want with such tacky shoes?" Teb asked with a world-class sneer. I gave her a hundred points right off the bat.

"What do you mean?" I asked, filling my voice with the sound of righteous offence.

"Look at them! They're like… two quid?"

"I know – bargain!" I said, clinging tighter to the beautiful shoes.

"You shouldn't buy clothes just because they're cheap," she said scornfully. "You should buy them because they're nice and flatter you… And those shoes so would not!" I could see her casually checking out the size inside – we were the same shoe size, but I wasn't going to let her know that – she was a good seven inches taller than me, and let's just say the proportion imbalance was on my side.

"I think they do – I tried them on," I lied.

"And *Ally* told you that they looked good?" She raised an eyebrow. She had this terrifying expression when she wanted to look stern, thanks to her thin, elegantly curved eyebrows – she could probably make grown men cry with the careful application of one raised eyebrow. I glanced at Ally, who looked sort of terrified, unable to tell what was going on, only knowing that when Teb looked like this it was time to hide behind something and wait until it blew over. She was immune to fashion insults by now – she was wearing cracked and twisted plastic flip-flops in two distinct colours and styles, united only by extreme age.

"What do you think?" I asked Teb, deferring to her excellent advice, which was going to be predictable enough.

"You'd look like a slag in those because you're too short for heels."

Okay, *rather* more offensive than I'd anticipated… I felt anger bubble up inside me despite my attempts to coolly control the situation. Any field operative would crack under this treatment. "What the *hell*? Heels are *made* for short people!"

"When you want to be as tall as me, you're going to end up with a huge collection of hooker heels!"

"But these aren't hooker shoes! They don't even have proper heels – they're wedges!"

"Slippery slope, Alana dear… There's a head rush in being this tall… Look me in the eye – if you can reach – and tell me you'd find a way to make violet shoes work with everything you own…"

I looked her in the eye. It was strange – I always almost expected to see pixie in there, her body and her whole aura screaming of those lovable magical miscreants. But eyes don't lie, and that was all Teb in there. The same dark brown eyes as she'd always had. It was maybe more unnerving than dealing with a changeling.

She raised her other eyebrow, her expression turning to one of sheer pity for poor little me.

"Maybe you're right," I said sadly.

"Mind if I take those then? I look good in heels," she said.

"Since when?!" I protested.

She grinned, and took the wedges from me. "Yoink!"

"But… but you're already a huge great giant!" I protested as she headed off to pay for her ill-gotten goods.

Tanya patted me on the shoulder. "That was a very good thing that you just did."

"My poor, poor ego," I sighed.

In Which Alana Somehow Goes Dress Shopping

I knew the day was going to be irretrievably bad once we were walking down the high street again, arguing over the music shop versus Waterstones, when Tanya's wonderful big mouth blurted out, "What about prom dresses? Do any of you have one yet?"

"Mum's making mine," Ally said at once, perhaps unwittingly backing up the "Ally's Mum sewed the Awesome Coat" theory.

"*You're* going to the prom?" I asked, barely believing it. I hadn't bought a ticket, and was sort of vaguely thinking I'd end up with at least two out of three of my friends sitting on Ally's living room floor, watching old 80s movies with her Mum. None of us had talked about it. At least not in front of me.

"Um, yeah… It's on midsummer! You never know what might happen! I'm not missing it for the world!"

"Some of us aren't going to it for *loopy* reasons," Teb said, then added with a smirk. "I'm going to have a date for it, anyway…"

"Seriously?!" Ally cried, coming to a halt because she believed it was impossible to have a dramatic conversation on the go. The amount of times she fell over in surprise, I was thinking that was actually quite wise. "*Who?!*"

"I don't know yet," Teb giggled. "A load of guys have asked me… I've got a couple of months to stalk them on Facebook and decide which one won't get stupid-drunk, puke on me, then fall in the lake."

"Pah, who needs a date?" I contributed.

"You, apparently," Teb said, taking my cynicism for actually *caring*. "Hey, take Ally — you can be lame and dateless together."

Ally turned and grinned at me, "Yeah, go on Alana — take me to the ball!" she giggled, faking a princess swoon at the sight of me. She stumbled back a few steps when one of her flip-flops fell off.

I opened my mouth to argue, but nothing came out – my throat was all caught up with the weirdest feeling… a date with *Ally?* It worried me in a way I couldn't place… I clung to the first logical thought that flew by – I respected her too much for a phoney date – after a moment of bumping into a wall over several other confused thoughts that all jumped into my head at once. Like… "What the…?" or "That idea is not…" or "Ally dancing…" or worst of the lot, "Did Teb have any idea…?"

Why the fuck would Ally care about a fake date, though? She didn't! I'd be making far too much of a deal of it just for complaining… A fake date was the best I was going to get when these three people were the only girls I talked to in all the world, and the Piper was my only other friend. And if he was getting asked to the Prom, then he and Ally would… I stopped thinking, swallowed, and said, "Yeah… Whatever."

Ally smiled, still scuffing around in circles trying to get her sandal back on, and I felt my stomach clench – I had to look away, struck by the strange notion that I'd start crying if I kept looking at her.

"W-what about Tanya?" I asked. "Shame about your drunken idiot on Facebook, or you could go with her, Teb!"

"Oh, I have a date already," Tanya said airily.

"You don't!" Teb said, surprised. I think she was offended that anyone could possibly have a confirmed date before she did. The whole reason she'd ended up giving herself to the Green Man in the first place was jealousy over Ally going all squishy-eyed for the Piper, it had seemed.

"Yeah… Warren Spiggs asked me back when we were on Yearbook together. Then when our *coup d'état* against Jess on the Prom Committee failed, we agreed to go together anyway!"

For once the rest of us agreed on something as we were all shaken from our personal musings (I doubt Ally's were very dark, but mine and Teb's certainly had been) to give each other very worried looks.

"Well," Ally said, the trademark cowardly waver in her voice, "Let me assure you that we are one-hundred percent behind you…"

"Now, as your friends," Teb cut in, "we need to know *exactly* what you are planning to sabotage…"

"I was going to wear my fairy dress," Tanya said, in her same unconcerned way. "But then I realised I'd already worn it to school a few times, and it's bad luck if he sees you in a dress you've already worn…"

"Pretty sure that's just weddings," Ally said helpfully.

"*But we'd love to help you find a new dress,*" I added hurriedly, glaring at Ally. Tanya's dress was already something of school legend (I was surprised to find most people thought Tanya was 'indie' and 'kinda awesome' rather than mockable – not that I would have, but I would have been far too scared to wear what she did, thinking I would be mocked). Her fairy dress, complete with wings, was a new acquisition since her adventure, and was swooshy and pretty and, after a mere few hours of being worn to lessons, in the most dilapidated state ever. The wings on the back had torn, the skirt was muddy and the sleeves filthy from trailing over inky pages as she wrote. The fact she wore trainers with the silky fabric hadn't helped the look at all. "Can't hurt to be too superstitious, eh?" I knew that would be a winning point with Tanya.

She nodded.

Ally mused on this. "I suppose if you had so many ankhs and lucky rabbit feet and horse shoes that you were weighed down to the point of falling over..?"

"Sounds like you at exam time," Teb scoffed. I suddenly found myself looking forward to exam day a tiny bit. Ally was *cute* when she was over-prepared.

"Contrary to popular belief, you *can* make luck," she said haughtily. "Well, shall we to Debenhams go?"

"Aye aye! Lead the way, cap'n!" Tanya said excitedly.

"I wasn't doing my pirate voice," Ally protested. "Not that time…"

"Just go," Teb said, starting us moving again with a nudge to both Ally and Tanya to set them forwards again. I followed the three of them, who fitted together so well, and somehow, more than ever since I'd got to know them and worked my way into the group, felt like an outsider.

*

In the department store I browsed idly, not sure I should be buying a dress at all — did I *really* want to go to the prom? Answer, quite easily: no! But… they sort of expected me to go now… Would I feel worse sitting at home doing nothing? Isolated and separate from my friends… Plus the nagging feeling that whatever amount of joking Ally had taken that proposal as, would she feel stood up if I didn't come? Would I feel that I'd wasted the evening just as much as if I'd gone to stand in a corner watching Ally dancing with her friends and enjoying herself? Or would she enjoy herself, even if I wasn't there, and didn't mind about not having a 'date'? The other two both seemed paired off, though uncertainly in Teb's case, and the only certainty I had about Tanya's date was that destruction would follow… Did Ally want me to go with her so she'd have someone else to talk to? Would an evening standing around in pretty dresses, complaining about everyone else in the room, be worth the extortionate fee?

I sighed, rustling through a rail of dresses at top speed, bored out of my mind, then headed off to see if I could find the café that was promised somewhere in the building. I could get cake now and buy a dress at the last minute once Ally had bullied me into buying the prom ticket. She was going to have to work to get it.

There was another goblin going into the changing room in the guise of a dumpy old lady. I was on a hyper alert for them now, though I was sure many slid by my notice in day to day situations. Until now I'd thought Ally's Mum was the only person I knew who could see them (she tended to nod to them in the street and unnerve them quite a lot once they put two and two together on why she was so friendly to them). Why could Teb now see them? It was probably Cathy's fault, bringing up more suggestions of memories that Teb should have buried. I added it to my list of pressing questions to ask the Piper next time he bothered me. It was getting to the point where I had to grab him and demand answers before he dare give me anything else to worry about.

The café was found near the Home and Garden part of the shop. This nook of the building had a dozen goblins all sitting around little tables sipping tea and taking dainty bites of cake. I realised they must all retire here, or *something*. I'd never seen so many in one place before. I did an about turn and went to find Teb, to try and annoy her so much that she wanted to go somewhere else. Somewhere *far* from here.

I stumbled across Tanya first – she grabbed me by the back of the shirt and yanked me behind a display of extremely tall shop dummies in swish suits.

"What gives?" I grumbled, straightening my clothes but maintaining the secrecy she'd enforced on me with some respect – it paid to listen to Tanya. She merely pointed, and we peered between the legs of Mr Burgundy Suit to see Ally messing idly with a group of female shop dummies in tweed trousers and loose, baggy tops – twisting their hands around so they looked like they were all shrugging. I guessed she was off in her own little world.

"Shop assistant coming?" I asked, feeling like I should probably go rescue her if there was.

Tanya shook her head. "Teb's behind that rack of dresses on the other side," she said.

I wondered what that was about, but at that moment Chris King, class heartthrob, Romantic poet wannabe and guitar player, appeared around the corner, spotted Ally and grinned. I clenched my fists, scowling at him for looking so intently at my friend.

"Hey, Ally Guardian!" he said. I had no idea why everyone in the sixth form used full names for everyone, but it had taken me a few weeks to figure out that most of the side people I'd been quickly introduced to weren't called Jessstanderwick or Oliveravery or whatever. I wished I'd signed up under a fake name within a few days… Being "Alanalarbie" isn't very fun. Especially when half the idiots managed to turn it into "Alalalarbie".

"Eep!" Ally replied, startled out of her thoughts and knocking over one of the shop dummies with her flailing arms as she leapt back. Chris caught it and set it upright before he was in the middle of a disaster scene that would get them both kicked out.

"Whatcha doing here?" he asked. I felt Tanya patting me on the shoulder, and realised I was making a low hissing sound under my breath.

"Trying on hats!" Ally said, a note of fear in her voice I'd not heard before… Was she intimidated by him? Flustered by his mere presence? Blushing because he deigned to *talk* to her? I'd never seen her act that way around any guy before…

Including Chris.

He borrowed a hat from the dummy nearest, and dropped it on her head. "Nah, you're cuter without," he said. Ally sort of wobbled and burbled from under the hat. "So, uh, do you have a date for the prom yet?" he added. Tanya's hand that had been resting on my shoulder turned into a powerful grip to stop me jumping between the row of shop dummies and breaking that little scene up.

"Yes!" Ally squeaked. "Sorry! I just found out like ten minutes ago, but I can't go with you!"

"Oh… Shame," he said, as Teb tripped out from behind her display, clutching a long purple dress.

"Hey Ally! I found a dress!" she blurted out. "Hi, Chris King!" Tanya cracked up beside me while I stood in utter bewildered confusion, the reset button hit somewhere in my head. Everything was booting up again after the sudden stop. I could not enjoy Teb's intervention like Tanya intended me to, even if I would normally have been almost wetting myself at her opportunistic butting in.

"Hi Teb," he said (the "full names" deal doesn't apply to Teb – Ally and Tanya were the only people apart from Teb's parents who could say the whole thing off the top of their heads). Chris looked startled from her sudden appearance, but his charm didn't falter, merely switched targets.

"You're going to the prom, right?" Teb demanded, in full rampage mode. "Good. I'm wearing purple," she pointed to the dress she was holding, "so try and match, or at least don't fucking clash, or I'm ditching you."

"Um, yeah… okay. Um… Give me your address over Facebook, and I'll come pick you up…"

"No, I'm going with my friends. I'll see you at the Prom. Don't be late!"

"Oh, um, okay… I'll see you around, then?"

"Maybe," she said, grabbing Ally's arm and marching off in the direction of the changing rooms.

"Shit," I said, remembering why I'd come back down to the fancy dresses department. Tanya let go of me as Chris wandered off in a daze and I legged it across the shop floor. I got to the changing rooms just as a shrill scream echoed around the department store. In the changing rooms the scene was frozen with the chubby goblin lady standing, topless except for a hideous frilly bra, holding up two shirts to a store assistant, caught in the act of debate and looking deeply affronted now.

Teb turned on her heel, dropping the dress. She fled from the shop, tears pouring down her face.

"Well!" the shop assistant exclaimed. "How rude!"

Tanya tried to field her as Teb fled, but now I grabbed Tanya and held her back. "You and Ally had better not go after her," I said. "She won't be able to cope with either of you telling her that this is all normal."

My poor weird friends looked at each other and seemed to agree. "She left all her bags," Ally said.

I picked them up, and the dress as well, handing them to Ally for safekeeping. "Buy the dress," I said, looking through my own purse and finding a twenty pound note. "She can pay us back later."

"She didn't even try it on!" Ally complained.

Tanya shrugged. "It's the right dress."

I pressed the twenty into Tanya's hands, since she knew best, and ran after Teb.

Familiar

I'd already lost her by the time I got onto the little-more-crowded high street. Students from the sixth form were showing in force, taking advantage of study leave. I skidded to a halt in front of an alarmed couple of boys I vaguely recognised – more importantly, if I recognised them, they'd definitely know my fleeing friend. "Did you see Teb?" I gasped as they looked at me with consternation.

"Ran off that way," one of them said. "Is she okay?"

"Bad day!" I called over my shoulder, already legging it in the direction they'd pointed. I repeated this a couple of times, but by the time I was past the bus stop we were into the kind of neighbourhood with diddy little primary schools, occasional corner shops and rows of identical semi-detached houses. No one to ask if they'd seen Teb (except the surly lollipop ladies, who I wouldn't dare talk to if you paid me). I slowed to a walk, feeling a mite ashamed of how fast I'd run out of puff. I should have been in shape after all the work the Piper put me to.

A large raggedy grey dog, sort of like a massive greyhound (probably some sort of mongrel mix of pretty much all the breeds of big ugly skinny dogs) came padding up to me, bumped me firmly in the hip with its nose, and turned and trotted off with a sort of looking over its shoulder and rolling its eyes look. I followed, recognising the Piper on the inside, though not the outside. I wish I could say it was the weirdest way he'd appeared to me.

He led me on at a fair pace, and we went down a short road that felt more like a driveway, then onto a country footpath that led away through the fields that ringed Bilsworth.

"Oh!" I said, recognising the walk at last – I'd wandered up and down it a few times in the past. It led roughly back in the direction of Troutespond, cutting a fairly straight line through the countryside until it reached the high street somewhere a few hundred metres away from the school. On the way it jumped over the old train station for Troutespond, unused since the sixties. "She's gone to the train station?"

"Yes," the dog replied. I wished, as with many things, that I lived in a world where that would have scared the crap out of me. "I wonder why you didn't think of it yourself."

"Because I didn't think she wanted a three-mile hike?" I suggested. I was regretting my choice of flimsy footwear already, and I hadn't even started on the footpath yet. I wondered if Teb in her own literally cardboard shoes was going to give up halfway there and save me some walking, or if she was just mad enough to walk the whole way.

"Wishful thinking," he replied. He wasn't actually a dog. I mean, not even right now, as I looked at him and saw this beast. It was still bloody convincing even when I knew better. It put the glamour the goblins used to shame. I literally couldn't convince myself he wasn't a dog even when I knew exactly what I thought the Piper looked like.

I glared at him (and got a wounded puppy look in response — like he cared what I thought about him… Clearly just abusing the advantages of this glamour form). We set off down the muddy path, wide and worn down to the gravel in some places by endless streams of dog walkers, joggers and cyclists. We walked between hedgerows in the hot sun now, but this path went through just as much woodland as exposed fields, and there the ground was so muddy I could see myself sinking knee deep if I didn't watch my step. It would be quite pleasant to walk with supplies of water and snacks, walking shoes and someone for company other than a terrifying entity of balance, justice and beating up rowdy fairies with an oboe (I'd only heard stories, but they seemed strangely plausible). Seeing as I'd already written up a hefty list of things that I thought needed his attention, I asked, "Why the hell can she see the goblins anyway?"

"Probably Cathy's fault," he said right out of my inner monologue, and didn't elaborate, which meant my own spurious theory was still the best answer.

I gave him a minute and tried the next most important thing on my list. "So what do I do now? Or are you going to fix it for me?"

"This is not a problem to the laws of the universe… At least the ones I worry about. Human problems should be solved by human people… Though with the right leverage a non-human person might be helpful."

"So you just don't like heavy lifting then?" I asked darkly, thinking of the very inhuman problem I'd dealt with in the wee hours of today. And also wondering just what point he stopped classing things as "human" problems. I would have bet he had full authority to meddle here, that he could have waved his magic whistle, played a few notes and we'd have Teb all back to normal. But he was going to make me do it the hard way anyway.

He laughed — it was *really* creepy seeing a dog laugh, by the way. I wished his voice sounded more… doggy… but it was the same well-mannered voice he always had. "I ask you to do the things that are important for you to do. 'Fixing'

Teb is one of those things."

"Well… Can I *tell* her why she's seeing all this? I mean… it's a lot to take in…" I wished now that he *hadn't* offered her the mind wipe after the whole adventure… Or I wished that Ally and Tanya had taken it too, for what good it would have done on those who already believed in fairies and magic. Having just one friend who didn't know what was going on was awkward, but now that she was the one whose life had gone down the crapper thanks to the pixies, I *really* wished that she already knew why. Or that I wasn't going to have to break her into a conspiracy right after seeing how she reacted to us planning a fucking shopping trip behind her back.

"You would be best served in explaining at least a portion of it," he said. Dogs that use long words and old fashioned phrasing? Creepier than laughing dogs. Though it didn't suit his punk-rock look, I couldn't stop imagining a top hat and monocle.

"Why *are* you wandering around like that anyway?" I demanded. He was a lot easier to handle when he at least pretended to be a normal human person.

"I had some other business in the area… This shape is easier for surveillance."

"Then why weren't you a doggy when Ally first met you?" I asked, breaking my own rule of "never mention Ally to the Piper". D'oh.

He gave me what I think was the dog equivalent of a mysterious smile. Dogs are not really known for their thoughtful and secretive ways, but there you go – he managed it somehow.

"Teb is trapped in a situation that only she can truly mend now. You must help her see it through to that end. No burning things, no fighting. Just keep her sane. Now perhaps is the time to finally be a friend to her."

I looked down at the dog lolloping along at my side to ask what the hell that was about, but he'd vanished.

"Pfft, mysterious mumbo jumbo doesn't work on me," I said out loud, in case he was still listening, then doubled my pace, heading towards the old station.

Last Train Out Of Here

My only consolation as I traipsed on down the long and slightly winding path through the woods and fields, over hills and under bridges, was that Teb was only about five minutes or so ahead of me and the station was drawing close. She had longer legs, as well as a head start.

I wished the Piper had stuck around to chat, weird and annoying as he was. But he had work to do and he trusted me to do this on my own – he might not see me calling him as a sign I was bored so much as one that I needed help. We didn't really chat outside of work.

I considered calling someone else, Ally most likely, but I had nothing to report except that I was tired, and I didn't want to call them until I could reassure them that everything was okay. Ally was presumably freaking out and the last thing she needed was me to say, "Still don't know anything!" to her.

It took a while, but at last I got into the valley between one town and the next, and saw the mouldering wooden towers that stood for the rail bridge, stairs going nowhere. As trains still ran under it the main part of the bridge had been taken down and there was a crossing much further down the footpath, the station closed off from public wanderings. The footpath led, in a much shorter, more direct way, down to the village. It would be easy for us to get home but I hoped Teb wanted to talk for a good long time so we could both get our breath back and recover from the epic hike we'd just taken.

She *had* to have cooled down by now, I decided. No one walks for something like two hours and doesn't walk out at least the best part of their rage, fear and confusion.

It was easy enough to gain entry – thanks to a tiny bit of vandalism on the fence that surrounded the station an opening could be made between the big loose boards to admit anyone. And Teb had got there first. I hauled myself up, careful not to step on the exposed nails that Teb had left behind after she'd torn her way into the station as so many disaffected teenagers had done before her. If she was in the mood for ripping out planks with her bare hands, maybe I've been a bit optimistic about walking as therapy.

The platform was rubble under all the plants that had grown on it. In the fiftyish years since it had been decommissioned several small trees had sprung up on the platform and, apart from a chainsaw taken to anything that grew out beyond the yellow line (now crumbled and washed away like all other clear features of the station), the woods had spread freely across the platform in undergrowth and bushes. Some people might not notice that the train was passing through an old stopping point even if they looked directly at it.

Two large trees had grown into what had once been a quaint little wooden ticket office, clearly constructed of cardboard if the utter destruction of it as the trees pressed in from either side was any indication. All that remained, by some odd twist of fate, was the sturdier beam that had been part of the counter, balanced tentatively between the trees. You could stand behind it and sell tickets same as ever, if you really wanted to play at stations.

A bench survived, though not the wall that it had once stood against – it now resided in the middle of a thicket of saplings with bricks under their roots, piled around the edges with takeaway cartons and bottles and cans. Sitting on the heavily-carved wooden bench among the hundreds of local initials was Teb, curled up and watching the track over her knees.

"Nice day for it," I ventured.

She raised her head and turned her eyes to me. They narrowed to the kind of look that would have had a lesser person fleeing at once. There was definitely hatred there. "Why did you follow me?" she demanded. I'd never heard loathing quite like it before. It was kind of intimidating to realise she'd probably happily rip my throat out, but I went and sat next to her on the bench anyway. My stomach had clenched up with a mixture of all sorts of wonderful types of fear – of her, of what I was going to have to tell her… What she might tell me in return. This wasn't going to be your average heart-to-heart.

"Wanted to make sure you were okay," I said, trying to sound as light as I could.

"Where are Ally and Tanya?" she asked, her voice a little shaky now – she was losing the battle not to cry in front of me. She was determined not to look away, though.

"Probably making *terrible* decisions about what prom dress to buy for Tanya," I said. "And they're going to buy you that purple dress you were carrying around."

"But… but…" she gave up, looking back down at her feet. They were bare – there were blisters on the tops of her long toes. Her shoes lay forgotten on the ground amongst all the junk food boxes.

"Let's assume for a minute that you aren't crazy and all the weird stuff you saw today is real stuff that anyone might have seen if they'd just been looking the right way… That all those dreams aren't a sign of some inevitable breakdown, but something that you just happen to be seeing," I suggested.

"'*Just happen*'?" she quoted scathingly. "Are you just trying to pretend like you know what's happening to me, so you can use it to mock me? Do you have *any* idea what I'm going through?"

I shrugged. "I can guess. Maybe I can't relate well enough to please you, but I know."

She snorted – it was meant to be derisive, but she was snotty from all the crying, and it didn't really come out that way – more like a choked-back sob. "Did you ever see the film *The Terminal?*" she asked, after a moment.

"Is it possible there's a Tom Hanks film in the world anywhere that Ally's Mum *hasn't* made us watch?" I asked, wondering where on earth she could be going with this. A crappy metaphor for teenage existence? A surprisingly astute summation of what the hell was up with her body?

"Heh… Well, I'm like the guy in that… Trapped in this station. In my dreams I fell in love with the stag guy…" I saw a blush quickly appearing on her face, and her words became more rushed – she was forcing it out. She didn't want to tell it to me, but she recognised, maybe only subconsciously, that she *could* tell me. It wasn't easy on her, me being me. I swallowed hard, feeling suddenly just as uncomfortable as she did, wondering how I could tell my own life back to someone like this.

"But then last week the me in the dreams just… ran off. I don't know where he… The Green Man… was, but where we'd been living… it was empty… I got chased here, and I got into the station, and I can't go back out or they'll get me… But…"

"They didn't hurt you?" I butted in despite myself.

She took a deep breath, running out of strength before she was out of story, tears bubbling back up to the surface and gripping her throat so hard she could barely speak, and my stomach clenched so tight I thought I was going to throw up. "No."

I breathed out hard.

"But I'm *stuck*. I don't feel right. My skin feels all wrong on me in the dreams but when I wake up it's like an itch, and I just know that if I took the train I might be able to fix this… But I can't get on the trains either. They stop here but they won't let me on! There's no way that I can pay the fare, so I just sit on this platform and cry!" she wailed, as if the irony of where she was sitting crying right now had only just struck her.

"You came here to try and… Get off the platform?" I suggested, my head still spinning with relief. I hated to trivialise how she must feel to not be in her own body, but seriously. Best of a bad situation.

She nodded, and I felt moved to look through my pockets for a pack of tissues I carried around. They were a bit battered, but she took one without a snotty complaint and blew her nose.

"The dreams and… and those *things* I saw… they're linked, aren't they?"

"In the same way all the world is linked… I'm linked to that tree as it's linked to cake as that's linked to… whatever. There's another side to the coin – the weird side. Fairies exist, and they're right arseholes a lot of the time."

"Oh… God. A world where Tanya makes sense?" She sounded like she'd been half expecting my explanation. I suppose it was believe that she was seeing fairies or assume she'd cracked from exam stress. With what she'd seen, she'd have to have been leaning towards wondering if what she dreamed and saw was real in some way. I mean, there was only so far you could take it, and she was a very rational, scientific girl. An answer was an answer. We'd been through this conversation before, but when the burden was all on Tanya and Ally and their nonsense.

I nodded gravely, swallowing back the relief and offering my thanks to Tanya for preparing everyone for this so wonderfully. "Tanya never stopped believing in it, but you and Ally did. A-around the time you met me," (this was going to be *so* hard to say – I could feel myself chickening out at every turn) "Ally noticed a ton of weird shit going down – dancing girls who vanished into thin air, the links the Piper has with this town – the *Pied* Piper. He's a real dude who's done an awful lot more than you'll ever read about. She wasn't the only one who noticed the magic in the air – Tanya was so excited by it that the Piper accidentally banished her to the fairy world at the same time as Cathy. His magic couldn't really tell fairy from freak. He got her back before you missed her – I don't know if you'd even bother to remember that time when you bought Ally ice cream in the March weather to stop her having a panic attack, before Tanya showed up again?"

Teb frowned. "That was the *day* we met you…" even in her selfish (and rightly so) state of mind she was watching me closely. "You're responsible for this."

"Only incidentally. To Ally I was one of many odd things happening to her that week. I was sent by the Piper to protect her after he met her late at night…"

"That guy with the dreadlocks she was so excited about seeing was the Pied Piper?!" Teb snorted. "What happened to the weirdo in the tights and pointy shoes?"

"Fashions changed," I said calmly. I'd never done this before. Almost half a year in the service of the Piper and I'd never had to tell people crap like this existed – the bad exposition scene in a movie – was I phrasing this like I was explaining to a stupid audience? My natural assumption was that everyone seemed to be a little credible to begin with and at the point where I met them they were well on the road to fully believing, and just needed background details explained. Most of the victims of demonic possession we'd sorted out had been Christian and knew full well what was going on.

And then there was Teb.

"So… So he does his piping thing for fairies now?"

"In essence, yeah. He's been tasked with keeping the world in balance... I think maybe he was even doing it before the story we all know him from. He came back to Troutespond in March because of Mr Brooke and Cathy..."

"She *is* a fairy then?"

"Did Tanya say something she shouldn't have about her?" I asked, rolling my eyes. Hardly surprising. Tanya couldn't be trusted with any secret, except she spouted so much nonsense that it was impossible to pick out what you needed to know from the flow. I'd either got the same thing from Ally about Tanya or at the very least assumed the same with her similar conversation... Never mind the *first* time I'd rather more casually talked to Teb about this.

"She might have done... So... Why am I seeing them? What happened in March?"

"Tanya broke into the fairy world for a day trip, which was when she vanished for over a day, and you and Ally got all excited about finding her with news crews and police search teams in the woods and all that drama. Which apparently you've done before, so maybe that seemed old hat to you as well and stopped you thinking of that week as particularly strange. You were more concerned about which one of us got on the news to make the appeal at one point. At the fair the Piper told Ally that Tanya was too far gone to be anything less than counter-kidnapped, and at the same time you cornered me, demanded to know what the hell was going on, and I told you all this..."

"Bullshit."

"Listen to the story, Teb. It explains why you don't remember this as much as anything."

"But I remember stuff that *did* happen that day!"

"And how boring and repetitive and the same as last year it was too, huh?"

She frowned, trying to pull up memories she'd filed away in the sort of box that gets shoved under a bed and left for the dust bunnies. I took the time to distract her from the futile task. "We agreed to go with Ally – well, it was my *job* to go with Ally, but I let you think you'd spearheaded it and we "agreed" and stopped Ally from running off, and went to the fairy world. There we found Tanya, but, more importantly, witnessed the awakening of the Green Man. You were rather taken with each other – he kissed you and, from Ally's reports, the fact you didn't knee him in the balls just goes to show that you liked him more than your average joe."

I took a deep breath.

"Well, to get Tanya back... I'm sorry, but after that moment and considering how nice you'd been to me so far so you're going to have to believe me when I say this because it doesn't make me look great..."

"*What.*" It wasn't a question so much as a threat.

"I had this nice elaborately planned scene where I'd con you into trading your virginity for Tanya's guaranteed freedom or something like that – don't look like that, you were obviously happy to give it and it was exactly the sort of thing he'd have seen as a fitting tribute to make everything we asked of him seem reasonable. You ruined my plans by jumping up and yelling that you'd like to be traded – straight out – for Tanya. Two months in the fairy world with Mr Green Man. Never mind you'd have only got back last week, and missed the coursework deadlines and revision sessions and stuff… You knew all this and went and offered yourself anyway. Still think there's a total freak in you waiting to get out if you do stuff like that…"

She slapped me – it stung like two months of bitter rivalry, and I had to bite back even the mildest swear, let alone my desire to jump on her, knock her flat and slap her silly for that. Maybe pull out a handful of that shiny hair she was always flicking around. I turned back as calmly as I could, and continued like it hadn't happened – though perhaps a little more respectfully to her. Don't provoke a panting, furious woman with murder in her eyes and eyeliner smeared down her cheeks.

"The Green Man decided that as he was keeping you he'd make a changeling – to make things fair in the eyes of the Piper, to fill a gap that we could all pretty much see wasn't left in the case of Tanya, who's hardly in this world, *ever*. You have a greater presence here, a gap you'd leave in this world if you were not here. So he got one of his pixies out, and demanded your full name…"

"That's bad, right?"

"You know it. Ally told him your name is Tebster Magee. I *used* to be sure you needed a proper name to do magic on someone… But perhaps a god's power is better than that, or perhaps enough people recognised it as your name that it had some effect – but he made a changeling. It wasn't perfect… It'd have had none of your personality, no hope of passing for you except in appearance, because that was all it could remotely copy without your proper name, and the shape it took was hardly you either. A good changeling can replace a person almost imperceptibly until little tricky details begin working themselves out and it starts doing evil shit.

"We went back to the doorway, where Cathy met us. Ally gave her your *real* name, and she did some insanely powerful magic once she had control of your name – she swapped your mind with that of the changeling. So it had your body, and you had its currently-identical-to-yours body. The Piper suppressed all the magic when you got home, and wiped your memory – you're as likely to turn into a pixie now as I have a hope of being the Queen. All that's left is a link because you can't leave your body behind completely. And you're dreaming your way down it so…"

"Fuck! All those dreams were *real*?!" Teb seemed horrified – and if her blush had subsided any, it now zoomed back like a well-thrown paper plane, landing square on her face.

"Yup," I said. "You're not more freaked out that you're not *you*?" Maybe my priorities were skewed, but I'd rather have my own body than a "pure" one… (Come on – getting with the Green Man is hardly an impure thing to do and even I can see that – he's a freakin' *god of sex*.)

She shook her head. "I've been freaking out about being in the wrong skin all summer. It's not surprising. You just… put a name to what I've been feeling in the back of my head the whole time. I mean, I feel like me. I'm *sure* I'm me… The fact that my body is off being possessed by some… monster… doesn't really…" She held out one of her hands and looked at it – the same long fingers and slightly-chipped nails. The tiny scar on one of her knuckles that she had probably had forever, the doodled smiley face that had to be Ally's work… (Maybe that hadn't been there since March, but we all bore the marks of Ally's love perpetually. We may as well have got them as tattoos.)

"Perhaps you're the best changeling ever – even you can't tell the difference."

"What do I do now?" she asked flatly, and I retroactively agreed that this wasn't the place for sarcasm.

"What do you mean?"

"I can't keep on like this forever. Tell me it's real all you like – I'm still going to go crazy, even if it's just because of the dreams…"

"Yeah, you get used to the goblins really quickly," I said.

She gave me an excellent "shut up, Alana" look. "You said it was your *job* to look after Ally?"

I nodded – she was *fast*, even when she was in the middle of a breakdown. I became about as aware of the outside world as a potato is when I was stressed.

"Well, is it your job to help *me*? Are you going to do anything about this? Or do I have to break into the fairy world right here and now and do it myself?! I'll find a way! If Ally can do it then I fucking can!"

"We are. Ally and I were going to plot how to help you this afternoon… Kidnap the changeling – the one in the fairy world – or something. Now that you're in on the plot though and told us its last known location… That makes it a *lot* easier!"

"So what's the plan?"

"I don't have a clue," I told her, grinning.

"Oh come *on*, I am right on top of the fucking changeling; it's just in a different dimension to me or something!"

"Technically that's not accurate… It's fairer to say some sort of Other World or…"

"Shut up, how do I fucking get there? I'm doing this now!"

"Er, well…"

"Come on! You've been there, everyone's been there! I feel like the only person in town who doesn't know the password! What's the magic word? What do I have to tap and say 'open sesame' on? Where's the goddamn *door*?"

"There are three of them in the village and –" I had to repeat myself loudly over the beginning of another shout, "– AND you won't be able to use any of them."

"Why the hell not?"

"The stone circle is for fairies only. The pond in the graveyard of the church lets you in but doesn't let you back out again. And... Tanya's the only one who has the magic word to use the one at the top of the biggest ramp in the skate park."

"What? The *skate park?*"

"Long story. It's built on an ancient site... It still channels the energy if you know how to use it, but you *don't*."

The funny thing was that she totally did, but I wasn't going to tell her that. Tanya had used the real actual name of the fairy world – the password, if you will – as part of their childhood games. While nothing bad had ever happened to them at the time, before the memory wipe it was Teb who had remembered the name and opened the doorway for us. I was sure of two things: the Piper hadn't erased the name from her mind because it would involve destroying all her precious childhood memories, and another, I finally had a reason to be glad she was so hazy on the details of those past events.

"Well, I have a fucking changeling body... It's got to be good for something. Why *can't* I use the stone circle?" A good question that I didn't want answered. She leapt to her feet, all memory of blisters and fear of broken glass gone.

"Sit down," I sighed, patting the rotted wood beside me. "It won't work."

"I don't see why not!" she yelled, and, feet now jammed back into her pumps, she set off quick march out of the station.

"Urgh, Teb, don't do this," I groaned, dragging myself up to follow her, and feeling the complaints from my feet far too loudly.

She shoved the displaced wooden boards aside and hopped down from the platform, which I had to take as, 'Screw you and an easy life, I'm doing this.'

*

I caught up with her several hundred yards down the path, panting and with my legs burning. She was still striding along, fists clenched, teeth gritted, head held high.

"Are you really going to walk all the way to Troutespond, then *all* the way back here once you're in the fairy world? The distance isn't any less," I said, pleading with her rational senses. "Come on, think about this a bit. No real human body can be worth all the running about! Let's go back and get some walking shoes and bottles of water at least... We're both wearing freaking ballet flats!"

"You forget," she said, not even looking down at me, "that all pain is completely temporary and soon I'll be trading in this body."

"Well I won't!" I moaned. "I'm not going to be able to *move* tomorrow."

"Good. Maybe you'll stop following me everywhere."

After that I shut up because I could tell that I was going to have to save myself for the walk. Also I thought of a good comeback several seconds too late.

It wasn't so far from the station into the village, obviously since it was Troutespond station. But there were branches on the vast network of public footpaths that could keep a rambler rambling for days without meeting civilization, and Teb chose to keep on rambling, turning onto the path that led behind the houses and back up into the hills. *My* house to be precise: I could see its roof from a couple of points at the beginning of the walk.

"Can we please at least get some lemonade?" I gasped as the path began to slope at an obnoxious, ankle-crunching angle. "A glass of water?"

"No," Teb said, her voice still burning with the sort of determination that I knew her older friends would be scared to go near. I was beginning to see why. She didn't even bother to argue with me or go into deeper detail about why she was right and we should keep walking. I had to admit, that was sort of scary; Teb never normally resisted an opportunity to find a way to put me down or drag out an argument to get as much chance as possible for snarky lines. This was my first real experience of the rampaging Teb that Ally and Tanya had warned me about, but far from the last.

Legs wobbling, sweat rolling down my face, I almost crawled to the top of the hill after Teb. She quite easily strode up it. I had a feeling pixies were stronger than us, and she was unconsciously channelling this. I had to be grateful she wasn't interested in sports, hadn't already pushed herself to what she thought were her limits and gone way beyond… We might have had to do this weeks ago.

She stopped, panting but not showing any of the unsexy signs of the hike. "Well?" she demanded, perhaps to me, perhaps to the few standing stones that were still visible after all the thousands of years that they had hung out here.

I made it to a stump of a fallen tree and since I was already grimy from the bench at the station, I didn't even check my seat before I flopped down onto it. "Try knocking," I suggested, not enough wind for any longer smart-ass comments. I ran a hand over my face and looked at the sweat dripping off it. My hair was plastered flat to my forehead and I scraped it back, feeling lines of wet running through it. Along with the humming heat in my face I could tell that I looked fucking amazing.

She made a move forwards and then hesitated. I gave her points for rightly doubting my advice.

"Alright, fairies, open up!" she demanded, striking a hands-on-hips pose of authority that clearly impressed no one. The little clearing in the woods remained still and quiet, barely a breeze rustling the thick green canopy of oak and hawthorn above us. Near the hilltop, my phone buzzed a couple of times, collecting messages.

She turned to me. "Seriously, Alana. How do I open it?"

"You really think that I'd tell you? I was hoping that you'd wear yourself out with the walk and all the fight would go out of you. I clearly underestimated your ability to be stubborn."

"Thanks."

"But I think that we should take a while and work out a plan. Let them know that you're okay. Ally and Tanya can help us think of something which is a bit more subtle than just charging around. I know fairies love someone who tells them what to do in a bossy voice, but this is deep magical crap you're tangled up in. Even the changeling might not have the power to change you back again on its own. We're going to have to figure out how to make the switch as well. Since I know the Piper isn't just going to line up and do it for us, we'll have to find someone who could… Are you even listening to me?"

She was standing on the big slab of stone in the middle of the circle, a table for all the lost rituals that had happened here, or perhaps just a fallen stone from elsewhere in the circle. No one knew. Anyway, it was the focus of the circle now, the centre point where all the magic was coming from. And now Teb was dancing about on top of it, trying to annoy some fairies.

"Come on, come on, come on!" she complained.

"Get down from there," I groaned.

"Is it working?"

"No, but the fairies probably think that you're a massive idiot now."

"They can hear me?"

"You're yelling loud enough for people to hear you down in the town, so probably."

"Then give me my bloody body back!" she yelled into the sky.

There was a rustling in the undergrowth to our left. Teb gasped and froze. "They're coming!" she hissed to me.

I rolled my eyes.

A mud-splattered white Westie dog came snuffling out into the clearing, saw us and yipped happily. Teb was so alarmed she almost fell right off the stone, and hastily scrambled down.

"Not a fairy dog, is it?"

"Come here, Wuffles!" we heard a voice call in an unnaturally high dog-pitch. Crunching footsteps announced the approach of Wuffles's owner. "Wuuuu-ffles! Wuffly Wuffly Wuffly!"

"Guess not," I said. "Come on. The moment's been ruined and any suspension of disbelief has been broken now. Let's get out of here."

We hurried to take a path that would get us away from the embarrassing moment where we pretended Teb hadn't been yelling odd stuff, and the lady had to look like she didn't mind yelling "Wuffles!" every few minutes without any shame.

Once we were a good way away from the stone circle, Teb picked up our conversation again. We made a slower journey home.

"So what do we do now?" she sounded dejected. Once her initial resolve had failed she hadn't got any reserves to keep it going, thankfully: despair and confusion were so much easier to fall into.

"I figure I'll go home, talk to Ally and Tanya… We'll work something out.

Tanya knows everything there is to know about fairies and stuff like this. She's probably got a dozen solutions worked out already; I bet she's been thinking of them ever since this happened to you. We will just have to pick one which sounds best for you..."

"I'll be consulted too, right?" she asked, sounding alarmed. "I don't like the idea of Tanya deciding what's best for anyone..."

"You will," I assured her. I glanced at my phone. "We've been away from the others for hours. They must be going spare – well, Ally will be. Do... do you think you can face the real world again?"

"Maybe," she said. "I think... I think I'll just go home and have a bath."

I nodded. "Hiding from the real world is also good."

"Do we *have* to walk *all* the way back?" Teb complained as I opened up my phone to type the necessary reassurances into the group chat.

I was going to find a brilliant sarcastic comeback, but I found that I really couldn't bear to, even if I did think of pointing out in no uncertain terms it was her fault for making us walk all the way up here in the first place. Instead, I found that I was saying sorry.

*

We set off along the footpath that pointed homewards. It may not have been even a quarter as far as we'd already walked but that had stayed with us, the huge push to get over the hill piling on top of the long hike from one town to the next, and we limped along. I kept my eyes fixed to where the skyline occasionally opened up between the hills, searching for the tiny tower of the church in the town square.

I felt like I needed to be as responsible for Teb now as I had been for Ally back in the early spring. Would she appreciate the stalking that would involve? Ally had barely tolerated it, and she *liked* me. But she hadn't seen anything wrong with herself either...

"You know, in a way I'm glad this is all real," Teb ventured, shaking me out of my musing.

"Oh?" I asked, having not pegged her as the optimistic type.

"I feel less crazy for falling in love with the Green Man in my dreams... Now I know it was real it feels so much more –"

"Ooooh no, no no no," I said quickly. "Do not go justifying falling in love with weird magical guys. They're not worth it. *Don't* go down that road any further than you already had to."

Teb gave me a very strange look, and I eventually identified it as concern. Hey, there was a first time for everything! After a moment she asked, "Why not?"

"You're a lot more ignorant of these things than I thought, in that case... Never mind the obvious flaws in being sexed up by a *fertility* god, there's the terrifying wife to worry about. Or the whole Persephone factor. Do you *want* to be routinely kidnapped by pixies?"

"No," she said, "but…"

"They were just dreams, as far as you were concerned," I snapped. "Think of them that way and don't you dare wish for anything more."

"Why are you so *hostile*?!" Teb cried, furious and blushing again. "You're not jealous, are you?"

"Ha!" I snorted. "Jealous of someone who got to fuck Mr Manliest Man of the last eight millennia running? I think not!"

Teb opened her mouth to reply equally emphatically, but something stopped her. Her mouth slid closed into a frown before she tried again. "Was that actually sarcastic?" she asked with considerable disbelief, apparently far too used to my snarky ways to catch the odd comment that wasn't.

"No," I said, trying to sound a bit calmer before she started asking too many questions about my personal life. "Have you really not even guessed that I'm gay yet?"

Her jaw dropped. "Seriously?"

"Well, if you ask my mom, I just do it to piss her off, but by all other accounts, yes."

"Oh," she said, caught suddenly off-balance between pixies and normal personal drama. "Oh."

I smiled to myself as we walked on in silence, conversation squished roadkill flat with the awkwardness. Sure, I could have spent our acquaintance so far with a much more unsubtle attitude, made Teb way uncomfortable around me (or at least worried that I was making them all uncomfortable), or I could have kept it up my sleeve to stun snoopers silent, as I'd done now. I did miss the days when that had been my biggest secret, and I'd lain awake for weeks at a time with the horror of anyone guessing. I couldn't help but hope that Teb would tell or confirm it to Ally, and I wouldn't have to do the same to her. That didn't seem quite as fair.

"S-so, why were you so angry that I like the Green Man?" (She sure could be persistent!)

"Did you not hear me? You value your life too much to throw it away on him!"

"Oh… Well, thanks for caring."

"You're welcome," I snapped.

It was only belatedly down the path that I thought about how hard it must have been for her to admit she loved him, that she'd have felt like she was giving away a huge secret… To me of all people! And I had flat out refused to listen, attacking her instead. Maybe her dislike of me was a lot more justified than I normally gave it credit for.

We carried on our silent march until we were on the main road. I smiled, feeling the safety of the town bubble around me. To be honest, Troutespond was anything but safe, especially to Teb and I, marked out with glowing neon signs saying, "We've spent far too much time poking magic things and being poked back!" It really screws up the aura or something. Teb picked up the pace again and I knew what she was excited about. The promise of relaxing, soaking her feet, watching a comforting movie, getting the extended version of her Life Since Changeling Times from Tanya…

Me? I still had plenty of work to do…

I turned the corner for my street, and found that Teb had instinctively followed me. "Hey, go home," I said, too tired to bother putting better words to it.

"I *am*," she said, never too tired to be haughty at me.

"You can't seriously live this close to me," I said, surprised. We were in the realm of comfy-looking two-storey houses with big drives and a usual vast number of kiddies on bikes and scooters, or with footballs and Frisbees, or else just in swimming costumes enjoying a sprinkler on a modest front lawn. I lived up a *seriously* posh avenue that pretty much doubled back into the countryside from the way we'd come, lined with trees, the houses hiding behind long drives and thick hedges. "I *must* have seen you around before…"

She pointed to the only dark-skinned kid in a group of about twenty zillion white kids all playing an intense game of football at the end of the closest cul-de-sac. "We kinda stand out in this neighbourhood," she said. "Well… See you… later."

"I'll let you know if Ally and I come up with anything to help," I said.

She was already heading off down her road. The little brother of hers I'd never known she had came running up to her, totally letting in a goal while he was distracted saying hi to his big sis and declaring loudly that there were ice lollies inside. She went into one of the generic houses along the way with no more hesitation after that welcome bit of news. I realised I was staring when the squirt, heading back to the game, gave me the finger. He'd almost certainly learned it from his sister. Right. Not stalking her or anything. I turned and carried on my way.

Home. Whoopee.

The Last Word

I found Mom watching TV in the kitchen, stirring something in a fancy bowl. There was a spread of chopped and diced things on the black marble kitchen island, a display of many bright colours in bowls. She was a bit of an OCD homemaker — I think I'd need to properly have it out with her before she'd stop cooking huge fancy meals that the two of us couldn't finish on our own. She always cooked for three. Like Dad might just happen to wander in one day, ruffle my hair, kiss her on the cheek and say, "Oh hey, dinner!"

She gave me the slightest glance to assure herself I wasn't an intruder, then went back to slicing. A laugh track echoed from the TV.

I went to the fridge and opened it, wincing at the cold air prickling on my skin and betraying fresh sunburn. I took out a can of Pepsi and held it to my cheek, biting my tongue to stop from yelping and, seeing as Mom wasn't paying any attention to me, rolled the can all over my hot face before I went to get a glass.

The kitchen was so soulless — something out of a magazine transplanted exactly into the room. The floor was smooth lino over some original, personality-filled brick tiles that I vaguely remembered from my childhood. The bricked-up fireplace had been seamlessly incorporated into the design, the oven sealed into its place, sleek and shiny in black and silver, and somehow so *cold* despite the blue flames hissing under a slow-boiling pan. I wanted big merry red and yellow flames crackling in there... but I was not going to let myself get into contemplation of a fire any time soon.

Gulping down half the glass at once, I saw Mom wince out of the corner of my eye, as if this was some new horror I'd contrived of to embarrass her. I figured it was time to get out of the room before she decided to express it.

"Alana?"

I froze with my foot on the bottom stair, that same horrible dread squeezing my stomach that I always felt when Mom opened her mouth. I hiccupped slightly from nerves and downing too much soda. Trying not to belch made it even more awkward.

"Yes, Mom?" I eventually called when she didn't say anything else. I was beginning to wonder if I had imagined it.

"Alana, when I want to talk to you I expect to *see* you."

I groaned and dragged myself from the hall to the kitchen again. "*Yes*, Mom?" I sighed, with another hiccup to punctuate it.

She briefly glanced up at me, then looked right back at her chopping board. Hypocrite. "Did you hand in all your coursework?"

"Yes."

"Was it finished?"

"…Yes."

"You're home later than normal."

"I was out with friends; we went shopping."

"Oh, your *friends*. Who are they again?"

"Just some people from college. Mom, I'm not going to ostracize myself. This might surprise you, but other people like me and ask me to go places with them sometimes."

"You know I have every reason to be concerned about the sort of friends you make. You should invite them over: if you can't let me see them, then I'm going to have to say you can't see them either."

That scared the hiccups right out of me. "I'm basically an adult! You can't just *stop* me seeing people!"

"I can and I will, even if I have to get the police involved again. You're lucky I agreed to even let you go to the college. I still think it would have been better for you to learn at home. Far fewer distractions."

"*Mom*, you're not being fair. How can you let me prove I've changed if you keep me on such a tight leash?"

"I'm sure the *other* mothers totally support their daughters going out at one o'clock in the morning to God knows where!"

"You know what? God *does* know and since you're such good friends with him, ask him yourself what I've been up to! If He does exist He'd tell you I'm good. I'm doing half my penance just from putting up with you!" I turned on my heel and stormed back out of the room.

I stomped all the way upstairs, not slowing down until I reached my landing, despite my exhaustion from the day. I had the attic pretty much all to myself; a huge, spacious room with the rafters poking out of the slanting ceiling. I'd pinned a load of things like wind chimes and dreamcatchers to them, and I caught myself smiling as I imagined Ally coming in here and setting them all off; being so much taller than me that she'd walk right into things I hardly noticed anymore.

I collapsed onto my bed, kicking off my shoes and stretching out, getting comfy on the big pillowy duvet. I still had a *Sabrina the Teenage Witch* bedcover, because A: I was far too lazy to go buy another one, and B: well, until I hit twenty, the irony was more than enough to make me giggle every time. Besides, Melissa Joan Hart was still sort of cute even after years of staring down her silly grinning face, and had been one of my first girl crushes. Hmm, if I'd got into Buffy, would I be off fighting vampires instead? Maybe Sabrina had more of an influence on my life than I'd thought.

As I got settled back against my pillows, the covers warming up under me, I wondered if falling asleep at four in the afternoon was a little strange. *If this was another time zone, I'd be asleep already,* I told myself.

Or, with twelve hours of the day still ahead of you. Face it, you're in Hawaii.

I wish!

I rolled off the bed again and retrieved my phone and the glass of Pepsi from my nightstand. Taking a rather more measured sip of the Pepsi, not wanting to make any calls with the hiccups, I looked up Ally's home number.

It rang once and was snatched up. "Hey howdy hey! Guardian residence!"

"Hi, Hester," I said, smiling to myself at the story I'd been told of how the school had needed to call Ally's home for some sort of trouble she'd been in... They'd thought she was pranking them right up until they had her standing in the office with them as they made the call, because they couldn't believe it wasn't her picking up the phone with "Moshi moshi!" in a fake Japanese accent.

"Well met, sister," she said, and I wondered how it had taken Ally so long to realise her mum was a practising Wiccan.

"Is Ally back yet?" I asked, even as I heard a faint, "Mum! Stop bugging Alana and hand me the phone!"

"She'll be right with you," Ally's Mum said sweetly, then I heard a beep and insanely cheery hold music began trickling down the line. I think it was *Greensleeves*, but it cut off as soon as it started (thankfully – I did *not* want that stuck in my head all day) and I caught the tail end of another, "Muuuum!" before Ally turned her attention to me. "Hey Alana! Sorry my phone ran out of battery. I kept checking it to see if you had messaged yet. Last thing I saw was on Tanya's phone. You found Teb?"

"Walked her safely home and everything. Why didn't you tell me she lived so close to me?"

"You live near Teb? That's cool! I never knew that!"

I smacked my forehead. How was it possible that I'd been friends with them for two months in a tiny town where they were in and out of each other's houses constantly, and I still appeared to be a mystery to them? I was going to have to be less secretive. Not that I wanted a slumber party any time soon. The thought of Ally hanging out here, sitting on Sabrina with me, bubbled into my mind. I quickly shook it away.

"So – to business! Teb needs body switchin' back again. How do we do it?"

"Pixies have a sweet tooth, right? We could lure the changeling out with some of my mum's homemade cookies!"

"I totally approve of her making cookies, but waving them in the fairy world would get us mobbed by pixies… And no changeling. It's stuck in the old station. I found Teb there this afternoon."

"So we know where it is? Let's go get it then! I suppose we'll need Cathy to switch her back?"

"Uh – yeah! That hadn't occurred to me!" I laughed. "I was so concerned with getting Teb home safe and sane I never stopped to think how we'd actually *do* it…" I think the Piper had probably hinted we'd need Cathy – quite strongly too – but like I said, awareness of a potato when I was stressed. It made sense that Cathy would have to undo it… Spells were undone best by those who'd cast them.

"What I don't get is how they let this happen in the first place," Ally said. "I thought the Piper would *fix* it, and that would be the end of it…"

"Either he did a shoddy job so he could keep stalking you, or he just didn't know that would happen," I said, and kicked myself for not only encouraging discussion of the Piper to Ally, but reminding her that they'd had a thing. Not that she probably ever forgot it – I still caught the little hesitation as she said his name. "Neither would Cathy – she seemed to think she was helping, and she wouldn't have any reason to make sure we kept bugging her… She's *not* going to be happy when we show up and ask her to undo what she thought was her amazing favour to us. She's going to take it like we're calling her wrong for doing it."

"Shall we give *her* some of my mum's cookies?" Ally suggested.

"Ally, I hate to say it, but not *everything* in life can be solved with cookies," I told her, with some regret that this was so. "Come on, you seem to be all friendly with her… What does she want?"

"Well…" Ally paused, and thought about it, probably doing that cute scrunched up "I don't know anything!" face.

Finally it occurred to her. "She's pretty worried that the Piper didn't put any protection on Mr Brooke – nothing lasting, anyway."

"Yeah, he probably has another exorcism scheduled next March in his diary," I sighed. Annoying thing about messing with *anything* supernatural was the great big "come possess me!" sign it hung around your neck. I'd followed Ally around at first because the Piper had been worried she'd get possessed, seeing as when she'd bumped into him, her inner eyes had suddenly been opened to all the magical happenings of the world… Tanya probably still would have been borrowed by fairies whether Ally had been investigating or not, but the fact she'd *known* had made every moment looking at fairies, or Tarot cards, or whatever else she'd done, all opportunities for that door in her mind to be wedged just a little further open. Maybe it was just a lifetime of slow exposure to Tanya, but it hadn't happened for her – and maybe Teb would have coped the same, had she not been changeling'd.

Mr Brooke, on the other hand, as an average member of the oblivious public, was a firm non-believer in all this, and even put his possession down to a brief mental breakdown from stress. I was sure even after nearly a year living with Cathy by the time March came around again he wasn't going to be any more receptive to the idea of pixies – while living with one would be quickly wearing down his mental defences against the uncanny and unnatural. When Cathy had to return to tend her Queen, Mr Brooke was in for a kicking.

"So look up a way to protect him from demons!" Ally said excitedly, "If all your Catholic education doesn't help, then you're still the champion of random Google searches!"

"Yeah… I'll give it a try," I said, trying to sound as uncertain as I could. Ally wasn't to know what was chalked on the floorboards under my bed.

"Right… I'd better phone Teb and make sure she knows I care – I probably have a lot of apologising to do as well!" I could hear Ally wince.

"Yeah," I replied. "Okay, you can call her."

"Great."

We sat in awkward silence for a few beats.

"Right, well, see you tomorrow! We can arrange times later when my phone is charged up!" There was a click and then silence on the line.

I sighed, dropping my phone onto the pillow beside me, then flopped back as well, staring up at the elaborate embellishments in the ceiling plaster.

I wouldn't be doing any Google searches. I'd been taught all there was to know about demons a long time ago.

*

I decided it would be a bit extreme to shove my (king-sized and extremely heavy) bed aside and lift the carpet up just to check a few details, no matter how cinematic it would have been. So I went to my bookshelf and idly examined my old Nancy Drew collection. I'd long since disposed of the works, after they were done shaping my formative years, and replaced them with rather more useful content. There had been a time I *cared* what my mom thought.

I took out one of the big omnibus books and slid the jacket off to reveal my "Magic sparkly book of awesome". It had been renamed lately after Ally had been complaining about how ominous everything sounded in witchcraft. Book of Shadows? No way! I felt the usual pang of guilt for not writing in it lately. I figured I should at least write an update on how best to fix a wonky ley line and the resulting dangers of pixies. This book basically chronicled my adventures working with the Piper these days. I didn't learn new magic half as fast as when he was bossing me around, and the learning curve was steep. I'd pretty much given up on books from stores that smelt of incense and had dragons in the window, or covens full of mopey teenage witches from my old school (and a few boys who were mostly in it for said mopey teen girls but were too weaksauce to actually do any magic and call themselves witches). A few discussions with Ally's Mum had helped me pick up some strange and interesting tips, but mostly what I used these days was on the big epic "fixing the nature of the universe" level.

None of that was very helpful though. The book fell open on the latest page, where a ballpoint pen was crammed into the spine to remind me to write new stuff in it. I wanted to go way back though — back beyond when it had been a Book of Shadows, back to when it hadn't even had a name and I hadn't fancied myself any sort of Goth or Wiccan or whatever. I had just been very easily led, and taken a few extra lessons on the side. Lessons that had carefully stripped away everything I'd been taught in my religion classes, Sunday school and anything the Church had ever told me. A mixture of lies and hidden truths long buried and things that were genuine truths, but twisted until it was far easier to just say it was a lie that could be backed up with tons of factual reference. And dark magic. So much dark magic.

I had once wished that I'd thrown away the book and burned it, but the Piper had said to keep it. He'd said that one day I would need it. And that I needed to know this stuff still, even if I didn't use it. He is balance — good and evil. Maybe you stay on the good side, but you hold the dark as close because a being of pure good has no place in the world, no comprehension of how to fix what is wrong. No understanding of what that even is. There's no good without holding back the evil. He said there are no villains, only people who do bad because they think it's for their own twisted ideas of good, people doing good for their own bad reasons, and that there is no pure evil in humans, no way to define whether anything is right or wrong. He can only see a balance of the two powers, and he keeps the world to that, but can't explain why some things happen and why some don't.

"Besides, it's character building," he'd added, laughing at my little emo sulk. Like he didn't see how close to crazy being in a constant struggle with both very literal demons, and my own personal metaphoric ones, would bring me.

Fuck him, he might be right about everything, but that didn't mean I couldn't resent him for it.

Actually, I reflected as my slow turning of the pages brought me toward the beginning of the book, demon warding was one of the first things I'd been taught. My old friend had been a jealous kind — didn't want to share me with anyone. I didn't normally go back and edit the spells, but I'd added a few notes and an amended design to his lessons. A circle that kept *him* out too.

The pages I'd been looking for turned at last in my shaking hands, and a folded piece of paper fell out from its long entrapment between the covers. I leapt up instinctively, dropping the book, and backed away to the other side of the room. I knew sure as anything that I hadn't put it in there; I'd only been back to that page a few months ago to write in the amendments.

Maybe it's from Mom? my optimistic side suggested. Gods knew I couldn't lock my bedroom door and had suffered for it before, but I'd figured Nancy Drew had been about as safe as anything, and that had certainly always escaped Mom's notice before. Besides, I *knew* it was from *him*.

I could just leave the paper there, folded, and bin it. Or lock it back up in the pages once I was done copying the spell out. There was absolutely no reason I should read it. It would only encourage *him*. He'd *know* I'd seen it. He'd probably known exactly when I was going to have to turn to that page. That paper might not have been there yesterday for all I knew.

It could be a warning. Or an apology. Or something harmless. He always looked out for you, I found myself thinking. Right back to idiot sixteen-year-old logic, like he would really be able to have someone's best interests at heart. Or, a heart.

I picked up the paper and sat on the floor by my bookshelf, holding the folded square closely, taking steadying breaths. Maybe I should have called someone – Ally, The Piper, *someone*, but by the time it occurred to me someone else might be able to help me out, I'd unfolded the paper and was reading the contents.

My love, Alana,

I congratulate you on losing the battle not to open this letter.

I may not be able to touch you now – not a curl on your head, a kiss to your hand… Nor to hold you in your dreams, and I know you miss our night-time wanderings of the Other Worlds as much as I do… Maybe more, for I still visit those places, and think of you, while you have only fragments of dreams left to cling to. Do you remember the pools? The mountains? The expanse of the skies of eternity? All that you would have been Queen of, if you'd stayed. I ache to think of you trapped on that earthly plane, running messages and errands, engaged in lowly tasks I wouldn't demean my least minions with. And working for that two-faced whistle man! He has no honour in his task – not the passion for his work you could find in the most irresolute corners of my kingdom!

But I am not here to complain or to wallow in what we once had, merely to point out that no one can deny me temptation, for that is my right and duty, as much as it is his to walk away and leave you when you are in the most danger. The fact you chose to read this, and I know you did not hesitate, proves I can still tempt you. There is a path before you that you can once again walk toward me. I won't work any dark arts, nor lay out wave after wave of delights, no attempts to lure you back to my side shall be offered. I just wanted to remind you… I'll be waiting.

I think that is all the temptation I need to offer.

My love is as eternal as…

I read through it three times, screwed it up, and missed the bin. Tears had been running down my cheeks since the second reading, but now uncontrolled sobs burst from deep inside as I remembered it all.

Damnation.

I'd been hoping through most of the day that I'd actually get to rest and sleep, but finding the letter had shaken me up badly. As had the subsequent stages of putting it in the bin, taking it out again, reading it, putting it back in, taking it out again, etc. I finally folded it up a bit more carefully and put it back into my spell book to worry about later. I ignored every messenger except when Ally sent a message around six to tell me that she'd meet me on the corner of Teb's street at ten the next morning, seeing as I knew where Teb lived but would get murdered if I went in to wake Teb up in the morning… The stupid petty details washed over me and I nodded numbly to what she told me and then went back to my curled up position, running slowly through that time when I thought I'd found true love and friendship.

Gods, I'd been stupid. I had to keep forcing the first words the Piper had ever said to me back to my mind, over and over again, countering every moronic thought with his mild voice. "Stop and think about this for a moment. You still have a choice." Kind of underwhelming for what had dragged me back from the brink, but in the end a very reassuring mantra to remind me that I had chosen and I was very safely on the other side of it, no matter what anyone else might say.

When Mom called me down to dinner we sat in silence, picking our way through the sumptuous feast she'd spent so long preparing. It was weirdly flat, despite the impressive display she put on, and I reached for the pepper mill. I began grinding a ton onto my cheesy vegetable squishy thing that made up a good third of the meal. Mom winced. I grated some more. The squishy thing was getting rather dark with pepper…

"Alana…"

I gave the pepper mill a final shake for luck and put it back. My eyes were watering a little from the smell. I ignored her, and reached for the spicy tomato sauce she'd set out in a little stoneware bowl.

"Alana, what are you doing?" The protracted grating sounds had drawn her attention, and she looked angrily into my plate from across the wide dining table. There was no third place setting. She'd never been overtly *crazy* — but the big old dresser with plates in was almost within arm's reach, should the need arise.

"It's bland," I said.

"It's not. Scrape off that pepper and stop wasting food."

"There's plenty more," I grumbled, layering on the tomato.

"You're not going to eat it now," Mom said, but then went back to ignoring me, as if realising she'd risen to the bait that I hadn't even intended to set. It was just that everything between us became a confrontation.

I ate a bite. It burned like hell. I held it on my tongue until my eyes ran and

I was sniffing, and swallowed when I realised I was crying, not just reacting to having stuck about a thousand degrees of hot food in my mouth.

Mom made a tutting noise under her breath. I remembered how that used to drive me mad. I couldn't even remember noticing her doing it in recent times… I'd been so sucked in with my life as one of Ally's friends… Had it made me a better person? At first I'd been so grudging about being dragged back to the good side, so taken in by what I'd seen on the bad side that it seemed a punishment to have to go through redemption.

But when I'd finally reached that point where it no longer bothered me and I actively looked forward to doing good again, I hadn't even noticed. It must have happened at least a month ago – I'd finally put enough behind me that I was looking ahead again. But… But I was still stuck. *He* still had the power over me to throw me right back off course. I was as stuck as Teb was, between one world and the next. Only hers was Earth and the fairylands – mine was Heaven or Hell. For eternity. Because fuck it, I'd been Catholic once, and Christianity still believed in me, still had a claim on my soul from when I'd been christened, and I was powerless to resist it, no matter what the Piper said about working off my sins during my life to make things easier for me later. All I was doing with him was avoiding the square which said "Go straight to Hell, do not pass Go, do not collect £200."

Was saving Teb the same as saving myself? Would that be enough to prove that I was good and break my service with the Piper, to return me to normal life, just one of billions of drones trudging back and forth, blissfully unaware of what the higher order had planned for our latest string of screw-ups?

As I slowly picked the vegetables out of the cheesy mess, I realised with a horrible, chilling certainty that now I'd equated our current Teb-saving mission with my own fate… If I failed, *he'd* call that a victory.

At least Persephone got to leave for half a year at a time.

"Well, Tanya texted me your address this morning but this is more fun."

I woke up to the buzzing of my phone – someone was calling me. I think they had been for some time, if my dreams of angry hell-bees was any indication. I fumbled for the phone, knocked it off the nightstand, grabbed it from the floor and finally answered it.

"Hey?" My voice sounded terrible. I *felt* terrible. My eyes were puffy and glued shut, my head throbbing. Don't go to sleep crying, kids. It's not good for you.

"Morning, Alana! What's your house number?"

"Who is this? Go away and leave me alone…"

"It's Ally, silly! I'm on the corner of Maple Drive and Barn Road… Where do I go?"

"Why? Just… Stay there. Is Teb there?"

"No… I was going to get you and then we could get Teb together!"

"Seriously, I need a shower before I can go anywhere. Get Teb and I'll meet you on the corner, like we arranged."

"But I wanna see your house!"

"You are not allowed *near* my house," I said, slowly heaving myself upright and looking around. I spotted jeans on the floor, grabbed them, then staggered to the closet.

"Well tough. I'm on Shepherd Drive… Am I getting warm?"

"I dunno, what's the weather like out there?"

"Another fiiine sunny day!"

I grabbed a t-shirt, even as I winced at her cheery attitude. Misery clothes don't tend to be the type you can wear on a hot sunny day. Not without frying. I dropped the jeans and looked around for a skirt.

"You can wander around the neighbourhood all you like, I'm not telling you where I live."

"Is it this house with the big old-fashioned American car in the drive?"

"No."

"The customised number plate says otherwise… Unless there's another Larbie on this road?"

"Fuck off."

"I'm ringing the doorbell!"

I heard a trill of the bell and swore again. I hung up and barrelled down the stairs, rubbing my eyes and running my hands through my hair, though I knew it was pretty much standing on end and beyond hope until it had been beaten into submission with scalding water. Mom was coming out of the dining room as I crashed into the front door after jumping down the last stairs. She was already dressed up in her nice housewife outfit, ready to look immaculate should she need to take the Cadillac out to go grocery shopping… Or maybe just to impress the sofa. I was wearing baggy tracksuit bottoms and a t-shirt so large it was sliding off one of my shoulders and hung to my knees. It was stained from my hair-dye adventures – considering the colours I'd been, it wasn't pretty. Green, red and black splotches covered it, so it looked like I'd been slaying zombies in my sleep.

"Alana, go get dressed," Mom said, horrified both to see me and at the thought of anyone else seeing me standing in the door, bringing down the neighbourhood. I ignored her and pulled open the door to reveal Ally standing on the step, grinning at me, eyes sliding quickly past to inspect the airy hall behind me.

"Nice house."

I grabbed her by the arm, dragged her inside and hauled her off upstairs before she dared even say "hi" to Mom. I guessed Mom might warm to her a little for that comment, but I don't think she'd be very pleased that I had any friends at all, especially ones who looked as weird as Ally.

"How many floors does this building *have?*" Ally panted as we reached the attic landing.

"I'm on the third," I said. I took her into my room while she was still counting landings in her head and sat her down on my bed. I picked up my dropped clothes from the floor. "I'm going to have a shower. Sit quietly, don't touch stuff, and don't listen if my Mom offers you cookies – it's all just a ruse."

With that I hurried to the upstairs bathroom, locked myself in and leaned, shaking, on the door, waiting for the adrenaline to pass. My heart was thumping in the back of my head, and the exhaustion loomed back up and flopped heavily over me. I turned the shower on and climbed woozily in, ready to try the slightly more normal approach of waking up in the morning.

A few minutes of being pummelled by hot water later I went back to my room, purged back to freshness, to find Ally sitting on the bed where I'd left her, looking around with fascination.

"You have a lot of DVDs," she said, gesturing my floor-to-ceiling shelves that lined the only wall in my room that *was* floor-to-ceiling instead of tapering off into the shape of the roof at hip height.

"I like movies," I replied, towelling off my hair then dropping the towel in a laundry basket.

"I guessed… Did you tell Tanya we were doing this?"

"No. She usually comes along anyway, doesn't she?"

"I think *someone* has to tell her… She can't get *all* the details just from guessing…" Ally shrugged, watching as I combed my hair and put earrings in at the same time. I could see her looking at me with her usual kind of "surprised by everything ever" expression. "Anyway, I don't want her knowing what we're doing. We're pretty likely going to the fairy world today, aren't we?"

I shrugged. "Maybe," I said, switching to eyeliner. It hid the mess my face was after a night of quiet crying.

"Well… it's all very well asking her for information and stuff – I got a ton from her about changelings last night, but… I don't like the idea of her coming with us. She actively wants to live there. I don't want to have to rescue her, or for her to trade herself right back again for Teb or something stupid like that."

"The fairy world owes us Teb," I said. "The deal was for two months, and now it's time for Teb to come home. Over time. The only reason she hasn't is because it's a pixie in her head… All nice and caught between worlds for us. Tanya couldn't trade herself for Teb if she tried."

"That's still not very reassuring. She finds ways to do stuff you'd never have thought were worth trying."

I nodded. "Don't worry, Tanya doesn't know a word about it from me." I looked around, spotted my red shoes, cleaned up from the mud and fairy drool I'd managed to coat them in the night before. I pulled them on, picked up my bag and raised my eyebrows expectantly at Ally. "Come on then – what are you waiting for?"

We went downstairs. I spotted Mom lurking in the lounge, trying to catch more details of who my friend was.

"See ya, Mom," I said pointedly as I opened the door again, pushing Ally through as her eyes boggled, taking in everything she could of my disappointing home life.

"Will you be back for dinner?"

"Probably not… Bye!" I got Ally through, darted after her and slammed the door.

Out in the sun, as we walked down the driveway, I aimed a kick at our car. I think I dented a hubcap, and grinned to myself as we carried on down the road. Ally giggled.

"That was fun… Now I know all the secrets of the mysterious Alana!"

"You don't," I said at once, sounding far harsher than I ever meant to be to

Ally. I was pissed off that she'd invaded my privacy after I'd told her not to, but it was Ally. You didn't get mad at Ally. Teb I'd probably have slapped already since I owed her one, but Ally... Bleh.

Her expression wavered in the face of my anger, but it jumped right back to demented smiling. "I could totally work out some secrets from your house." I think she'd taken it as a challenge.

"Huh, right. Ally the great detective. Tell me one thing you worked out you didn't know already." To be fair, the boggled expression she kept permanently warmed up did not seem to lend itself to suggesting an astute, perceptive mind. Also I'd heard her open her mouth.

"Okay, so... I didn't know your mum was Catholic."

"No shit, Sherlock... I went to the *Catholic* school. What else did you work out?"

"Hey, my Mum knows people who have kids who go to that school who aren't Catholic and just like it because it's *not* the other school and gets really good results... If you really want to know..." Ally frowned as her brain slowly collected together all the impressions she'd picked up and ordered them into a reasonable set of facts.

"Well it's like eleven in the morning and even though your mum was dressed nicely she wasn't at work. My mum does the same: puts on her nice clothes around the house when she's sad. And your mum's really sad. I guess whatever happened to you the Piper never fixed your home life... She was really suspicious and angry and you don't talk to her much. She cared about you being home for dinner... I don't know why if she doesn't want to spend time with you... It's not like your Dad lives with you. I guessed that *ages* ago." Ally glanced up, checking my expression. I'd jumped right into the kind of pained neutral expression that one uses when they realise their face will be eaten if they show fear. "Your Dad... Your Mom still has their wedding picture up in the hall, so they're probably not divorced..."

"Okay, that's enough," I snapped, stopping. We'd reached the corner anyway – it wasn't a long walk at all between the slight class divide Teb and I lived either side of. "Stop fucking assuming stuff about me and go and get Teb."

"Yeah... I kind of assumed it was a sensitive issue..." Ally said, sounding apologetic, and like a flaming idiot too.

"Why the fuck did you *say* anything then? No, don't answer that – I'm going to the shop. See you in a bit." I turned and doubled back – I needed alone time and a big bag of cookies for breakfast.

That fixed everything, right?

Fuck.

Cookies and Cream

I regretted yelling at Ally more than anything by the time I got back to Teb's street corner, munching chocolate chip cookies. I could only hope that Ally regretted prying into my life just as much. Yes, she was curious, and could be very observant when she put her mind to it – she wasn't a total ditz like she'd have everyone believing if she could. But there was a big difference between observing and pointing out.

Maybe it was my own fault for making my life such a mystery. I wouldn't tell a thing if I didn't have to… I know we were all meant to trust each other, although I don't think that Ally would hesitate to tell anyone about *her* family situation, and people could be an awful lot worse about revealing mental instability in the family than a death…

There'd been a horrible moment last month when I'd gone around Tanya's house for the first time, and seen the photos of her mother dotted around the living room, and Tanya had told me, as she got us drinks of Sprite from the fridge, casually as anything, "That's my mum. She died of cancer when I was three." For a moment the big bridge of trust had opened up over the yawning chasm I'd dug around myself and I could easily have said something – let her in. *Trusted* her with a fact that should really be quite insignificant about my life. Maybe not me as a person, but it wasn't like I struggled with it every day… Not directly. Maybe he'd have probably been a bit more cool with me as *me*. Influenced Mom not to snip me neatly out of her life until I was nothing more than an irritating lodger in her house…

"Crying and eating cookies? Can you *get* any more emo?"

Ah, Teb was gracing us with her presence. I gave her points for managing to make snarky comments when she looked about as sleepy and dragged from her bed as I felt, and so plainly dressed that I barely recognised her. She looked like she'd put *effort* into looking that bad, because no one could possibly find such boring, awful clothes as that within easy reach, unless Teb had a secret fetish for dressing drab in her spare time. She wasn't even wearing purple.

"*You* don't get a cookie now," I said, wiping my eyes, wondering when I'd even started crying. As my vision cleared I spotted Ally bobbing around behind Teb, looking kind of shaken and scared of me.

"Do I get one?" she asked in a voice that would have sounded playful to Teb, but to me conveyed so much I found that I was wiping away another escapee tear. I shook a cookie free of the pack and held it out to her. She bit it from between my fingers with skill and a giggle, clearly feeling everything was forgiven. She looped an arm through Teb's and said, "We're off to see the wizard!"

"It's a pixie," I said, looking up from my hand, which had been hovering in shock where it had been when Ally's lips had closed so briefly over my fingertips. I dropped my hand and held it behind me as I followed them, rubbing my fingertips together to dislodge some crumbs and shake away the sensation.

"Same difference," Ally scoffed as we cut into a path that led through the woods that lined the northern border of the village, behind the neighbourhood Teb and I lived in, with Ally's a short way to the east. It was cooler under the trees, the shade patchy over the footpath that ran behind lines of fences of the back yards of Troutespond. It was nice after the bright sun that had assaulted my fresh-from-the-dark-of-sleep eyes.

"Is it the same?" Teb asked.

"No," I said. "Stop confusing the poor thing, Ally." I might not manage snark this early in my day, but I could sure patronise for England.

"God, this is rare – *Ally* getting the upper hand on me in a battle of the wits," Teb said, clearly unable to admit I frequently did it to her. "Just you wait – I'll learn all there is to know about pixies!"

"It's good to see you're taking this in your stride," I said, not wanting to stop while I was ahead.

"I'm serious!" she protested, looking over her shoulder to give me a proper glare. "No way am I letting *you* know more than me."

"You did, like, six sciences at A Level," I pointed out. "I don't think there's anything *more* you could know that I don't."

"Fairies and Physics bear little resemblance to each other…"

"Pity," Ally mused. "I'd have got far better grades if they did…"

"…And it looks like I'm stuck having to face up to fantasy," Teb concluded. "So I might as well do it *better* than you."

"Hey, I'm not the benchmark in weird just because I work for the Piper. It's Tanya you want to be challenging for that crown."

"I didn't say that I wanted to be weird – just to know a lot."

"Listen, love," Ally said in a kindly motherly way that seemed oddly suited to her even if it was just an act, "One goes with the other."

"Just you wait," Teb repeated, unfazed by Ally's concern. "You see if I can't do it."

"I'm not placing any money on it," I said.

"Me either," Ally nodded. "You probably *do* have the strength of will to stay true to yourself, but I *do* like the idea of us as one big weirdo happy family."

"You already *have* one of those," I said, accidentally letting my bitterness from earlier into the conversation.

Ally turned and gave me the sweetest smile, forcing me to stop in my tracks because it was either to stop walking or to stop breathing (which I did anyway for a moment). I suddenly saw why Ally kept dramatically stopping because the other option was falling over. The dappled light that filtered through the trees landed in patches on her hair, picking out spots of the rusty gold colour that usually hid under a mousey exterior, and her eyes sparkled in an almost unworldly way, that strange turquoise green shade of speckledy hazel I'd never even have said was possible until I'd met her…

"Can I have another cookie?" she asked brightly.

*

We emerged from the woods into the most unremarkable neighbourhood ever. It was the sort of place that was so ordinary it didn't even have whatever weird twist "normal" neighbourhoods had that harboured serial killers and had neighbours standing in front of news vans shaking their heads and saying, "It's such a quiet place… you just don't expect this in your own back garden!" It didn't stand out for being normal. It was too *normal* for people to even notice this. It was just, like… road, houses, trees, whatever.

I stress this because in the six hours between meeting Ally and seeing her house, I'd quickly convinced myself she lived in the weirdest house on the planet, all painted Mr Blobby style, crazy garden gnomes and a clown car in the drive and I don't even know what else… But she lived in about the most average house ever. She had some pretty funky curtains in her upstairs window, but her neighbour had a collection of meerkat ornaments in the front room window, so I don't think anyone could point fingers. The point was, apart from a few basic signs of human habitation, the house didn't stand out with any special personality. There was a big blue car in the drive – a businessman's car. There was a row of pretty flowers lining the walk up to the front door.

Ally caught me by the arm as I almost walked up the drive. "We're going to Mr Brooke's, remember?"

"Oh, right," I said, carefully removing her hand from my arm before she forgot and it got awkward. "Too used to going in there already…"

"You don't want to go in today," Ally said with a roll of her eyes. "Dad took the day off 'sick' from work."

"Did I catch inverted commas?"

"Don't ask," Teb chipped in. "Poor Ally is still scarred from the last time she came home too early on one of these days."

A few paces later we were standing in front of Mr Brooke's house. Once again it was entirely unremarkable. I'd never passed it and wondered who lived in it, because it was, like every house on this road, a total non-entity of pastel paint and pebble-dashed front. If the Guardian family failed to stand out, what chance did a history teacher – and if rumour was true, his dear old mother – have?

We stared at the bland house front for a while. I rubbed my arm where I could still feel where Ally's hand had closed around it. Her huggy friendly touchy-feely ways were going to get old fast until I'd had a chance to angst out all the weird feelings I'd got myself tangled in.

"Go ring the bell, Ally," Teb eventually said. "They're *your* special friends, after all."

"Oh!" she said, like that hadn't been obvious. She hurried up the drive and pressed the bell. Then she turned and gestured frantically for us to join her, not wanting to be caught alone. We shuffled up the drive and stood by her. A long moment passed, filled with the vague dread our insular society has instilled in us for knocking on strangers' doors. Finally the cheap plastic door opened. Cathy peered out with even more fear at having to *open* the door. She brightened up when she realised who it was.

"Oh goodness! I was worried it was the milkman!" she said, stepping back and letting us into the house with a casual wave that still betrayed her nervousness about getting us in and closing the door on the outside world.

"What's wrong with milkmen?" Ally asked at once.

"Your hear things," Cathy said darkly, which made me think that she was getting her experience of human culture from crappy daytime TV comedies… What did I say about fairies only wanting in for some of the lamest human experiences?

As we walked through the house I tried to have a good look around, very aware of how easy it was to read someone's house after Ally had glanced around mine earlier this morning. But the glimpse of living room through an open door in the hall was very dull and old-ladyish, with ugly, high-backed brown floral chairs and actual pictures of cats on the wall, which was something I thought was too ridiculously stereotypical to be true. Cathy led us hurriedly past this room, almost like she was scared of it, and into the kitchen. Though the house was similar to Ally's there seemed to be more walls in this house, somehow. The houses were already cramped, and even with a conservatory knocked into the back wall of the kitchen to make the whole room feel airy and light, there really weren't enough surfaces for all three of us to all lean coolly on as we were wont to do, being lazy teenagers.

It made sense that we were in the kitchen, anyway. Fairies in houses were household spirits most of the time – or rather, much less often connected with the rest of the house unless they were evil and lurked in the scary door of a wardrobe or something. The dynamic of a house had changed a fair bit since the good old days when fairies were in their heyday, but Cathy would still strongly believe this was her place… In a totally nothing-to-do-with-feminism way, I hasten to add. Though thinking that made me suddenly feel resentful towards Mrs Brooke – I could imagine her quite easily feeling smug that Mr Brooke had landed a girl who preferred to be in the kitchen.

She didn't seem to be spending her time cooking, though – she had a laptop on one of the clean white kitchen counters and a pile of books taking up a lot of space in front of the toaster.

"Open University?" Ally observed, peering at one of the books on the table. She would know that logo well – her mother had almost every kooky degree offered by them.

"Environmental Sciences," Cathy said proudly, swirling over to sit on a stool pulled up to the counter. "Ian's mother prefers it if I'm doing something with my time…" she actually looked sort of… *tamed*. She was wearing her impressively long and beautiful hair pulled back into a low ponytail that hung flat down her back, only fanning out when she spun – and that seemed less than before, like the dance was flattened out of her as she mooched about the house in baggy tracksuit bottoms and a white tank top. She looked happy, but she was beginning to seem *ordinary*, all the stunning beauty and otherworldly eyes aside.

"Tea?" she asked, as the kettle suddenly clicked behind us – Teb jumped, though I guess Ally was expecting it and I just hadn't been paying attention, so quickly decided to play it cool when I saw Teb start. We watched Cathy get out three mugs and put them on coasters, even though it was just the kitchen counter, then she carefully made the tea. There was something forced about her movements – she was trying so hard to do everything right, in a completely alien culture, and that meant lining up the tea bags so the tags all hung out at just the right angle to the handle, perhaps copying to the letter the first cup of tea she had seen made. Then the water was slowly poured in just to a point, as she bent over and squinted at some imaginary line… The milk and sugar ritual took twice as long as it should.

We all took our tea and for a moment the four of us stood in the kitchen, us girls watching Cathy as she blew on her tea, looking at us, waiting for an explanation for our visit. Teb's presence must have either been totally throwing her off, or she'd worked out that Teb was staring at her in a whole new "how on *earth* does Mr Brooke get a stunning fairy girlfriend like you!?" kind of way, unlike their first meeting since the mind wipe, when it had just been, "how on *earth* does Mr Brooke get a stunning girlfriend like you!?"

"Uh, where is Mrs Brooke?" Ally asked. I think Teb had elbowed her to remind her to act again. She was far too used to Teb and me leading the way whenever we did something serious.

"She went into Bilsworth today," Cathy said. "You don't want to see her, do you?" She sounded suspicious, like she wouldn't put it past Ally to want to see

Old Mrs Brooke.

"No! We wanted to talk to you!" Ally hastily reassured her, smiling earnestly, "Um… it's about that favour you said I had…"

Cathy beamed at Ally. "Anything I could do for you… What is it?" Her bright amber eyes danced over us again, still trying to work out the key to the conversation.

"Well, the fact of the matter is that things haven't worked out so well for us as they did for you. Teb's trapped in all sorts of weird and wonderful ways, and wants out. We need you to, well, put things back to how they were."

"Not," I interrupted, "to change the situation in your own life; the balance ended up way more in your favour, actually. You said yourself you felt you owed Ally something more. You're unsettled about the balance *somehow*, right?"

"So you… You want me to *undo* it now?" Cathy asked, setting down her tea squarely in the middle of the coaster by the laptop.

"Well, *yes*," Teb said, straightening up and likewise setting down her tea, though with no respect for the countertop. I shuffled a little aside, to where Ally was already poised by the fridge, ready to dive for cover if needs be. "I'm awfully grateful for what you did to save my future and not have me – or the changeling – sent to prison or sectioned or whatever would have happened if things had run their course, but… but my bargain was to stay as long as the Green Man was there, and the spell was meant to break last week already. Now I'm just having nightmares about being trapped in a station, and it's boring, and if I keep dreaming it the rest of my life I *will* go properly insane. The changeling wants out as badly as I do, and I'm sure you'd rather help another of your kind than me, but…"

"Hah! *Help* one of the Green Man's minions? Not likely…" Cathy scoffed. "I'm *pleased* it's suffering!"

"But so am I!" Teb protested.

"I thought you were happy with what I'd done for you," Cathy said petulantly. "I fixed your whole life and all you can do is come complaining to me…"

"Cathy, that's not fair," Ally said, peeking out from halfway behind the fridge. "It's not really on of us to ask you to do this now, but… Until now everything's been brilliant. We're all so grateful for what you did. Now things have fouled up, and it's not your fault… Or anyone's really. Just that things change and become rubbish sometimes. Like… Sequels to really good books…"

"We're willing to negotiate payment to you," I said quickly, before she rambled on about the declining quality of various series she'd read lately. "We figured you wouldn't want to do this for us just as a favour…" I held out the packet of cookies to her.

"You're suggesting I do this for cookies?" she snapped, although she also grabbed the bag from me, shoved her hand in it and pushed two cookies into her mouth at once. Fairies seriously had issues with sugar.

"No, that was just to calm you down."

"Well what else can you offer me?" Cathy snapped through a mouthful of crumbs. I thought of light and dark, beautiful and ugly. Sure, Cathy seemed lovely, but she had a fairy's temper, a fairy's manners. "I already *have* Ian."

"I don't know about that," I said. "Maybe for the summer, but in the winter you have to start returning to the Lady, and come Spring you have to leave for two whole months. You *know* that one quick fling with Mr Brooke last winter left him vulnerable enough to become possessed by demons… Imagine what almost a year of living with you will do to him when you finally have to leave him and surrender the protection?"

"That won't happen," Cathy said fiercely. "The Piper wouldn't let it."

"We all know how great his quick fixes for things are," Teb snapped. "Look at me! I'm a fucking *pixie* just like you, and I don't see how by any natural order *that's* right! But it passed some friggin' test that Alana can't even explain except that it just *is*, so we're having to go through all this two months later! Can you really imagine someone who thought it was a good idea to do this to me would have remembered to… do whatever the hell he's meant to do to protect Mr Brooke?"

"You need powerful witchcraft for that," I added, filling in the technical side. "Even the Piper didn't know the spells to keep me safe when he saved me – I was beyond any of the quick rebalancing he did with Ally and Tanya in March. Fortunately I already knew them, so he didn't have to go wandering the country looking for another witch to do it for me. I have a spell that anyone can do, even a pixie. Something that will protect Mr Brooke as long as he lives. I'm willing to give it to you if you fix my friend, okay?"

Cathy bit her lip, frowning deeply. She picked up her tea and took several long sips from it, breathing in the hot, calming steam before she opened her eyes and looked straight at me.

"You promise the spell works?"

"Am I swearing in tongues and spitting pea soup? Of course it does." This was somehow weirdly validating to my *other* issues, at least.

"Okay. Let's go find Teb."

Teb raised a hand. "Uh, hi?"

"*Other* Teb," I said.

"Not-Teb," Ally contributed.

"Oh, *her*," Teb said darkly. She cracked her knuckles. "That pixie's fucking lucky it's in my body, or I'd break all its teeth when we find it."

Two Tebs is More Than Enough

Mr Brooke's car sped down the twisty country roads that connected our village to anywhere. To get to the train station by car was far more confusing than on foot, but Cathy had insisted. She was very proud that she'd passed her driving test first time without any lessons. Whatever she'd done to fool the driving instructor, it wasn't fooling us. Teb was actually clinging to me, though perhaps more with the plan of using me as an air bag than for friendly comfort.

Ally kept glancing at her phone. "Waiting for a call?" I asked, leaning forward to peer at the screen. She turned in the seat (of course she got to call shotgun) and shrugged. "Tanya should have left a comment by now that said, 'Meet you at the station!'... You know how she is."

"There's no way she'd know where we're going if you didn't tell her," Teb said, pulling me back so she could carry on clinging as we screeched around another corner. A truck coming the other way ploughed onto the verge to avoid us. Cathy didn't seem to notice.

"That's never stopped her before," Ally said. "It's been bugging me all day... but this is the least we've ever seen Tanya when *anything*'s been up with fairies and stuff. Normally you can't take a step out of your house without her showing up and being all, 'Hey! Let's go!'"

"Any particular reason you make her sound like Navi from the Zelda games?" Teb asked.

Ally giggled and shrugged, making irritating high-pitched fairy noises for the rest of the drive. Cathy presumably didn't get the reference, which is probably good because that was probably quite unintentionally racist to fairies if she had known what Ally was doing.

We finally came to a stop, hearts racing, knuckles white from clinging, at a layby with a Public Footpath sign pointing into the woods. A few other cars of determined dog walkers were scattered around the layby as we squeezed through the annoying gate designed to stop just about anyone entering thanks to the complex mechanism, but especially people who had to squeeze through it sideways because they were too wide, and then we set off down the path. Cathy pulled her hair free of its ties and shook it out. She danced a few steps, breathing in deeply.

"Mmm, trees," she said. The sunlight took on an odd quality, sort of... Much more mellow and sparkly and serene. All the colours were turned up a notch like someone was fiddling with the contrast and saturation controls on the telly.

"Ooh," Ally said, even as I rolled my eyes. Urgh, fairies.

So we went along in a merry procession until we saw the footbridge of the station. We all instinctively slowed and looked up at it warily, like the changeling might be watching us from one of those wobbling towers. But of course, it was a whole dimension away, and we could have sat on that platform all day without letting it know we were there. That was the problem.

It didn't take long to break in again given no one from the council had come by and fixed the damage that Teb had caused. We stood on the platform, looking about. It was as grotty as it had been yesterday. Nothing potent of the magic that was taking place under our feet.

"Um, so how do we get into the fairy world?" Teb asked.

"Turnstile?" Ally suggested, as Cathy pointed, heading off that way.

It was a battered old thing that stuck out from the folds of the bark of the tree that had grown over the ticket office. It clunked rustily as Cathy pushed on it. But it seemed to be working. We hopped over the barrier, then queued up to reenter.

"Hold my hand," Cathy ordered, holding out a hand to Teb. She took it, Ally took the other hand, and I grabbed Ally's spare hand. Cathy pushed the turnstile until the old bars creaked around with a heavy metallic groan and thud. I tried not to look surprised as they began slowly spinning around and Cathy stepped through. We were pulled after her, each of us barely hopping through the turnstile without receiving a whack to the butt from its twisting bars, and I felt terrified for a moment I'd get stuck until I was pulled through.

The world blurred around us – mostly I was concerned with the horrible dropping sensation like we'd fallen an immeasurable distance. I looked down at once to see the ground still under my feet, same as ever. I looked back up as I emerged on the other side of the barriers to find myself back in the eternal night of the fairy world once again.

Here, things were orange today. (You could never tell what colour anything was going to be, though they did like their themed colour schemes. Don't go visiting on Halloween aka the night when the veil was thinnest.) The platform we'd been standing on remained much the same in its general state – run down, rotting into the ground. But now glowing lanterns in twisted, dirty glass shaped kind of like squashes stood on top of poles just a bit higher than I was tall, and filled the whole scene with their deep orange light. The two towers of the footbridge glowed with fairy lights all the way up them, like Christmas time. It wasn't bright – merely that the darkness was given an orange colouration, like the night sky above a city. It seemed sort of misty here, the edges of the world cut off far sooner than they were meant to be, turning into a black void of nothingness, given a token shape of the outline of trees before the weird stars of the fairy world appeared above. They crawled over the ceiling of the world, close and far, bright and dull, always shifting into new systems and constellations.

"God, it's just like my dreams," Teb murmured, taking a cautious step towards the ticket office. A hole opened in the side of the tree, the bark swinging aside to reveal a large window through which tickets were presumably sold. A goblin was standing behind this opening, and looked down at Teb with a strange sort of expression. Mind you, now we could see the goblins for what they were every expression seemed strange on their alien faces. This goblin was a weird sort of animal/human hybrid, long hair and drooping ears framing a sharp face that was as much human as it was vole, a big moustache under the pointed nose. The sharp dark eyes glittered under thick eyebrows and, rather than a beard, fur crept around the edge of its face, blurring the hairline. It wore a formal sort of uniform, a matching cap with antennae poking out of the top.

"What train?" he asked. He was giving Teb a very suspicious look. She was staring off down the far end of the platform.

"We're not here to get a train," Cathy said firmly. "Just to collect some lost property."

"The office is down there," he said, gesturing with a paw.

"We've got it," Ally said as we all turned to see that Teb had already set off down the platform to where a dark-skinned figure in a gold dress sat on a bench, looking sulkily down at the floor. Teb walked towards her/it dazedly, and finally stopped in front of it. The changeling looked up, meeting the eye of the one whose image it had stolen, only to be trapped in the original body.

I followed cautiously as Ally stopped to ask the goblin ticket master a question about his job, Cathy hovering nearby to intercept any stupidness whereby Ally might accidentally sell herself into his service for thirteen years or something. I was more curious in the scene down the other end of the platform.

Teb took a little involuntary step back – I could see her gasp. I stopped a few paces away, close enough to hear everything, but not so close they'd draw me in and ruin this as pure entertainment. Her eyes were wide and she was shaking hard. I'm sure confronting yourself is one of those big literary themes that Literature professors dork out over, and this in particular would have them squealing in glee at the symbolism and blah… Pretty sure it was just super nightmare fuel for Teb. It was creepy enough watching it from the side.

They weren't perfectly identical and after a first initial moment of "woah!" I began to see differences. The changeling, in the long golden dress, hadn't been treated the same as Teb over the last two months. Despite the nice dress it looked ragged and thin in the body – I don't know if it would have bothered to eat anything, but it was supporting a human body, whereas Teb could have stopped eating entirely and not damaged herself for two months in the real world with that new body.

Real-Teb had carried on tending to her hair as well, but on the changeling the thick fringe that hung perpetually just in her eyes had grown out and was now swept behind her ears, showing off the curve of her forehead and elegant, arched nose in a way that made her look much older. Her eyes sparkled with something dark and vicious, and that made her unfamiliar despite the fact that whatever else, it was still freaking *Teb*. The Real-Teb (in a borrowed changeling body) looked round-faced, young and outclassed in her plain clothes and body frozen in time two months ago.

"I can't believe you got this far," the changeling said, looking up at Teb with a sort of incredulous gaze, sounding half-stoned, like it was weary beyond belief. "I thought I had at least another month of plotting to get out of here and far away before you'd work up the nerve to challenge me."

"You're trapped here," Teb said, although a waver in her voice revealed her uncertainty that this was the case, despite how haggard the pixie seemed.

"Oh, trust me, I've been working on plans aplenty to escape." Its voice didn't sound much like Teb's at all – there was a coarseness to it, a hoarseness. If we'd taken it back as intended it wouldn't have tried to blend in like normal Teb at all. It *couldn't* have. It didn't have her name.

"Well, I'm not here to challenge you," Teb said, trying to sound diplomatic. "We're here to switch us back. You can go on your way in your proper body once we're through."

"That's great for me, but are you sure *you* want to go through with this?"

I'd been watching pretty neutrally until then, liking the idea of Teb bitching out herself instead of me for a change, but I took that as my cue to step in – I was going to have to intervene before this got messy. "Alright, alright, let's get on with the switchin'."

Real-Teb turned to me so quickly I heard the *fwip* of her ponytail lashing around. "What does it mean by that, Alana? What did it mean?"

"Nothing. It's trying to trick and tempt you. Trust me – I know it when I hear it."

"Do you really want to sever the only link you have to this world?" the changeling continued over the top of my warnings, its voice rising in pitch, jabbing at the nerve it knew it had uncovered. "Your only link with *Him*?"

"He's dead!" I said quickly, putting a hand on Teb's shoulder now, trying to comfort her and draw her back to her senses. But fairy trickery is about as powerful as it gets when they desire it. Demons give you a fighting chance and enjoy the internal battle as much as the mischief that may result from it. There is always the option to walk away and say no with a glowing clean slate. Pixies don't draw the same pleasure from the temptation and corruption – they live for the end results. They're not evil. Don't ever think they're evil. They just often have a very warped sense of fun. Teb *could* have walked out of the Green Man's grove back when the choice first came to her, but since she didn't, she'd been bespelled into complacence lest she change her mind. I remembered the Piper's words to me about my own choice.

"He was killed in a *human* ritual! How are you to know what happens to Him in His own land? Did you *see* it?"

"Cathy!" I yelled over my shoulder. "Get over here and fix Teb!"

"Right," Cathy said, and I saw her take Ally by the shoulder and march her over to where we were standing, cutting short the conversation with the ticket goblin. I spotted a new light on at the end of the platform – a glowing white beacon. A goblin stepped out of the office behind us, wearing the same uniform and cap. Cathy winced, passing him right as he bellowed out, "Twelve fifteen to Waitington!"

She and Ally drew to a halt by the bench the changeling sat at – we were encircling it now.

"Hey, it's the dancing traitor!" the changeling said. "Does the Queen know you're here now? Do you *really* want to free me? I could run off and tell her as easily as –"

"You wouldn't dare cross me if we were on her land," Cathy interrupted coolly. "And you don't scare me even away from it. Stand up and face the girl whose image you took."

The changeling got up slowly and looked firmly at Teb's face; Real-Teb looked down quickly, but Cathy reached up and pushed her face gently so she was looking her clone in the eye. I could feel the first wisps of fairy magic reaching out from her before she'd begun whispering the words to an old spell. Ally and I stepped back and her slow circling of Teb and Not-Teb turned into a dance, her fairy magic suddenly spinning into the most raw, powerful form. All her illusions of being a pretty human girl faded, leaving her as the strange, wide-eyed, doll-like winged creature she actually was, wild and dangerous – there was the hint of sharp teeth in her round mouth.

The words to her spell were drowned out as a train pulled into the station. Despite the spectacle of magic in front of me I had to turn to look, curious about what made the train so loud. It was a proper old-fashioned thing, steam pouring out to mix with the mist that pooled around the scene. There was a violent green glow from the front, where a fairy fire burned within, and its lantern echoed the colour, sending a beam into the murk beyond that only illuminated seemingly miles of green-tinted tracks to the horizon. The engine was deep purple, the carriages orange and green, with gold trimmings and many swirly designs in thick wooden ornamentation disguising their state as mere boxes on wheels.

This seemed to be a goblin-run operation, for a creature that was only pixie-height, but the ugly mismatch of creature parts that marked the common goblin, hopped out, wearing a cap with "CONDUCTOR" embroidered on it in threadbare gold. It looked at us expectantly. I shook my head and quickly turned my attention back to the spell-casting.

Both Tebs had an oddly blank expression now, drawn into an unnatural daze. Each was being slowly coaxed from the body in which their soul or essence of being (or whatever it was that made up the inner of the shell of the pixie) resided. I could feel it loosening in each of them. This was the dangerous part; we may have ended up with an empty Teb if Cathy screwed up and allowed one soul to fly free. There was an eternal pull on a human soul drawing it one way or the other, and once it was twisted free only a strong grasp could stop it floating away like an errant balloon. Or dropping like a lead one. I wasn't going to comment on Teb's chances, though there was a background radiation of Christian upbringing on us all in this country, even though all four of us were non-practicing except sort of me and witchcraft. And, hey, she wasn't even religious — though she was agnostic, who's to say her soul wouldn't go a-wanderin' and find some new berth to stop at, as per her ancient religious heritage, though she might not know Ganesh from Vishnu in practice. In any case myths showed us the precedence — if we lost Teb's soul, no amount of questing would get it back, though we might lead it to the doorstep of whatever realm it settled in. Those were the rules. Rules that goofing around with souls and bodies in a fairy realm could not possibly compare to.

I shivered as I felt the moment of parting — two empty bodies stood frozen in front of us. For a moment I could have sworn they were speaking to each other, a whispered *"You could stay if you wanted..."* in the air, and then...

"Hey guys! What did I miss?"

Tanya was standing at my side, looking half-wild and completely barmy (as per usual, I suppose) and giving the most insolently smug smile I'd ever seen.

"Tanya!" Ally shrieked. "What on Earth are you doing here?!" She looked furious — I couldn't believe Ally had it in her, though she hadn't looked forgivingly on Tanya since March.

"I came to see Teb re-Tebbed," Tanya said calmly.

"How did you get here?" I asked. She sure didn't look like she'd taken the easy ride like we had, her hair messy and lank, her eyes dark and wild like she hadn't slept since I last saw her.

"There was a cairn in a field just north of the village — it wasn't very well sealed."

"Oh for fuck's sake! Do I have to go fix it now!?" I moaned.

Before Tanya could answer me a rather more interesting argument broke into a scuffle, and a moment later one of the Tebs — the one in plain clothes, and now sporting long bloody streaks down one cheek to match fingernails grown long and sharp on the other Teb's hands — darted around the other and fled onto the train.

"Yeah, thanks for stealing my body, bitch!" the Teb in the gold dress yelled as the conductor hopped back in, blowing a whistle furiously. The carriage door slammed and it began pulling out of the station at once, like they had been waiting for the final passenger. The Teb in the carriage watched us for a moment with a weird, detached look, as if it felt it should be drawing more importance from this parting than it actually did. Then it turned haughtily away, no longer our problem.

Texts from Last Night Dot Com

As we left the station the ticket goblin gave Teb an irritated look. "Please remember our facilities shouldn't be used for claiming sanctuary *next* time you visit, thank you."

Teb looked innocently at him, as if to say "that wasn't me!", and I had to grab her hand as Cathy pulled us back through the barrier. A moment later we were standing out in the midafternoon sun on the cycle path. Teb looked up at the sun and breathed in the hay-fever-inducing air deeply. "Mmm, the real world and a real body," she said. Then, "God, I'm so *hungry*."

Ally was digging in her bag, and pulled out a pair of rather nicer jeans than the ones Teb had sacrificed to the changeling, and a t-shirt.

While she changed behind a tree I noticed I was getting a rather impatient look from Cathy. Right, I still owed her. I took a rather scrunched up bit of paper from my bag and handed it over. "All the instructions are on there," I said, hoping she would definitely tell it apart from the class notes I'd scribbled it on the back of. "Thanks."

"Great!" she said brightly, all sunshine now we were paid up. "Well, let's get back to the car. I'm sure we all want to be home soon… Like, before Ian finds out I borrowed his car!" she giggled.

"Um, you said you *had* a driving license," Ally pointed out as we started walking back down the path.

"I do!" Cathy said. "Ian just doesn't like me driving his car for some reason and I'm still saving up for my own…"

"Um, on that note… I'm sure we don't *really* need to rush home," I said, glancing at my watch. "It's only two o'clock, somehow… I'm sure Mr Brooke won't be home yet."

Cathy frowned uncertainly, like she didn't quite believe there could ever be a time when one would drive without speeding. Still, once we got in the car she relented a little and went from breakneck speeds to merely pixie-racer speeds. Nothing had to mount the pavement to avoid us, though.

We were back in Troutespond in a jiffy, and pulling up outside Tanya's house, seeing as she lived closest to the main road. As she unfastened her seatbelt she called, "Bye, guys!"

"See you later," Teb and I said automatically, and even Cathy turned in the driver's seat and smiled as Tanya got out. Ally didn't say a thing, sitting with her arms folded, staring straight ahead, down the road.

"Uh, we might as well get out here and walk," I said, elbowing Teb gently, really not wanting to try and be sociable with Ally when she was like that. "It isn't really far for us from here."

"Right… See you guys later," Ally said, now that Tanya was out of the car.

I leaned closer to the back of her seat, and talked quietly to the headrest as Teb hastily unbuckled her seatbelt. "You can't really be angry with her. She's probably just feeling left out."

"I can if I like," she replied petulantly.

I rested my hand briefly on her shoulder, then realised I had no idea what that gesture was supposed to mean, so I pulled my hand back and got out of the car.

"See you, Ally. Thanks for everything, Cathy."

"No problem!" Cathy replied as I got out and closed the door. I turned to see Teb and Tanya having an awkward conversation as the car pulled away.

"Not reeeally, no," Tanya was saying, glancing our way.

"Um. Right. Well…" Teb shuffled and looked helplessly at me too.

Was *everyone* annoyed with Tanya today? I figured I might try and say *something* nice to her.

"Well, we really ought to get going – I'm sure I have a cairn I need to be fixing." *D'oh.*

"Sure thing! Sorry about that!" Tanya said brightly, waving and skipping up to the door of her house. She made it too easy to be mean to her – she just let it slide right off. If she used her cuteness to its full advantage she could make people feel terrible for talking to her that way. I didn't really know what side I was meant to be on – really I was meant to be the neutral fourth party between the others, but I was just as divided as they were. If they had a proper falling out, I was going to be really badly torn.

"Oh, Alana?" Tanya said, hovering on her doorstep. I turned. "Thank you," she said. "You've done such a good job with Teb you won't believe it. But you did. I'm really grateful for it."

"Calm down, dear," I said, feeling my cheeks warm up.

Okay, so maybe I could pick Tanya's side and not feel too guilty. She was lovely.

"Sooo," Teb said, as I hurried to catch up with her. "Where do you live?"

"Never you mind," I grumped. It was bad enough that Ally had found it. "You're not ever going there. Shouldn't you be running off to spend time with your family?"

"Um, to be honest, I was expecting to feel more different after the switch than I do. I just feel really hungry. It's not like I was *away* from them."

"True," I said.

"Anyway, you live right near me. I'm curious. I want to knooow about you," she sang, flouncing along beside me. I recognised it as an uncanny impression of Tanya.

"Look, I've done my part and fixed you up. Can you leave me alone now?" Jubilant Teb was not something the Piper had trained me to deal with.

"I thought you wanted to be friends?"

I snorted, though as with most things Teb said to me, there was a tinge of sarcasm to her words.

"I was just doing my job, not looking for approval."

"Isn't that what you want, though? To be the fourth musketeer?"

"Look, there's your turning. Just take it and go home." I couldn't bear her much longer. I was conscious that shouting at her and parting in a huff wouldn't be a good way to end the day. But with Ally's sulk at Tanya, and Teb's only moderate enthusiasm for the good result, presumably because she still had so much else on her mind, there was a less than festive mood in the air. But damn it, this had been a victory that the four of us (sort of) had shared in. It should have helped seal me into the group. I'd done all the hard work. And even if I didn't seek Teb's approval, Ally had to at least think that I got on with her other friends.

I forced a smile onto my face. Teb was regarding me with a cool stare, a sort of detached fascination with whatever external show I'd been putting on over that angry internal rant. She found me pitiable. Mockable. I felt a muscle twinge in my cheek as I struggled to keep the grin in place.

"I'll see you later then," she said. She stalked haughtily away, head held high, without waiting for a reply from me. I had already pretty much decided not to give her one anyway.

It came back to what she'd said earlier: very little *did* feel different. I hadn't got any of my own closure either.

I mooched home with my nose pointed much closer to the ground.

And damn it, no, that was not a comment on how short I am.

*

When I got in Mom was actually not in the kitchen. I supposed she was working upstairs on one of her little editing jobs or something, so I went to take advantage of our milkshake machine.

About ten seconds into watching it blend up half the contents of a massive bowl of strawberries I'd found in the fridge, my phone rang. Ally. I answered it, sucking strawberry juice from my fingers. "'Lo?"

"And behold?"

Well, she sounded cheered up from not too long ago.

"One cup of tea and you're chirpy again," I guessed. See? I could do detective work too!

"Yeah. I think mum's burning her 'special incense' again as well. What is that horrible whirring noise?"

I reached over and clicked off the milkshake machine. "The kettle," I lied. As much as I liked seeing her, I wasn't keen on my house having the same open door policy as her and Tanya's. Letting her know there was a milkshake machine would not help me out with a hot summer pending (trust me on that, Teb had seen to it). For another thing you could see the swimming pool from the kitchen window.

"Sounds like it's in pain."

"So what's up, aside from you?" I asked, hastily moving the topic on as I poured my milkshake into a tall glass.

"I wanted to say sorry for annoying you today. Um. I think you were, anyway? You didn't like me barging into your house."

"Ha-rumph," I said, somewhat self-mockingly, now I'd had several hours and new dramas piled on top of it all. There was a pause as I wandered through the tall glass doors in the lounge and stepped down onto the warm patio, soothing on my bare feet. I realised that she was waiting for me to say something… Like accepting her bloody apology. I cringed. "I wasn't mad at you," I said, hoping she'd take that pause as confusion over why I was supposed to be annoyed with her, not me being too annoyed to reply. I wasn't… exactly.

The point was, I definitely wanted to stay friends with her. "Bleh, sorry, I think the hot weather is just making me grouchy."

"It's okay."

"So we're still good?" I asked, padding across the patio. "Still friends?"

"Yeah, of course. How cruel were your friends before if you're worried we'll stop liking you over something so silly as this?"

I wanted to have a good response to that, but instead I hissed, "Damn!" I'd spotted a huge floppy sunhat, my mom's new one for the summer, from behind. She'd taken the very pool chair I'd been aiming for. I sincerely hoped she was asleep, getting a book-shaped pale square in her tan. I backed away, then when I'd put enough space between us, turned and quick-walked back through the doors and into the dark living room.

"Alana? What was that?" Ally asked, while I was busy trying to remember exactly how loudly I had been talking until I'd spotted Mom.

"Never mind," I said, heading up the stairs instead. My hand gripping the chilly glass was beginning to feel a little blue, and the prospect of drinking this whole thing sitting in the shady house seemed suddenly a lot more daunting, potentially riddled with brain freeze. "What were you saying?" I prompted.

"Well I actually called to say… Argh, Tanya! She drives me crazy sometimes! Always running off when you need her or showing up when you don't… I can't believe she came to the station today! I swear, I was half-testing her to see if she would and what do you know, she exceeded expectations. How did she even know? No one told her!"

"I think she just does… If chaos will result from her being there. It was like everything happened at once when she turned up." Safely in my room, I sat on the edge of my bed, still holding my milkshake in front of me, not sure where to put it down without spilling it. I didn't want to make slurpy straw noises down the phone after already making the effort of lying to Ally about something so stupid. There was clearly something wrong with me.

"Urgh, yeah. Well, at least we got Teb back and got home without too much fuss."

"It was suspiciously easy," I admitted. It had been bothering me as much as anything else here. "I don't know Teb as well as you, though the changeling was a poor copy. You think we definitely have the right one? I know none of us really talked to her aside from me, and I can't really judge…"

"Well, you saw the changeling. It didn't act anything like her." Ally sounded deeply uncomfortable.

"I suppose it didn't have any good reason to try. We had the real Teb right with us. Who would it be fooling pretending to be her?"

"Um…"

"Maybe," I prompted, since she was having some trouble, "you should phone her up for a chat, you know, just to congratulate her on having her real body back and all, maybe ask her how she's doing her hair for the prom, I don't know. If anyone could say they were talking to the real Teb it's you or Tanya."

"Blah, Tanya."

"Okay, seriously Ally. I know she's weird and disruptive, but you've been her friend so long *surely* that can't bother you or you'd not have stuck it out for fifteen years."

Ally heaved a sorrowful sigh, then coughed because she and drama don't go well together. "No," she wheezed. "But since… Since the thing with the fairies when we met you… She's been different. I don't feel like I understand her anymore. She's playing a game and we're not in on it this time."

"These are weird times, Ally. I know to you I sound really collected and knowledgeable, but I have just had more time to get used to it. All of you, even Tanya, need some time to adjust to a life where magic is real. Teb's another whole step behind, and you're running second last thanks to Tanya having always believed in it. There's something about her, like she has a sort of psychic edge or something, a sense of everything way more than we can feel, and I don't think she realises that none of us have the same feelings as her. And then she might have only just got her confirmation she was right, but I've been through the wringer for years more than you lot. And while none of us are on the same page with each other, we'll never realise that all of us personally feel overwhelmed by what we know and do and see… You have to build a whole new sense of self around these facts. I quit wearing emo clothes, you know? I mean, Teb only just found out, so she's barely going to be herself for a while, even if she really is literally herself again."

"What?"

"Uh —"

"Oh, right, I see."

"Point is… Don't get too jumpy around Teb and assume she's a changeling if she's a little odd to begin with." (That probably had not been my original point or the thrust of my argument when I began this conversation, but it still felt like a pretty important thing to say, so my shaky rhetoric could be excused here.)

"Should I be phoning her up to give her a Q&A about Teb's likes and dislikes then?"

"If she *is* a changeling, then she'd know all that stuff anyway. She has access to everything Teb."

"What about all the stuff that's happened since the changeling copied Teb?"

"Oh, you are asking all the right questions today, Miss Guardian. Even that weird dream link aside, the changeling can't be that clear on what's happened these last two months. Why not phone her up now for a pop quiz on What We Did Last Month?"

"Will do!" Ally chirped, and a moment later the line went dead.

"Yeah, goodbye," I sighed.

I switched hands on the milkshake, after throwing my phone onto my pillow, and slowly unclenched icy white fingers fixed in a death grip around an imaginary glass. By now the ice cream had separated out, floating in a dull peach-coloured layer above thinner red gloop from the strawberries. It looked deeply unappetising, even after I gave it a whirl around with the straw. I felt cold and sad all of a sudden.

Everything about that conversation *should* have cheered me up, I felt. So why did I feel utterly rotten? I flopped back onto my bed and stared up at the ceiling.

There came a knocking at my chamber door.

"Go away," I complained, but not loudly. Mistaking my mumble for some sort of permission to enter, Mom came in.

"Where've you been?" she asked. It wasn't an outright accusation, but I could hear it in there.

"Just out with my friends," I complained, not looking her way. She was a lot taller than me, and wider too. Her shadow filled the room, darkening all but the far corner of the ceiling, standing in the way of the slanting window as she was.

"I thought we agreed that you weren't going to give our address out anymore."

"It's not my fault she tracked me down. It's a small village and we have a *really* obvious car. Ally might be daft as a brush, as they say, but she certainly has eyes in her head."

"Well then, if they want to come over here, maybe they should. I should meet your friends."

"Oh Go-odie," I said, catching myself mid-blaspheme before I gave her something to be angry about.

She was less than thrilled with my tone anyway. "What are they like anyway?" she snapped. "Are they good girls?"

I cringed, better than saying "Ha!" or something. She only meant something along the lines of, "Please say they are at least *some* denomination of Christian. I can live with that."

"Good as gold," I said. "Nicer girls you couldn't meet. One's a bit of a hippie, one's a bit... away with the fairies. Teb's pretty normal, though, for someone mostly raised as an atheist."

I saw Mom shudder a bit, like she was only just allowing herself to come to terms with the horrors of the sixth form that picked up all the dregs of the comprehensive school she'd sent me to. "It seems I have to meet them," she said, adding afterwards in a rather unconvincing way. "They sound delightful."

"I'm sure Ally will have told the other two how boring it is here and put them off coming... There's no need..."

"You're being ridiculous, Alana. Invite your friends around — tomorrow if you like. You're all on summer vacation now, so they should have time to spare... Since they find so much time for you *out* of the house."

"Aren't I supposed not to have any stress now I'm on holiday?" I grumbled, realising too late that was an open invitation for her to tell me to go get a job.

"You be grateful that I'm letting you *have* a vacation. I was this close to sending you to your grandma's for a summer school." She held up two fingers which were pinched together instead of showing a valid measurement.

"You would never have been able to make me go."

Mom gave this long aggravated sigh she always used in conversation with me. I used it as a standard for when I needed to wrap things up or we'd be shouting at each other through slammed doors for the rest of the afternoon.

"Mom, I *know* what psychopaths look like. Ally is about as far from that as anything can possibly be. The rest are alright. You don't have to worry about me making bad judgement calls with my friends again. I've learned my lesson." The Piper had seen to that very well: he'd pretty much assigned me these friends for one thing.

"Well then you have nothing to worry about when they come around for dinner."

"Mom, please... Just leave me alone." It was that or get back to telling her not to invite my friends around, and if I said it again, there *would* be a fight.

The thing about Mom was that she always sounded this weary combination of sad and passively angry... Mostly she just sounded depressed and neutral, like she'd given up on expecting any good to happen. She never took any pleasure in a victory against me. She felt no humour in inflicting suffering on me. It was just a resigned sort of acceptance that this *had to be done*. The only problem was she was completely illogical and unfair and tyrannical, and had a firm set of beliefs of what *had to be done* that didn't correspond with anything compassionate about accepting your only child for who they are and the fuck ups they make.

The shadows drew back from my ceiling and I heard her close the door behind her. Not slamming it. Thank God for that.

This wouldn't be the last I heard of that crazy idea of hers. I could feel it in my bones. Maybe I was kind of psychic like Tanya as well.

*

For a couple of hours I cleaned up my room. I wasn't confident enough to recycle all of my notes left over from the A Levels. I was pretty sure I'd have to retake something, if not all of it. But I packed everything away into a storage box and shoved it under my bed, out of mind for the time being, shutting away the horror that I was going to have to stay in this stupid place under my stupid mother's thumb for another stupid year while all my friends left for brighter futures.

Once I'd done a search for laundry I realised that I was retroactively making my room fit for Ally to see it. That deflated my zeal for tidying. I sat on my desk chair with a creak from the wonky back, and for a while I just cringed over and over to think that she'd been in here, seen my room in the state it had been after weeks of hard study and accumulating cans of energy drinks.

That was where I'd ended up when Tanya called, around about seven.

"Hey!" she practically yelled down the phone.

I cringed again, but just because she made my head hurt. "Hello? What's up?"

"You fixed Teb, right? We should meet up to celebrate!"

"Should we?" I asked dubiously.

"Yeah! Everyone's so gloomy, I don't know why..."

"I think we're just waiting to see if there's any fallout to having brought Teb's real body back. We can't just say, 'Everything's great! She's back!'... I mean, we barely know what happened in the fairy world, thanks to you, but if Teb had been physically trapped out there, mind and body, and then rescued, we'd have to be treading so carefully. Maybe it's just weird that we're not? I think I'm just waiting for a shoe to drop, and I hate that I'd be in charge of fixing it. The Piper should be all over this, but he hasn't said a thing to me about how well I handled this or if we fucked up somehow. I mean, maybe he showed up to decontaminate Teb and he just hasn't found a moment to tell me, or..."

"Alana. You're overthinking this. It's Teb! She'll be fine! Let's go to the pub!"

"Do we... do that?" I could not recall a single instance of anyone in the group so much as mentioning the pub, or drinking anything aside from tea.

"Sure, we've been going to the pub for lunch or whatever for years. Well, of all of us I'm the only one who isn't eighteen, if we're talking about drinking. Are you coming out or not? Everyone else is."

"Have you talked to them yet?"

"No, but I'll be able to persuade them." I didn't doubt that.

"What about me?"

"Peer pressure usually seems to work well enough."

"Oh, all right."

She had me there.

*

Teb showed up dressed head to toe in purple. There was a purple scrunchie in her hair and a one-shouldered top in dark purple like the last part of a sunset. A skirt which, in frilly layers, went from dark indigo to a delicate lavender. She wore dark tights and her battered purple ballet flats.

"Impressive," I said, since no one else was likely to call her out on it. Ally was too busy stressing over needing her ID to go into a pub, even though this was the most relaxed country pub ever, and Ally was old enough to drink *and* was only getting lemonade despite all that. Tanya was trying to convince her that she'd been in there a million times without being asked for ID, and Ally was countering that now they looked old enough to drink it was different. Somehow Tanya could keep arguing past that point instead of crying for the death of logic. She was wearing a pair of bear-paw-shaped earmuff-headphones around her neck, despite the heat. She was automatically disallowed from commenting on other people's clothing choices.

"I'm sick of wearing gold," Teb said. She flounced past me to the bar and demanded a bottle of wine from the barkeep. We were all dragged into showing our ID, despite Teb claiming loudly that she was going to drink it all herself.

"Are you sure you can even *drink* all of that?" Ally asked her as we headed to a table in the corner. Teb had a bottle of red wine by the neck, casually swinging it at her side as she walked.

"Of course," she replied scathingly.

"Have you even eaten yet?" I asked, seeing why Ally was worried. Teb was not a regular drinker, and her returned body looked frail and weak. I thought she was probably just stomping around so much from sheer willpower. In her place I'd have slept for a week.

"Oh... No." Teb seemed sort of confused. Perhaps Tanya had called her out after she'd showered and dressed but not before she'd had a chance to get food: months of starvation would make her a little woozy and confused, especially when it was just thrust on her like that, and by now the magic of fairyland would be wearing off and she should have been starting to feel it. She looked spacey, anyway.

"Get a jacket potato or something before you knock back too much of that,"

I advised. "Or it'll go straight out your head…" Not to mention right back out of her mouth a few minutes later, more likely than not.

She nodded. "Silly human bodies, am I right?" She strode back to the bar, ponytail swinging behind her.

"How *did* you persuade her to come out tonight?" I asked Tanya.

"I just said we were going to the pub. It was Ally who was hard work."

Ally grinned bashfully.

"I suppose it's not like she's *actually* been anywhere, as far as she's concerned," I admitted. "It's not like she *needs* to cram in time with her family. She didn't miss any."

I watched Teb as she stood at the bar. She was fiddling with her hair, clearly tutting about the wait for service, if her expression was anything to go by.

"What do you think, then? Is that Teb there?" Tanya and Ally would know best, having known her longest.

"Almost certainly," Ally replied at once.

"Maybe certainly," Tanya said, frowning. "Teb is impulsive *sometimes*, but she's very self-conscious about it when she is. She never tried actually justifying drinking a whole bottle of wine, not even a 'ha ha, not like I'm an alcoholic now' or anything. She just up and bought it."

"I should have a glass of it maybe," I said. "She's going to be so sick. Changeling or not, she needs to remember that she has limits."

"It's not like she ever overindulged while she had the fairy body," Tanya said. She'd clearly never had to quick-march across several miles of uphill countryside after a rampaging Teb who had decided to ignore the complaints department in her legs. "This is new. New and Teb is a bad combination. It suggests what we have now is not entirely the same as what we had before. There's so many other things that could have happened to her in the mean time, if it is still technically all the Teb we knew when you add up all the constituent parts."

Teb came back before we could discuss it more. She plonked herself down, throwing a napkin-wrapped knife and fork down with a clatter, and scowled at us, clearly noticing we'd abruptly stopped talking when she reappeared.

"So how are you enjoying this realm?" Tanya asked cheekily.

"It will suffice, for the time being." Teb's face was stony. Then a wonky-toothed smile broke out on it, and she made an odd noise which I think may have been laughter. I'm not sure I'd heard Teb's laugh before that point. It wasn't lost on me how pathetically relieved even Tanya's answering laugh was, never mind Ally's woeful attempt at mirth.

*

A couple of hours later we helped Teb stagger from the pub. The night had come and the air was unexpectedly crisp. Unfortunately for me the rest of my friends were cold-resistant either through drunkenness or habitual poor dress. I was the only one hopping up and down rubbing goose-pimpled arms.

"Let the cold air do its work," I said through chattering teeth, since Ally looked utterly lost about what to do now we'd moved Teb. And Tanya… Well, she appeared to be stargazing. "She'll sober up enough for us to send her home, hopefully."

I had helped Teb over to one of the benches either side of Troutespond's war memorial and she was leaning right the way back, joining Tanya in contemplation of the night sky. Slowly, slowly, she straightened up, then flopped forwards, ending up with her head between her knees.

"Um, don't throw up," Ally advised, dancing a nervous step back. Of course she was wearing her ugly old flip-flops… Not the best footwear to have on around a groaning inebriate.

"I am still impressed that she drank the whole damn thing," I said.

"I'm fine," Teb said. "A little dizzy, maybe." She was swaying, even with her arms attempting to pin her head in place.

"You needed two of us to help you walk," I pointed out.

"Maybe we should go back to my place?" Ally suggested. "Mum's really understanding, and she'll know what to do as well."

"Oh dear… Calling in the responsible adults," Tanya sighed mournfully.

"Only you would think that Ally's Mum is a responsible adult," Teb hiccupped.

"Alright, let's go," I said. Not like I was trying to hurry them along or anything, but I was trying to remember the first stages of hypothermia.

"Easy for you to say… You're too short for her to lean on," Ally grumbled. We'd tried it, since Ally was hardly a reliable leaning post, with a tendency to fall over nothing even sober. But Teb had practically somersaulted over me the first time she'd begun a drunken meander and I'd put myself in her way.

I lifted Teb's bag. "I am upholding part of the sacred duty of looking after a shitfaced friend. See? All her stuff is safe, and her phone hasn't sent a single drunk text!"

"Who would she even be drunk-texting?" Ally asked, not meanly, but baffled.

"True, all her friends in the world are right here," I said, not baffled but meanly.

"Chris King!" Teb yelled, as if it were as much a revelation to her as us. "I can drunk text Chris King!"

I pulled the phone out of her purse and held it out just beyond Teb's reach.

"Alana!" Tanya and Ally cried, aghast as Teb swiped at it and completely missed by over a foot to the left.

"What?" I asked innocently. "It'd be really funny."

"Teb, get a hold of yourself," Tanya said earnestly. "Just because people are normally idiots when they're drunk doesn't mean that you have to be! Do you really want to be a *normal idiot*?"

Teb lunged at me. "I need to! Give me that phone!" she screeched.

One second I was standing there laughing and holding the offending device up, the next she had crashed into me and sent me spilling onto the paving stones. She was still so much taller than me that even as skinny as she'd suddenly become she had me pinned down as she struggled to grab the phone off me. Ally was making shrieking noises in the background; Tanya was at least quiet, although not helping because she was completely absent from this altercation.

"I don't have your freaking phone!" I yelled, kicking helplessly. Teb stopped trying to pry open my empty fist and looked down at me, confused. She wasn't angry. That was the scary part. I wrenched an arm free and shoved her off me.

As she fell onto her butt she saw where her phone had skittered away when she jumped me: almost as far as the curb. She leapt up, grabbed it and ran off.

There was a stunned sort of silence as her footsteps faded, except for the ringing in my ears. I rubbed the back of my head as Ally and Tanya blinked at each other, dumbfounded. Tanya had leapt back onto the bench, practically into the arms of the town hero's statue.

"She didn't see that the battery had fallen out," Tanya croaked. I was amazed she was shocked. I suppose there had to be a first time for everything. She pointed to a shiny black square on the ground halfway between me and where the phone had fetched up in the fight.

"Well, at least she won't be texting anyone," I said, picking it and the back of Teb's phone up and dropping them in Teb's bag.

Ally and Tanya said nothing.

"What, are you actually waiting for *me* to say it? You know her best. That was a changeling there, or I'll eat my shoes."

War Councils and War Crimes

We ended up at Tanya's, since it was closest. It was also far less suspicious for us all to lock ourselves in her room to talk. Her dad was a quiet, private type, unlike Hester. Ally's Mum would have been at the door trying to offer us all freshly-baked oatmeal raisin cookies. And that was if we got the door closed in the first place. Ally was only one step up from sleeping in a converted airing cupboard.

"I'm honestly amazed that she – it – fooled you as long as it – she – did," I said, swivelling back and forth in Tanya's desk chair. I was sitting in it backwards, leaning on it with folded arms. There was a reason the similar chair in my room leaned back like a limbo dancer and made alarming cracking noises if you tried to straighten it up.

Ally passed a stress toy, water-filled with hundreds of wobbling pink feelers, from hand to hand. "Well it made *sense* that it was Real-Teb," she pouted. "The stuff they yelled at each other when Teb ran off… What on *earth* happened at the station if we *didn't* bring Teb back?" She had her back against the wardrobe, long legs stretched all the way across the fuzzy pink rug to touch her toes on Tanya's night stand.

We both looked accusingly at Tanya. She was sat on her bed, looking through her text messages with a frown on her face. She glanced up, took in our dark expressions, and looked even more confused. "What?" For someone who always seemed to know everything, she did a good show of being ignorant of what we were annoyed about.

"It was your fault. You disrupted the ritual," Ally pointed out, mashing the stress toy.

"I did no such thing," Tanya said.

Ally bristled, but, bless her, words did not come easily to her when she was so furious and so it was a simple matter to interrupt before she found a coherent line of argument. Or twisted that toy so much it burst.

"If Teb didn't want to swap back and neither did the changeling, Cathy would have found it next to impossible to complete the spell," I said. "Fairy magic. It works on conviction. The changeling said a lot of things to Teb that I shouldn't have let it say. It seemed to have convinced her that she had a chance to go to the Green Man again... Maybe I should have listened more when Teb told me she was in love with him."

"She's *what?*" Ally shrieked, thankfully dropping the stress toy in her surprise. It bounced away under the bed, the feelers' movement giving it a strangely organic look, as if it were consciously running from her in fear. I didn't blame it. Angry Ally was a rare and terrible sight.

"I thought he was dead?" Tanya said, more joking than confused. Like ha ha, isn't Teb crazy?

"Off topic," I complained.

"Well if he's currently dead, then she has an awfully long wait until next spring for him to take her in again. So Teb's run off but she has nowhere to go. Isn't that a valid point to be making?"

"I suppose, but that leaves pretty much anywhere Teb had gone. We don't even know anything about that train, unless you have some mystical knowledge of the fact there's a fucking ghost train in town. I don't think we can do much about Real-Teb at the moment. The real question is what do we do now that we know we have a changeling instead of Teb here?" I used my best council of war voice.

"Go and find the real Teb and bring her back!" Ally said, no hesitation.

"What are we going to do about the changeling though?" Tanya asked, thankfully coming up with an argument for me so I didn't have to face Ally's wounded puppy look. She was already in such a mood with Tanya she merely scowled at this suggestion. "It's on the rampage!" Tanya said earnestly, and again for rare facial expressions from her, there was real anxiety present.

"Do you know much about changelings?" I asked Tanya, who was usually something of an expert, even if she hadn't weighed in with a "well, actually..." about the goblin express.

"What do you know?" she challenged, raising her eyebrows.

I bit my lip, racking my brains but finding authentic fairy lore was a pretty steep task because people had so many fanciful ideas and talked about them at great length online, and I wasn't sure what I had absorbed that was fact or fiction, because I just hadn't come up against the real things enough to start sorting through the nonsense. "I know some lore about *baby* changelings, but I've never even seen one. They're a lot more uncommon these days... Fairies don't seem to like modern babies, or maybe everyone using webcam baby monitors has put them off trying."

"Well, we know it wants to cause trouble," Tanya said, interrupting my attempt to puzzle out things with matter-of-fact clarity. I was annoyed she was interrupting me, but I was also sort of grateful. The eternal duality of being friends with Tanya. "And whether it was affected by the alcohol or not, it has issues controlling its reactions down to a human level, because wow-eee it flipped. Which means it's going to be wild and unpredictable, and hellbent on causing as much trouble as it can now that we've unmasked it. I'm pretty sure that it was trying to fit in before, but the prospect of sending drunk texts… Well, it's a reminder of our own ability to sabotage our lives without any help from the supernatural. It just proved too tempting when it *could* have done something destructive and we wouldn't have batted an eye. But it blew it."

"So have you got any good news?"

"It's still a fairy, even in Teb's body. They have rules and weaknesses aplenty. We just need to get close enough to exploit some of those."

"Trick it or trap it, right," I said, nodding.

"What about Teb?" Ally demanded.

"What about her? She's a tough cookie. And she *chose* to run off. We can deal with her after… The changeling on the loose is a much bigger issue."

Then I got those wounded eyes turned my way. I should have let Tanya say it: it must have been on her lips before I got my grouchy reply out.

"She's our *friend*. We should be helping her first! I'd run right after her if I knew the first thing about how to even do that. You two are the ones with all the knowledge of magic and fairies and Other Worlds and so on… Why are you still sitting here? Why don't you go after her?"

"Ally, honey," Tanya said in the most motherly voice imaginable.

"What?" Ally snapped. "Why are you taking that tone with me?"

"Alana already said it. Teb wasn't magicked away or kidnapped. Nothing happened to her except that she made up her mind to leave. You know what Teb's like when she puts her mind to something. Imagine trying to pull her away from anything 'normal' and you'll see that this is already running close to impossible. Let her get it out of her system a bit and perhaps she'll be more willing to talk to us and see that she has to come home. In the meantime, what we can do for her as *really* good friends is try and clear up the changeling mess, so when we bring her back the whole town doesn't think that Teb is a psychopath."

"You're unbelievable!" Ally declared. She looked around desperately, grabbed the stress toy from under the bed and threw it at Tanya. Then she jumped up and ran from the room.

Tanya and I sat in uncomfortable silence until a moment later we heard the front door slam.

"Thank goodness we went to my house instead," Tanya sighed. "Imagine if she'd stomped off and left us sitting in her own bedroom!"

"Aren't you worried?" I asked, swallowing hard over the snakes writhing in my stomach at the thought of Ally including me in her thoughts as she stormed away. Part of me wished Tanya hadn't brought me into it… An even madder part of me wanted to chase after Ally and take her to Teb right now. In just a few minutes we could be walking through the knee-deep golden meadow on the reverse side of the skate park, with weird fairy stars wandering about above us. Who cared about Tanya?

But I knew she was right. She'd been on my side in that fight, after all.

"Pfft, no," Tanya said. "We used to fall out all the time. Ally is terrible at holding grudges and being angry. She'll be crying already, and by the time she gets home she'll just be nervously fussing about how long she has to wait to call me and make things up."

I felt horrible that Tanya had confirmed that Ally would probably be crying because of me, but not much I could do about that right now, unless there was a more urgent problem. "She won't go running off into fairyland without us? She does know how to do that still, right?"

"Yeah, but no. Not Ally. She's a meddler but then she's also a coward, in a good, self-preservation instincts way. She might phone me up and ask me to come with her for back-up but I can say no. I think… I think we're on the same side this time."

That was an odd thought. "Well, if you're so sure about that."

Tanya just nodded cheerfully, a massive smile on her face.

"Well then… I guess, how do we stop the changeling?" I asked her.

"I don't know. We need to find where it's gone first. We really ought to have followed it when it ran off."

"Don't blame me… You and Ally stood there like morons. I was too busy checking myself for a concussion, so I think I'm allowed to not take the blame for once in my life. Which way did she even go?"

"Back up towards her house."

"Oh, *great*. She – it – knows it can't trick us, so it's gone back to people who'd be genuinely horrified if she started acting violent or doing whatever character-defaming stuff the changeling can cook up."

"Well, what are we waiting for?" Tanya hopped up and grinned at me again, offering me a hand.

"It's not a joke," I grumbled, letting her haul me to my feet.

"Oh come on. Don't say that you're not enjoying this."

I didn't say it.

*

We jogged through the dark town, Tanya leading the way with her long strides. She wasn't lanky like Ally. I forgot this most of the time, but she was pretty athletic and competitive. Ally had told me about how she and Teb used to sit and chat in PE classes. She'd never mentioned what Tanya had been doing during that time, but I was guessing she was vigorously warming up while Ally and Teb showed their forged notes to the teacher.

I huffed and puffed after her until we were stood outside a two-storey suburban building of modest modern design, identical to all the others in the little close I'd seen Teb disappear down the other day. The road was a recent addition to the village. Tiny square lawns, all perfectly mowed, lined a gentle U of houses. At the end of the cul-de-sac the road was less a space to turn in and more the neighbourhood playground. In the dull light the chalky ghost of a hopscotch game glowed faintly. This late the street was utterly dead. Aside from murmurs of televisions, the front windows all flickering with blue lights from a dozen sets all tuned to *The Great British Bake Off* or whatever, there was only the rustling of trees beyond the houses.

"Are you going to go ring the bell?" I asked when we'd loitered long enough to ascertain that no one was screaming or shouting in number eight.

"Hmm. Too risky. We could put it to flight again," Tanya said, frowning. "There's no light on at Teb's window. We should go into the garden and peek in through the patio doors. There's no curtain there or anything."

"What if they *see* us?"

"Not if we're careful. And if they do, well… Teb's my sister, and I am hers."

"*I'm* not!" I complained. "What if all Teb's done at home is slag me off for the last few months? You know she never liked me again after the Piper reset her head."

"I think she disliked you before that."

"Not helping!"

"Okay. Well, you're still *my* friend. There's nothing weird in you hanging out with me."

"Isn't there?" Approximately two minutes after Ally had run off it had become the longest amount of time I'd ever spent alone with Tanya. Ten minutes on I felt uncomfortable still, and knew if it were not for our business with the changeling then we would have run out of things to talk about *before* Ally had abandoned us to each other's company.

Tanya gave me a confused look. "Of course not," she said, giving me a rather pitying smile. I remembered her strange affirmation earlier: maybe she really did genuinely like me and just had a ton of problems showing it. Before it got any more awkward (well done, Alana) she sidled past Teb's Mum's big red car and wiggled the gate wedged in the space between their house and the one next to it. The latch jumped up on the other side. She did it so quickly, quietly and competently that I had a feeling this wasn't even the hundredth time that she'd done it. It made me feel a little better about being caught in their back garden.

"Are Teb's parents very strict?" I whispered, following close enough on her heels to kick her ankles a couple of times.

"They're very nice to her friends," Tanya said, but didn't comment further. It did the job of reassuring me about my own skin (if I could be counted as one of her friends), but then I felt selfish and worried for Teb, who might be in so much trouble thanks to the changeling…

Once we had squeezed past a set of wheelie bins we came out in an immaculate garden. A small lawn filled most of the square, its undulating border lined with a shin-high brick wall which I could imagine had taken huge chunks out of everyone's leg at one point or another. A grinning clay garden gnome sat on the wall, something which had Ally's Mum's handiwork all over it. A line of apple trees at the back of the garden were barely even taller than me.

"Urgh, this place is so suburban and conformist," I muttered, ignoring the gnome.

"Yeah, you can see where Teb gets it," Tanya whispered back. She gestured me forwards and I dared to peep around the pale tan bricks of the house's corner. Just a sliver of the scene beyond the French windows could be gleaned at this angle. I could see a disappointingly modern slice of an open plan living area: an inch of an archway into a room with TV noises coming from it. A corner of a dining room table with a flowery cloth over it. I could see a few fronds of a pot plant. To the right were a couple of counters of the little kitchen, where the little boy I'd seen the other day was standing on a chair, washing dishes and getting soap bubbles on everything. He had probably emptied most of the bottle of Fairy liquid into the sink.

Now I began to see what Tanya had meant. Teb did like trying to be "normal", at least as far as it was possible to be. This seemed to be a trait she'd picked up at home. Her deliberately boring, acultural, atheist family had stamped itself all over her. Could it be that embracing the weird magic stuff she'd found about, running off into fairyland, was actually a rebellion against *this*? Nothing to do with us or anything the changeling had actually said to her?

Well, the family seemed utterly at peace, not even in an uneasy state like they'd encountered the changeling and were now tensely wondering what had happened to their daughter and sister, unless her parents were out of sight scouring the evening news for reports of that new drug all the teens were doing these days or something.

"Hrm," I said.

"The changeling hasn't been here," Tanya agreed.

"Can we *please* get out of the back garden of some people who are basically strangers to me now?" I hissed.

Tanya shrugged. "Alright then." She backed off. I sidled after her until we were back on the road, then I set off for the corner so no one would see us loitering anymore. The quietness of the sleepy little close was making my skin crawl by then. I was not as good at wrongdoing as I used to be.

"Where else might Teb have gone? Er, changeling'd Teb?" I asked.

Tanya looked rather amused by my paranoia: she was still sauntering after me as I paused at the road sign on the corner. "I don't know," she cheerfully admitted.

"You know *everything* all the time!"

"Sometimes I'm guessing or pretending or you just *hear* it when I don't mean to actually suggest that. Um. I have a few blind spots. A changeling running around in Teb's skin is apparently one of those."

"Oh. Great."

"But can't *you* find it? Magic always works best on fairies and the like, especially in this world."

I nodded. That was true enough. Magic took a great deal of belief from everyone involved. You could even argue that curses were nothing more than psychosomatic. Not only did you have to know that you had been cursed but you had to *believe* it too. I supposed it was a failsafe built into the universe to keep order, since I was then far too deep in the inner workings to have a clawing doubt that magic wasn't real and *all* trickery and superstition.

No, *he* had seen to that, and now Ally and Tanya between them had proved that this was either the most intricate shared hallucination ever, or something that I was just going to have to accept. I was finding witchcraft a great deal easier of late.

And using it so often on fairies helped. As naturally magic creatures they didn't even need to know that you were about to use magic on them: the world just assumed that it would work. And so it did.

I can tell you this much: I would never be able to set a human on fire in this world, no matter how hard I tried. Maybe not even in the Other Worlds. The most fearsome witches were those who could talk someone into giving consent to let them do such horrible things to them. I was... less than fantastic at the rhetoric that would be required to trick someone into thinking that I had any special powers over them.

"Easier, yes," I said. "I'd need to go home to work any magic, though. I need my spell book and all my reagents."

"Okay!" Tanya said brightly, like we were just discussing the next steps of plans to meet a friend.

"So I guess this is goodnight?" I hinted.

"*Ally* saw your house," she pouted.

"Ally bullied her way in."

"Hah!"

"She did!" I protested. "In any case, I prefer peace and quiet for casting spells, and *privacy*. Mom would be all over it if I brought a female friend back that she's never even seen before this late at night. And then shut myself in my room. The last thing I need is her to burst in on me in the middle of a ritual on top of everything else."

Tanya giggled. "She needs to meet us, though! She won't be so suspicious when she knows how nice and harmless your friends really are!"

"Pfft!"

"Maybe me and Ally should come around some time tomorrow? All official like?"

My stomach clenched. I was never going to get over Tanya's ability to coincidentally say and know things that that she ought not to, like that my mum had also been putting this pressure on me from the other side. "No!" I cleared my throat and tried to sound more reasonable. "Don't you think we have much bigger things to worry about right now?"

"Well, maybe, but it seems things would be easier if we could use your house as much as the others… Especially since you have all the witchy stuff there. Very useful."

Suddenly I was wondering if I should be grateful for my Mom, keeping me from inviting Tanya over and having her paw through all my stuff.

"Urgh," I helpfully contributed.

Her amazing psychic powers clearly told her that I wasn't comfortable talking about this. "Well, we can discuss it another time. You go do your spells… Call me when you know anything!"

"Alright," I said, and backed off before she had any more clever ideas.

"Byeee!" she called, waving.

I turned and trudged home.

Worse Trouble

The house was dark when I got back. I stood at the steps fishing out my keys, feeling their jangling was obscenely loud in the utter still of the night.

I crept upstairs as fast as I dared, slowing when I heard Mom snoring. I was secure as long as I didn't noisily fall up the stairs. I took the rest of the walk up to my attic room feeling my heart slow down. It was the first time since Ally's incursion that morning I'd actually breathed easily. Even at the pub I'd been wary of everything, watching Teb with very well-founded suspicion, and since then I'd lived in alarmed suspicion that it would be watching us around every corner.

My room was dark, as I'd left it. I flicked on the light and scowled up at the dim bulb. It took forever and a day to warm up to a decent brightness. At that moment my room was barely even mood-lit.

As I dropped my bag on the floor, kicking off my red flats where I stood, I felt a vague sense of unease return, that same sense that something wasn't right making the hairs on my arms prickle. At first I attributed it to the confusion of seeing my room something approaching tidy for the first time in months, having to relearn it in the dim light. Guilt, I suppose, for leaving a pile of shoes and stuff on the floor. But it wasn't that; for one thing, there seemed to be other stuff on my floor that I hadn't put there.

My senses suddenly kicked in, the hairs rising on my arms and neck, crawling with the sense of not being alone. I spun around. Teb was sitting on my bed.

No, not Teb. Of course. The changeling.

It was half undressed and lying on its side, watching me with eyes that had become far darker and shinier than Teb's own, as if filled with the fairy sky.

"Hello, Alana," it purred, running a hand down its side to rest on a bare hip.

"Oh Jesus Christ," I sighed, hastily averting my eyes. "I thought you were supposed to be *good* at mimicking other people."

"I don't need to be in this body."

I hesitated, stopping on my slow attempt to bend down and take my phone from my bag (I knew the changeling got a little weird around them).

What was it even doing here? It ought to know the feeling between Teb and I. It wasn't even like the sort of rivalry you got from a misdirected, misunderstood girl crush, and I'd had enough experience of those from both ends in the past to know what that all felt like. So why would it even try this? Not to expect sympathy, surely? To win me over or convince me to stop the others from trying to catch it? A sort of, do you not prefer me like this? For all it knew it could have come here to walk into a trap. Though admittedly if it knew what Teb did, it knew that was overestimating me. Yet here it was, reclining on my bed without a single toss given for what I might do to it.

"You think I won't hurt you?" I cautiously suggested. Too late I realised I ought to have phrased that as a threat. I hadn't even thought to take my lighter out of my bag, just my phone for back-up.

"I can't know that yet," it replied cheerfully. "You don't care for Teb much, do you? Would you burn up this skin just to destroy another fairy? It would all be part of your job."

"Why would you even come here if you think I'd kill you, then?" I snapped.

"I thought it would be funny." It shrugged, rolling one shoulder lazily. A smirk bounced onto its face. "You can't even look directly at me! You're terrified! What if… You dare to look up at me, and you like what you see? This is Teb's real body right here. I'm *giving* her to you if you want it."

I shook my head, because there was literally no reality in which I'd do anything with Teb, full consent given or not, but because I'm an idiot and I *always* end up looking when I shouldn't, I turned my eyes on it as if to prove that I'd be able to ignore that it had taken most of Teb's clothes off. I'm ashamed to admit I don't even know what expression was on its face right then.

I wanted to find a million faults with Teb's body, the one she would be stuck with when we rescued her, the flawed, human one. It should have been easy, right? I wanted to look at her and come up with all the catty things that girls said about each other when they were only just out of earshot. But my brain kept translating it wrong. "Too skinny" became a rather more diplomatic "slender". "Pallid" could have been a useful word to describe someone whose winter skin had spent two months underground. But "Like creamy coffee" was the revoltingly bland and probably low-key racist description I found myself musing over. Even a faint sense of amusement that Teb was dropping a few cup sizes when we reunited her with herself was lost in, well… acknowledgement of the existence of her chest, which was more than enough to make my cheeks pink and my stomach tight because I'd literally never been in such close proximity with a girl lying sexily on a bed and actually inviting me to look.

Somehow along the way, whatever I went through, I'd failed to learn that I was just attracted to girls no matter how much I might occasionally not want to be.

Still, just checking Teb out was not a crime, I'd accidentally done it many times before, but then I sometimes accidentally did it to just about anyone, and it wasn't weird when straight people accidentally did it in similar situations like Tanya's bad choice of skirt on a windy day. And Teb wasn't going to know about this, ever, over my dead body, so I could pretend this had never happened. The changeling couldn't claim any actual *trouble* had been caused here, no sir.

"Will you please get out of my room now?" I said through gritted teeth.

"No. I could shout," it said.

"What?"

"I could shout and your mother would wake up, and here I'd be, looking like this, in your bed…"

Welp.

"You could," I admitted, heart sinking.

The changeling frowned.

"Is that it?"

I shrugged. "Do you want me to freak out? Would that amuse you?"

The changeling licked Teb's lips thoughtfully. "Yes. And yes. But this? It's the resignation that upsets me. You sound this close to saying 'alright then'. Where's the fun in doing what's expected of me?"

I shrugged again. "I've been in worse trouble with Mom. Literally get in line to ruin my life."

The changeling actually looked alarmed. "What happened that this isn't scary?" It was very Teb: the madly curious pitch on the end of the question, desperate for some interesting gossip, the look she got when promised something to think about which wasn't humdrum nonsense.

Fortunately, that actually made it easier to ignore her. "Like I'd tell you." *Or Teb*.

Somehow this was not going as badly as I'd thought it might have when I first saw it in my bed, running a hand absentmindedly over Salem as if petting a real cat (he looked very unamused about being half-squashed under its hip). We had a dialogue going and despite having had no plan at all for how to handle it, I'd managed to convince it through my utter misery that it could probably find a more fun alternative to entertain itself this evening that didn't involve dragging Mom into it. I mean, I was terrified and it was a stalemate I was going to do everything I possibly could to avoid it breaking, but… I could survive this. I could.

Unfortunately it *did* have other options available.

"You know what would be really funny?" it asked me.

"Excuse my pessimism, but what?" You'd have had to go pretty deep underground to find anything darker than my tone.

"If something did happen here. Between you and me. You'd never be able to look at any of your friends again! Hilarious!"

"Er, one, no. Two, *no*. I never would. I know restraint, no matter what you think that I might want…Which I don't, actually."

The changeling inspected Teb's fingernails, taking a moment to run a thumbnail under one before it said, "Well then it's a good thing I wasn't planning on giving you an option."

She lunged at me again. I'd seen it coming, and braced myself against being knocked back. Unfortunately it wasn't planning on taking me to the floor again. Instead one abnormally strong arm lashed out, grabbed me by the front of the shirt and yanked me forwards. Braced against toppling backwards, I was completely powerless to stop myself from nosediving into the bed, sprawled across the changeling.

"Heh, heh, heh, hello there," it said, its face just inches below mine. Suddenly I wondered if it even knew how to laugh. Maybe I had heard Teb laugh before and it had been an unremarkable sound, so I'd never even thought about it.

"Pathetic," I said, trying to seem tough and not totally freaked out about what it planned to do next.

It grabbed me by the back of the head and shoved my face down towards its own so hard I could have got whiplash. I struggled against the painfully tight embrace, now utterly revolted, and also, in the back of my mind, extremely grateful that the changeling was such a monster. This was probably enough to put me off Teb for life even if I had thought she was hot before. Like an inoculation against this ever getting awkward later.

My lips were crushed into Teb's pointy chin. I felt my lower lip split, warm blood mixing with my spit.

I managed to wrench myself away from it, pinning its arms down with both hands. It was still stronger than me, I knew, but it was squirming. It seemed strangely brittle, or at least worried that it was: it seemed deeply unwilling to try and twist free, like it didn't trust the body it inhabited not to snap like a twig under pressure. Kicking its legs seemed particularly pointless when I'd seated myself on its midriff.

Teb's shiny mauve lipgloss was smeared down its chin, and her eyes were sparkling with an impossible number of reflections for the actual lights in my room. It *hissed* at me.

"You're disgusting," I told it. "If you had any sense you'd hand Teb's body right back and leave. Because you would not like what I have to do to you otherwise."

"What's that then?" it snarled.

I had no idea. I couldn't hurt Teb's body (much). She'd kill me when this was over if I hurt the changeling any more than I had to. And my magical knowledge was far too weak. The kind of things that Cathy could do seemed utterly absurd compared to my meagre spellbook.

I'd hesitated too long. Taking heart from my uncertainty, it suddenly writhed fiercely, knocking me to the side. It tumbled on top of me, rolled, and sent us crashing to the floor. It was pinning me down. Again.

When it made a grab for my neck I clutched my own throat in sheer terror that it might try to kill me, but instead it took hold of my collar and tore my shirt open all the way down to the bottom hem. "Oh Alana!" it shouted gleefully. "Yes!"

My arms were free, so I managed to punch it in the chin. There was no remorse for Real-Teb, who after all had put me in this situation by letting the changeling trick us into thinking we had the real her. A split lip was less than she deserved.

"Oh yeah, I like it *rough*!" it shouted, loud enough to be heard on the other side of the town. I could barely hear it through the furious pounding in my ears, the tunnel vision of rage and embarrassment. I struck at it again, but I didn't feel like I really did much damage. It had barely flinched from my first strike: it didn't care much for this skin, and now it knew I couldn't kill it with one punch it seemed happy to take another.

It grabbed my arms again, this time holding me down with just one hand so it could begin tugging on my skirt. The material clung to my hips, and for once being curvy was sort of useful. But it wasn't a very sturdy item of clothing; it would tear soon.

"Piper!" I yelled. "Help!" I'd been out of my depth the moment I walked in through my door. I had not had the sense to realise it until then.

The changeling suddenly became extremely light – in fact it lifted off me entirely, scrabbling desperately to keep hold. I saw one white boot, one black, standing behind it as its bare feet kicked in the air.

"That's enough of that," he said.

It snapped at him, biting his hand. He fumbled his hold on it and it dropped to the floor, twisted free of his attempt to grab it and darted for the window.

"No!" I yelled, staggering to my feet, my head swimming. But it smacked the skylight and slipped right through out onto the roof. I heard the faint clatter of tiles as it ran away. I chased as far as the window, but I couldn't even pull myself up through it: my arms just turned to jelly and deposited me in a heap on the floor beneath it. It was probably long gone, clambering down the big sycamore tree in the yard. By the time I made it downstairs I'd never be able to catch it.

"You'll kill yourself if you go up on the dark roof," the Piper said, reaching up and pulling the skylight closed, perhaps thinking I was about to leap right back up for a second try. I felt rather more like wallowing in defeat instead.

He was bent over slightly, too tall to fit under the deep slope of my ceiling. It almost made me smile a little to see him looking so uncomfortable, absurd enough to cheer me up despite everything as a weird sense of relief hit me despite losing the changeling again. For one thing, it wasn't attacking me anymore. But the feeling faded at once when I heard footsteps thumping up the stairs. For a crazy moment I thought the changeling was coming back to get me.

"Oh God, it's Mom!" I cried, sense coming back too late. I had time to struggle to my feet again, but I hadn't even begun to survey the damage in my room when the door burst open. Then, in the long moment when she stood in the doorway, panting with rage, I had plenty of time to take in a purple skirt lying discarded on the floor by the door, a style and size I never would have worn. I could have kicked it right under my bed if I'd had the sense… Then I realised that I was standing there with my tits hanging out the front of my shirt and my skirt pulled down to show off a corner of the smiley face knickers I'd chosen in a moment of terrible misjudgement. I ran a hand over my mouth to get rid of a slick smear of shining lipgloss and blood.

Mom still hadn't said anything: I was sure she should have erupted by then. But she wasn't even looking at me. I followed her gaze to where the Piper was still hanging about like an unwanted imaginary friend, despite his well-exercised ability to appear and disappear as he liked.

He grinned sheepishly and raised a hand. "Well met."

Mom backed out of the room so fast I was amazed she didn't tumble down the stairs. The door slammed. It took another dizzying minute before she started down the stairs, slower.

"And *breathe*," the Piper said.

Right as my vision started to go white around the edges I realised that I'd stopped. I took a huge gulp of air and hastily sat on my bed, resting my head on my knees until it had passed. I stayed like that for a while. I had no idea what to say to him… Or to Mom in the morning, either.

Did she really think me and the Piper..?

Well, she must. I wondered how he looked to her. I didn't dare ask. Something that hadn't seen him thrown on the street, although I suppose after the fuss she made when I was forcibly outed to her, if she'd found me half-naked in my room with a hobo she'd still second-guess herself before chucking him out. It was one step closer to me giving her grandchildren, after all.

"I suppose there is nothing else to address here," the Piper ventured. Was he actually embarrassed? "I should leave."

"A second before she came in the door would have been better!" I burst out. "What part of 'It's my Mom!' did you take to mean 'stay here!'?"

He frowned. "If I had left you to deal with her on your own she would still be in here, searching for the other girl she would assume you were hiding. The changeling might even sneak back to cause more trouble if it sensed the house was in turmoil: revealing itself would be the last piece in the puzzle to make your mother throw you out the house, after all. Now that threat is neutralised and… I know how she feels about you."

"Just get out now," I croaked, waving feebly at him, like trying to shoo an irritating fly.

He kindly went.

I flopped back to stare up at the ceiling. My head was still spinning, my heart pounding with adrenaline. It was not every day that you were sexually assaulted by a changeling wearing a friend's skin, then instantly walked in upon by your mother with, for all I knew, a mohawk-sporting biker or whatever her worst fear of my taste in men had been before she found out I didn't have one.

I wanted to get up and change. Maybe hide the pieces of Teb's clothing strewn about my room. I *should* have called someone, but it didn't even occur to me. Instead I remained completely immobile, effectively paralysed, for what felt like hours. At some point my eyes ceased to be rigidly propped open. And then it was morning.

Same Colour, Same Weight, Same Size Feet

I woke up abruptly, far too early. The moment my eyes opened I knew that I would never get to sleep again, so I went to have a scaldingly hot shower, where my brain mocked me with the sort of mess of unstoppable thoughts that I'd thankfully not dreamed: confusing flashes of memories of the changeling attacking me; the way it had leapt at me in the street, pinning me down and tearing at me. I had long nail marks on my stomach and on my wrists that I hadn't even noticed or felt last night. They stung as the hot water pounded down on me. And then there were the times my mind fell onto the image of it posed for me, stretched out and inviting, wearing just Teb's bare flesh. Trying to make me *ashamed* that I might be interested.

I felt no less confused and messed up when I was dressed, although that was nothing new. What was new was a text from Tanya. *-Meet in village to discuss changeling @ 10?-*

I'd spent over an hour in the shower, I realised. That meeting wasn't far away anymore. I didn't bother replying but pocketed my phone and headed downstairs.

Mom was up and dressed as well. She practically leapt from the sofa, the newspaper falling to the floor, the pages scattering. She accosted me in the front hall.

"Alana, sweetie…" Her voice actually hurt my head. It hurt worse to feel her hand close over my heart and squeeze it. When had she talked to me in such a soft voice since I'd come home from Waitington? "Is there anything you want to talk about?"

"Not to you," I said shortly, and yanked the door open so hard it juddered on its hinges and almost slammed itself shut in my face with the rebound.

"Well, if you want…"

"Fuck off!" I snapped, and this time endeavoured to be on the other side of the door when it slammed.

I snail-walked to the centre of the village, my senses tingling with wondering if the changeling was nearby. I didn't see it and it may not have been anywhere close, but I felt like it may as well have been watching me the whole time.

I'd arrived early, but so had Ally. From the state of her you'd have thought she'd slept on one of the benches.

"Are you okay?" I asked with a pang of emotion, fear that the changeling had visited her next suddenly gripping me.

She blinked sluggishly at me. Finally she remembered to reply. "Oh! I haven't slept, but that's fine. I never sleep. Who needs sleep? It means I can be on time to meet you and Tanya!"

"Right," I said. Why don't you ask me how I am? I thought at her. But she didn't. I folded my red-lined arms behind me, suddenly feeling like she had no right to notice if she didn't care.

Though we were both twenty minutes early Tanya showed up at that point, having clearly anticipated our arrival.

"Ah, great!" *She* looked fine. As lively as ever, if not more enlivened by having something interesting to do. I hated her. "Alana… Did your spell work?"

"Huh? What spell?"

"To find the changeling? You *did* do it, right?"

I hadn't needed to. The last thing I wanted was to find the changeling now. I didn't even know why I'd come out that morning except that I'd have been sick if I stayed at home any longer. "No."

"What do you mean *no*?" Ally squawked.

"Um… I forgot."

"How do you *forget*? Teb is *lost to us* until you track down that changeling! Do you not want to find it? I know you hate her, but we care! You should have looked for it for *us* if not for her!"

"I'm sorry, I —"

"Sorry isn't going to bring Teb back!" Ally yelled, point-blank range in my face. Tanya had said she wasn't very good at being angry… This was *deafening* and I think she had it down pretty well.

I wanted to cry. I wanted it with almost every fibre of my being. Somehow I thought that if I cried everything would be okay again. If I hadn't been able to summon up a single tear for anything else that had happened, then surely Ally yelling at me would have loosed one tear? I begged it to appear.

But instead I found myself saying, "Well maybe I don't care about getting her back. I don't know why you care either when she abandoned you. Again."

And I turned and walked off.

A moment later a blackened flip-flop came hurtling past my head, but it missed. I deliberately stepped on it on my way past.

*

It took me a long time to realise where my feet had taken me. The first conscious decision I made was when I paused at the bottom of the embankment, then scrambled up it.

I sat on the long metal barrier that lined the motorway and watched four lanes of traffic rushing one way, four the other. There were hundreds of cars, lorries and coaches in sight at any moment, and the sound blended together into a huge roar, no individual car standing out, save a steady beat from the closest lane, *whush*, *whush*, *whush*, as they passed at eighty miles an hour.

Northbound, I thought. Heading to Waitington if they took Junction 83. Waitington… Huge, grey mess of a city. About as soulless as I felt that morning.

I remembered the first time someone had tried to take advantage of me. It had been in Waitington. The underpass beneath the library, to be precise, where I'd been sleeping. Where I had been left to sleep when my body couldn't be forced to go any further without collapsing. *He* had reached up through me, even as I was still waking up and wondering about the hand on my arm, and, calmly as anything, he had taken the man's head in my own hands and twisted it most of the way around on his shoulders.

I missed that strength. I missed the fearsome way *he* protected me, lashing out at even the smallest thing, killing without a thought if someone wanted to hurt me. I missed the perverse feeling of enjoying having him inside me, on my shoulder, whispering to me and holding me. I missed the shapes he took in my head to please me and make me compliant to being possessed. He appeared as the girls who'd dared call him in the first place. Who had *given* me to him because they thought it would be funny.

I was sure Nita's lips were not actually as soft as he played at her, or Del's breasts quite so smooth and pale, but I preferred his versions of them anyway. I thought about how he might try to be Ally for me… Would he fill her figure out? Airbrush the freckles into order, wipe the lopsided, nervous grin off her face into a classy pout? He'd drape himself around me with confidence, lanky arms bare and not about to accidentally elbow me in the kidneys because she'd fallen over her feet… I laughed and then felt horrible for doing it. None of that was why I liked Ally though. Most of it was the opposite.

At some point I'd managed to start crying, but I knew it was about all the wrong things. Here I was considering selling the last pathetic shred of hope that the Piper had bought for me, and all because I found it too hard to be yelled at by a girl who left the spoon in her tea and almost took her eye out every time she drank.

It didn't make any sense.

I knew I couldn't go back and give in to that power, though. Not when he was still lurking somewhere close behind me, just waiting for me to break.

I stood up.

The cars seemed incredibly close.

I carefully stepped out of my shoes. I nudged them with my toe so they were neatly pushed together.

I looked down at the road. An orange truck was powering its way up this lane, slower than the cars ahead of it, a little gap in the traffic moving quickly my way.

I felt the hot tarmac warming the soles of my feet, rough and prickly. I looked up at the blurry sun. I *did* hope that Teb found him, wherever she'd gone on her quest to locate her missing lover. It wasn't like I *actually* hated her.

I took a tiny step towards the white line between me and the cars.

A hand gripped my arm.

I whirled around, not entirely by choice, and Tanya yanked me over the metal barrier. I tumbled down the embankment with a shout, and for several seconds my world was filled with long grass bouncing past, taking turns with the sky to be on top.

Then the clouds were sort of still, if my eyes would have stopped rolling in my head from dizziness.

I heard a *crunch crunch* as Tanya picked her way down after me, and two small thuds as she threw my shoes at me. They landed not far from my head.

"Why did you take them off?" she asked.

"I dunno," I said thickly. In my state of mind it just seemed easier to answer her questions and deal with Tanya being Tanya.

"I do," she said.

"Why?" It was a pretty dumb riddle.

"They're Teb's shoes," she said.

That shook me. I sat up and looked at them. I hadn't even noticed this morning, but they were indeed purple instead of red.

"Oh. They are."

Tanya sat next to me in the grass, stretching out like she was at a picnic. "It's funny you have the same sized feet as her. I suppose you have to have something in common."

I curled up my toes, like clenching them would hide the length of my feet.

"Dad smoked a lot with me in the room when I was little. I think it stunted my growth. Like these feet… I should be able to look Ally in the eye. Not that I'd want to anymore. Why did you follow me? Why not Ally? She must have been upset. You've been friends longer."

Tanya shrugged. "I told you yesterday. Ally deals with stuff. You looked like you'd reached the point where you couldn't even lift the huge suitcase of baggage you've been dragging around with you and refusing to open."

"But… I'm not even your friend. Not like *them*. The three of you… It's perfect. I barely even fit in with *one* of you."

"You've been our friend for months."

"I've barely *known* you plural months."

"Well, we clearly made a snap decision, but we're not regretting it. You really think if Teb didn't like you she'd drag you shopping and share her popcorn with you at the cinema? When she makes her mind up about something she can't be moved."

"I thought she was humouring me… For Ally."

Tanya laughed at that. It was weird the Piper had assigned me to watch her in particular, in priority to guarding Ally and making sure Teb's head didn't explode. Tanya was the loose cannon, after all. I'd barely even *thought* about her for the past two months.

Yet if I wasn't as chicken as I usually was then she may well have just saved my life.

I had to think about something else. Like how normally she was taking all this. I clawed my way back to our conversation. "Aren't you going to ask me about how I ended up with Teb's shoes?" I asked suspiciously.

Her big blue eyes boggled at me, but it was nothing to do with confusion. "I think I can guess." She reached out a hand as if she were about to take mine, or put an arm around me or something, but I flinched away and then had to make it look like I was doing *something*, so I picked up the discarded shoes. I didn't have any other shoes with me, so I slid Teb's back on. They really did fit well. Hadn't her toes been bleeding into these two days ago?

I didn't want to think about anything: now was a time for action. "Fine. Let's go catch a changeling," I said.

Tanya sprang to her feet and offered me a hand. I looked at it suspiciously, then took it. She hauled me up.

"I was thinking we should go for lunch at yours!" she said brightly.

I wondered just how far back she'd been building that trap. For the changeling and myself.

How to Cook for Changelings

I don't know if Mom could have been more amazed when I traipsed in with Tanya and Ally in tow.

"We're expecting our friend Teb as well," Tanya said sweetly when polite introductions had been made.

Ally was still confused about the fast turnaround, not least since Tanya had barely explained anything to her. She only glanced my way a couple of times and hadn't spoken directly to me yet. Tanya, brilliant at getting stuff done, seemed less concerned about patching things up as worrying about the changeling.

She'd run home to announce on Facebook that she and Ally were going to mine and said something similar in a very loud voice in the centre of the village. I'd followed her mostly mutely as she hurried around enacting things. But I was thinking the same as her. The changeling seemed still strangely fixated on us and one way or the other it would know what we were doing. And it would more than likely drop by because it would put us in a situation where we knew what it was but couldn't call it out… It knew how scared I was of Mom. Tanya was turning my fatal weakness into the only strength I had to offer the group.

So we sat and made excruciating small talk about how well my friends were doing at school. Tanya had gone home to change as well as to broadcast our location, and she looked the straight A student she was claiming to be: a formal shirt with a light cream sweater vest over it, a navy skirt that came past her knees. Black lace-up shoes. Her usual pigtails actually went with the look she was going for. I was surprised she hadn't brought out a lens-less pair of thick-rimmed glasses.

Ally, of course, was wearing baggy jeans and a t-shirt with a hand-painted rainbow on it, her usual attire for anything. She seemed a little embarrassed of her flip-flops and kept shuffling them under the sofa.

As we were getting to the jobs they were applying for over the summer, the doorbell rang.

"Aha, that must be Teb," I said brightly, masking the terror I felt quite well, knowing Ally and Tanya would catch the sarcasm and be my back-up here. Mom beat me to standing up, so she went to answer the door. I sank back into the armchair and looked around for support, swallowing hard.

Tanya nodded encouragingly at me. "Just get through lunch and then we can get the changeling upstairs and away from her."

"You'll stay with me, right?"

"Of course." She smiled warmly. To be honest I had no idea how much she knew of what had happened to me the night before, but she was saying and doing all the right things, so I didn't really care.

After a moment of hesitation Ally gave a small nod. It seemed Tanya was right about her being lousy at holding grudges. My heart warmed up a little, and for the first time that day I began to have a little hope that we might be able to deal with the changeling.

Mom came back, leading the creature. It was smiling and dressed head-to-toe in purple again. I was beginning to wonder if Teb had an actual condition relating to the colour. No one should own so much of something they could make more than one complete outfit all in that colour (except black, of course).

"Hey Teb!" Tanya said, like nothing was amiss.

A much worse actress, Ally only mumbled something. I made an expression that was more of a grimace than a smile.

Mom didn't seem to notice our rather odd reactions to the entrance of our "friend".

"So, Teb… Tanya says that you are studying to be a doctor?"

The changeling settled itself into an armchair and reached across for one of the cookies on a plate in the middle of the table. Spraying crumbs out from a biscuit shoved into its gob whole, it replied, "No. I mean, that's one of the options…" Speech more tortuous than expected, it swallowed, continuing with only half a mouthful. "But I'm keeping an open mind. Maybe I'll go travelling? This place is so boring, isn't it?"

"Boring?" Ally demanded, hopefully intentionally leaping to the bait. Tanya, too, looked affronted.

"Come on, all the wide world is out there, no walls to stop you going where you like. I have always dreamed of seeing more of it than this. Didn't you know? I can't imagine being stuck in a shithole like this for the rest of my life."

Ally was practically bubbling over in barely-contained rage. I wondered how much of that was true to Teb's feelings. The changeling knew her best and was sitting there with a shit-eating grin: it had access to everything that made Teb. Sure, it might just know the best way to wind up my friends because of that… Or it was teasing us by letting us know all the secrets and things that Teb *really* thought of the world.

Mom, for her part, looked horrified. "I will thank you not to use language like that in my house!" she snapped. "I shudder to think where you learned to talk like that."

Ally and Tanya both looked affronted by that. While I might have had the worst vocabulary of them all, Teb came a close second, swearing more than those two put together. But that didn't mean that they hadn't been the ones to introduce her to all the words. I shrugged innocently. I hadn't been instrumental in teaching Teb English slang at a young age.

The changeling seemed to decide that it ought to play it safe for a while after that, and it made reasonably pleasant, if deeply disturbing to us, conversation about parent-friendly topics until Mom went to check on lunch.

The moment that she was out of the door the three of us bristled like angry cats and turned on the changeling.

"Well, isn't this fun!" it said.

"You be grateful we can't do anything until after lunch!" I hissed.

"I'd be a bit more careful about what you say," Tanya added mildly, leaning over and putting a hand on my shoulder. "You seem to be making Alana quite angry..."

The changeling laughed. "Oh no! What is she going to do? Cry at me?"

I just about reached for my lighter then and there, but managed to stop myself by imagining what Mom would say about all the ash on her clean cushions. Also, I suppose, Teb would not be happy if I lost her real body in a moment of anger against its current occupant.

My friends didn't get a chance to come to my defence, if they were going to at all, because Mom came back. "It'll be ready in a minute, so why don't you girls go wash up and sit at the table?" Her manner suggested she'd composed herself a little in the kitchen... Or maybe just preparing food was a great way for her to destress.

"Yes Mrs Larbie," Tanya said, all simpering obedience. In my anxiety over the changeling I'd actually forgotten that this was all Tanya's ploy to see inside my house for the first time.

Still, she and Ally were a lot more on the ball than me. I had yet to stop drifting about with a brain mostly off, and it was down to them to form a guard around the changeling, marching it into the dining room so it never got a chance to slip away, the damage done by its visit more than adequate already. I was going to have to be explaining all my decisions to leave the house for the rest of the summer.

The dining room also had a view of the swimming pool. I resigned myself to a summer of sitting around my own pool with the others practising divebombing when I saw Ally and Tanya both take a step towards the window, smiles appearing on their faces. I sighed and pointed at a chair. The changeling sat.

Mom came in with a dish of greens in her hands, and the rest of us plopped down into seats.

"Yuk," the changeling said, eyeing the salad warily.

"Shut up and take some. They're good for you," I found myself saying.

"Alana!" my mom complained. I scowled. She had been happy enough to tell the changeling that it was being rude herself.

It just giggled, turning its eyes on me. The meaning behind its smirk wasn't lost on me. "Look," it seemed to say. "Here I am and I can ruin everything and you can't stop me."

I looked away quickly, turning my sour look instead at Tanya, who had dared to bring it into my house again.

Thinking of going into houses, I was being a little slow on the uptake here, but its clean clothes meant that it had gone back to Teb's house at some point in the night. I didn't like the thought of that, although I (and maybe Tanya) knew that was better than a half-naked Teb showing up for lunch. It certainly hadn't looked like it had somewhere to store its house keys. Perhaps it had climbed in the back way there as well then. It might have been under house arrest if it had gone to ring the doorbell wearing barely anything.

So unless it had found some time to terrorise the general public, something which took a bit of effort in such a small, quiet town, then it was still only Teb's immediate friends and the Piper (and now Mom) who had experienced any of its true nature.

Mom brought out a few more dishes and joined us. I'd wisely started serving up and encouraged my friends to eat before Mom had even brought out the last thing. Her lips pursed up, but she didn't say anything about being denied her chance to say grace.

The changeling was already halfway through a huge helping and busy gulping down more. Maybe it had been trying harder to fit in at the pub, or we'd excused "Teb" for how hungry she was at the time, but now I saw just how awful its table manners were. Food was splattered all around its plate, pushed off to either side as it inexpertly used the fork to chase morsels around. A trail led from the plate to its face, dribbles of salad sauce all down its front. It made me smile a little to think of Teb coming back to find her clothes ruined, strewn across the town and covered in food.

"So, *Teb*," Tanya said, neatly spearing a cherry tomato on her fork without even a little squirt of seeds, "what are you planning on doing next?"

Fun fact: the fair folk are incapable of lying.

"I don't know," it said.

Fun fact number two: they're also rubbish at forward planning. Trying to interrogate them is more than useless. I doubted it had been thinking anything more than "This ought to be fun!" when it heard about the planned lunch.

"I know where my counterpart is going, though," it said.

The three of us all jolted upright in a synchronised "Oh my god! It knows about Teb!" moment. Then we all sank back into pretending nonchalance, in various speeds of uptake on how silly we looked. I glanced at Mom. She seemed confused, if I was reading her frown right.

"*Where?*" Ally cut in, desperation ruining any attempt to sound tough that her slamming both hands on the table might have hoped to accomplish. The salad cream bottle wobbled then, just when it seemed about to settle down, tipped over. Tanya caught it just before it hit the table and popped the lid back on.

The changeling crammed more cold ham slices into its mouth and chewed for an irritatingly long time. Just as I felt like Mom was about to ask a question it spoke instead.

"After riding in an endless loop on the ghost train, first she went to enact justice on those who wronged her. Then she fled to the grey town to see a witch who could tell her about the stars. From there she crossed the haunted woods in search of the goblin market."

"How do you know this?" I demanded. Tanya could deal with the riddle. I needed facts behind the magic.

The changeling gave me a rather pitying look. "How do you think she got to see her lover every night until they killed him? I've been watching *you* for two months in return."

I suddenly lost what tiny bit of appetite I'd managed to scrape up for the sake of appearances.

"You know what, let's go watch a film upstairs," I said, standing up and leaving my cold cous-cous untouched.

"Alana, what *is* Teb talking about?" Mom asked. "Are you in a cult again?"

Ally jumped up too, almost overturning her chair. "I don't think Teb is very well," she said. "Let's go upstairs so she can lie down."

I cringed and waited for Tanya to stand and offer a third excuse for leaving, but she was just grinning.

"I'm still eating," the changeling said.

"Alana, sit down," Mom snapped, knowing enough to see I was trying to hide something from her. "You're being rude to your guests."

Suddenly it was all too much for me. I could feel the same swirling in my head as last night, exhaustion and stress pulling on me until I could hardly think straight.

"But I'm doing it too and *I'm* a guest!" Ally babbled as I wavered.

With not enough prior experience of Ally, that actually stumped Mom. She hadn't learnt yet to just ignore everything that came out of her mouth at that speed.

Tanya finally got to her feet as well, her plate miraculously cleared, knife and fork folded on it. I was surprised she hadn't taken it to the kitchen and done the dishes too in the time it took us to work through this latest tangle. "Well, come along, Teb!" she said, skipping the part where we agreed or disagreed about the actual going. She leaned across the table and picked up the bowl of freshly cut strawberries that were waiting for dessert. In amidst all the other stuff I don't think Mom even realised how odd that was.

"Why are you bullying me so much?!" it complained. "I've only just met Alana and even she is always telling me what to do!"

"*Please* come upstairs, Teb?" Tanya begged. I'd noticed her shooting almost as many glances at Mom as I had. I didn't blame her. While confused, she could still read our faces plain enough, and the changeling's odd behaviour was steadily getting me into a position of having to explain more and more after they left. Of course my house had made the perfect trap for that very reason, but I'd been assuming Tanya would have the changeling in hand *before* Mom had enough material for a first degree grilling later. I *hoped* this was a sign that Tanya felt properly guilty about it.

"Since you ask so nicely," the changeling said, once we had all sweated for a while. It stood, nodded to Mom and headed for the door. We stumbled after it, surprised by its change of heart.

Out in the hall, Tanya and Ally both clamped a hand on one of Teb's arms each, apparently without communicating first. I had no desire to touch the creature again.

"My room's upstairs," I said. Ally looked up as far as the second floor landing and quavered at the memory.

"What did you mean by all the stuff about witches and goblins?" I demanded from the changeling, as we headed up the stairs.

"Just what I said," the changeling replied.

"Yes, but… what does it… even mean?" Ally asked, panting by the first landing. Okay, she made me look in shape… At least I was fit enough to manage my own house.

"The first part is clear enough," Tanya said. "She's going around beating up any pixies who… were mean to her while she was with the Green Man. She must have rode the train back again but I suppose she realised that she couldn't stay in Troutespond. There's only one witch in the village and since that's Ally's Mum we'd have heard about it before now…"

"Unless Ally forgot," I pointed out.

"Hey!" Ally complained. "I *probably* wouldn't have!"

"And Bilsworth is very grey in the fairy world, I hear. There's not much there, but I wouldn't be surprised if there was a witch there who Teb could communicate with. It's a very human-influenced spirit world, so it's easier for those who know about it to peer beyond the veil. And that quiet a town always seems to have secret occultists living in it."

"And the rest?" I demanded.

Tanya shrugged. "I've never been beyond Troutespond, and just heard tales about what lies outside or down the train line. Mostly it's goblins who use it, and I was with pixies most of the time I was there. Goblin culture is a bit beyond me."

"Oh, *now* there's a limit to your knowledge," Ally huffed.

We got to my room. I closed the door behind us and did the thing with the chair under the handle, just like in the movies.

"Now what?" Ally asked, sinking down onto my bed. I quickly looked away from her.

"Trap it," Tanya advised, leaning over to put the bowl of strawberries on my desk. The changeling drifted hopefully towards it. "We can't have it climbing out of the window or something."

"How do we do that?" Ally asked, muffled by the pillows on my bed.

"Don't you have a spell for it?" Tanya prompted.

"Ooh… Yeah. Yeah." I shook my head and went over to my bookshelf, trying not to look too obviously like I was shying away from the changeling. Its eyes followed me and a shudder went over my skin on that side of my body. I gave it a dismissive look and pulled my spell book down.

"Do you have a spell for everything in there?" Ally wondered. I'd brought up the existence of this book before, but they'd never seen it until now. The Nancy Drew cover made it a bit embarrassing to carry around in public now that I wasn't eleven.

"No," I replied, then felt guilty for speaking so shortly to her. I didn't have time to ramble on about how I built up a spell book over time, I told myself as I flicked through it. Maybe I could explain to her later when things were a bit easier.

I'd had to bind creatures before, so at least this was not an unfamiliar spell. It was something that I'd picked up early on while working for the Piper when I wasn't brave enough to make any decisions on my own. At the time I had thought that the angels were watching me, maybe even wondered if he was one of them as well. At least I worried that they were hovering close enough to tell me if I slipped up. But if I ever broke the conditions the Piper had negotiated for me, they never told me. As I drifted further and further from Christianity and into what sort of paganism someone like me can manage, well… You remember what I did to the last fairy monster that I had encountered in the line of my work.

I spoke the rather unedifying words of the spell as I took a step around to where Tanya was sitting in my creaking chair, and touched her and the changeling on the forehead at the same time. The changeling realised how unceremonial it was and that I was actually already doing the thing way too late – it flinched away and I almost poked its eye out with my thumb, but I got it.

"What now?" Tanya asked.

"You're bound together," I said. "It's not going anywhere fast."

Tanya stepped away from the changeling. It was forced to make a faltering step along with her.

Then it wrenched its arm back, and Tanya practically somersaulted forwards.

"I think your spell has some flaws," she complained from the floor. She used the invisible rope between her and the changeling to haul herself up. Thankfully whatever weird Sight she had meant she could instinctively reach for it and see the threads of the spell.

"The important thing is that it can't get too far from you," I said. Very clever of me, forgetting how strong the changeling was. I suppose I'd been matching them up, trump card style, and reckoned Tanya's wily ways would best the changeling in any situation. Wily ways were a little useless if you were knocked out.

"Let's sit over here," she said, dragging the changeling along with her. She sat on the floor and took it with her. Then she handed over the bowl of strawberries… A portion for about eight people, I'd have said, factoring in Mom's love of overcooking. And she'd had that on hand *before* I showed up with my new friends.

The changeling tucked into it with handfuls of berries, and suddenly I understood what Tanya had been doing: if all else failed, fairies were stupidly easy to control with their love of fresh fruit and sugary things.

Ally straightened up, recovered after perhaps the shortest power nap ever. "What do we do now?" she asked.

"We have to find Teb," I said, looking away from the changeling with a shudder when I saw red rolling down its chin.

"*Now* you say that," she groaned.

"Well *now* we have a captured changeling, we actually have something to swap her for," I pointed out. "We can't have two of them running around this world."

"So more magic?" Ally asked hopefully.

I was tempted to whip open my Nancy Drew collection and start throwing spells around to show off for her, but I shook my head. "We're outclassed. Tanya might be able to outthink a changeling, but I can't outmagic one, let alone untangle whatever Cathy did in the first place. I'm going to make a phone call first."

The girls all stared at me as I found my bag, pulled my phone out and scrolled through my contacts. I glanced up to see them all staring. "What?"

Tanya looked put out enough that I could guess: whatever I was doing it hadn't been discussed with her, and she was all about making plans. She was clearly worried I was going to mess things up.

I put the phone to my ear.

It rang once, then was answered with a casual, "Hey Alana – just fighting off some vampires. Can I help?" Never claim that you've lived an interesting life once you've known the Piper any length of time. He'll put your whole life achievements in weird to shame in half an hour.

"Yes you bloody well can," I snapped as I heard a gurgling scream on the other end of the line.

"Sorry, what was that?" he asked innocently.

"I caught the bloody changeling! Now tell me what to do with it!"

There was a pause, filled with some loud bangs and thumps. Then there was a huge crack that made me jump and hold the phone away from my ear. Ally and Tanya were watching me with a mixture of alarm and amusement. As I tentatively brought the phone back to my head, I could hear the Piper again. "Phones are pretty good weapons, in a pinch."

"Uhuh. I thought you said vampires don't exist?" (I'd had quite a list I'd run through when we first started working together…You'd be surprised what does and doesn't make the final cut. Though clearly he could not be trusted to tell it plainly.)

"And I intend to keep it that way. If Teb ran off of her own free will I can't do anything to bring her back."

"She *belongs* here."

"Not in her mind. Something convinced her to leave, and that has sealed the changeling's place in your world. We went over this with Tanya. I brought her back when I accidentally carried her in. When she ran into the fairy world of her own choice, there was nothing I could do. If you think bringing Teb home is the right thing to do, you're going to have to find her and talk her into it by yourself, on your own time. It's not my place to tell people what they should be thinking."

"Well, great. Thanks. Have fun with those vampires."

"What vampires?" he asked. I could feel his smug, cocky grin from where I sat safe at home.

Safeish, I thought as I hung up on him, and looked over at Not-Teb to see that it had finished the strawberries and was watching me intently.

I wanted to shout something at it for being so in the way, but Ally got there first: "*Vampires?*" she demanded. Tanya's eyes had gone rather wide and shiny with interest, I noticed, when I tore my gaze from the smirking changeling.

"Why is the Piper interested in them?" Tanya asked at once.

"What about the *changeling?*" Ally cut in, like she hadn't been the one to derail the conversation in the first place.

"He was, unsurprisingly, completely and utterly useless. Do you have any better ideas?"

"*Magic,*" Ally and Tanya said as one.

"Oh my *gods*, you two are terrible. Magic is not and never will be the answer to a personal crisis! I can't just magic up a solution!"

"Should we get Cathy?" Ally asked.

"You can try," I said. "We will need to find Teb again, though, and bring her to Cathy or Cathy to Teb."

"Well can you do some magic to find Teb?"

I almost barked out another "No!" but I realised that I was going to have to at least try something. They would march out and give up on me if I just sat and whined and said I was useless: I was walking a fine line to convincing them. Or, rather, making them realise it was true. But this was a council of war and we had to come up with some answers and plans.

I looked around and saw Tanya was leafing through my book. A chill ran down my spine and I rounded on her. "*Give that to me,*" I snapped.

Tanya smiled sweetly and threw the book my way. The changeling made a lunge but the spell snapped it back, and it sprawled on the carpet.

"*What?*" I demanded of it, hoping a burst of anger would make them forget I'd leapt back almost as far as the door when it moved, dropping my phone and spellbook.

It straightened up, rubbing rug burns on its elbows. Teb's elbows. "What are you going to do now?" the changeling laughed, dark eyes flashing with malice.

"Kick your ass if you keep being so obnoxious. Sit quietly while I try and find Teb, would you?" I approached cautiously and picked up my book.

"It's not going to work," it said, still rubbing fluff out of its scrapes.

I ignored it.

"Move it, Ally," I said. She slid off the bed and hovered awkwardly in the corner, stooped over as the Piper had been. My gods, those two. In his coat, out of the corner of my eye, she really did seem to mirror him.

I pushed my bed back a couple of feet, the better for negotiating out a huge portable chalkboard, something my old school had only got around to replacing with wall-mounted whiteboards in the last couple of years. I'd scavenged this one from a dumpster. The important thing was, aside from being great for drawing circles on, it was a free-standing object... If a spell went wrong, I was much more likely to end up with only a possessed blackboard that I could take out back and cleanse with fire, not a whole house of angry spirits. Now *that* would get me in trouble with Mom.

I withdrew to the middle of my floor and quickly flicked through my book of magiks until I located a Spell of Finding that had helped me a lot in the past. I'd used it to keep track of Tanya back in March, so I knew the fairy world was no barrier to it. Usually it was fairly unreliable when tracking something, because it only offered location, not realm. We knew full well which one Teb was in, though, so we weren't going to have to mount ten expeditions to cover all the bases.

"Let's see... What do I need? Something of Teb's... Her name will more than do... And... Some other stuff to help with the search..." I grabbed the box of notes I'd made while tidying and rooted out a stack of papers Teb had lent me – her long name was neatly printed at the top. Perfect.

I quickly sketched out the magic circle between the splatters of oil stains and candle wax. I opened my laptop and within a few minutes was printing out a train timetable for the Waitington-Severstrong Abbey route from the national rail website, since Teb was relying on the train to get around. They didn't carry the fairy timetables, unfortunately, but it had most of the stops on there.

Whenever I glanced over at Not-Teb as I made these preparations she was watching me impassively, a smirk on her face, or a sceptical raised eyebrow.

Eventually I had everything ready, curtains closed, candles burning, the smell of magic (that is, homemade incense that Ally's Mum sold me at an extortionate price) filling my room.

"That's not going to work," Not-Teb said when she saw I was ready to begin.

I didn't pay any attention, beginning to recite the spell.

"I could *tell* you why it isn't going to work," she added.

I started reciting the second repetition of the spell.

"...Or you could just keep talking, and not pay any attention to me?"

I said the spell again, then sat back to wait. Tanya and Ally leaned in to stare at the board.

Nothing happened. Okay, it wasn't supposed to explode or send an arrow spinning around to point at anything, but I remained utterly unenlightened about her location. The others weren't to know it was as boring as inducing a mild vision though.

"Did it work?" Ally asked.

"Heh," the changeling said. "Are you going to ask why it isn't going to work?"

I sighed, and slumped down a little, breaking my stance of what I imagined tense witchcraft should look like.

"*Why* isn't it working?"

"As far as the spell is concerned, I'm right here."

"I'm not *looking* for you. I'm looking for Teb. I know the freakin' difference — there's no fucking computer program that runs all the spells through a database and gets confused by two similar points of data. I'm looking for the one that's been Teb the whole time as far as I'm concerned, and it should fucking *find* her!"

"But *I'm* Teb."

"You're fucking deluded, that's what."

"Language, Alana!" Tanya giggled.

"Shut up," I snarled. "You're not helping. Just go sit outside or something."

"With Not-Teb here?"

I sighed. "Whatever."

"Um... I'll go phone Cathy," Ally said. She hastily exited the room.

"Just pretend we're not here," Tanya said, casually patting the shoulder of the changeling. I started to chant the spell again, but the changeling just laughed, the sound throwing me off my concentration, shaking me with memories I couldn't afford the time right now.

"You think *I'm* deluded? You certainly aren't one to talk!"

"What do you mean?" I demanded. "We know this spell is supposed to work!"

"I didn't mean that... You're so busy fighting to convince yourself you're normal and sane you can't even concentrate on the spell... Fighting off your demons, if you will. You've got it into your head that the Piper saved you, but you're as trapped as ever!"

I looked sharply up at her from where I'd been correcting little wobbles in my chalk lines, like that might help. She was holding a folded square of paper, the look on her face saying, *Got you.*

"Alana?" Tanya asked in a tiny voice. She was looking directly at me, but I suddenly wondered if she'd read over the changeling's shoulder. Had she made me send Ally away so we could talk? She hadn't said anything to her, but...

"You're not going to be able to cast that spell until you own up to your other side," Not-Teb said, fiddling idly with the love letter.

"What do you mean?" I asked, shaking with horror that I'd been stupid enough to let the letter fall, never mind been unobservant enough not to see it drop... Or had Tanya stolen it? How had she even got hold of the book in the first place? Was she working with the changeling? It seemed to obey her all of a sudden...

The changeling kept on talking and talking, though I'm not sure all the nonsense words sank in at first. "Teb made the same choice you're going to have to. She chose rightly, too. I *am* Teb now. I've been her too long, trapped in this body... Having the *real* body is very powerful magic. It stops me from being a pixie, and her mind stops my body being anything other than Teb. We are *both* Teb, through and through. The problem isn't that she's not herself. It's that herself is two distinct people now. I'm Teb as much as Teb is."

"What did Teb choose?" I demanded, surprised with how furious I was – the candle flames around me flared up and then several snuffed out from the stress, while the others shook and splattered wax across the chalkboard.

"Alana," Tanya said again, earnestly, raising a hand as if to calm me. It was the one the changeling was attached to: it raised its arm as well, mirroring her. I took a deep breath, trying to calm myself after the shudder of anger I had felt. Pixies *wanted* to get to you. I was giving it what it wanted. *Just breathe.*

"Alana," Tanya said. "You –"

"She chose to be herself," the changeling said over her, not done babbling yet. I couldn't stop myself from listening, wide-eyed. At a dozen points I could have interrupted or told her to shut up, put some tape over her mouth... Anything other than sitting cross-legged on the floor like a kid in assembly listening to a teacher.

"I'm Teb now. The side of herself that she threw away. She's cut herself clean in half, and like starfish, we each grew to fill the empty half to make two separate wholes. Didn't you wonder why you could never make friends with her afterwards when you won her over in two days before? She didn't have it in her! It was all in me instead. I was her passionate side. The one that would want to be with the Green Man. The one swayed by the body and its desires because that's all I had when she first left me with this hollow shell... She threw me aside like she didn't need me, and left me to pleasure myself with the Green Man... And in this body I *dreamed* and felt love, and all those things Teb tried to deny herself before.

"She was *jealous* of what I had with the Green Man, when she saw what she was missing out on. She thinks that because of the dreams she got of what I was doing, what I was *feeling* for the first time... she thinks that she's in love with him. She wouldn't want a dead husband and an empty fairy life if she had her own body. She's gone because she wants vengeance, to be a cold and horrible Queen just like the Lady, just like *her* body is telling her to do now she has what was once mine. She thinks that is how to be by his side when he awakens again, but the joke is when Spring comes around again… She won't even know what to do with him. She can't actually love him because that's for me! I was the one who was with him all summer!

"Just know that she wanted to trade places. She wanted to escape from people who'd try and make her feel the things she didn't want to feel. People like you trying to be friends with her. She wanted to go live in a world where the rules were simpler, and someone who knows how to work them could be a Queen in her own right. I appealed to her logic and she took the bait, and went for what would make her happy. She's more of a pixie than I am now – she's got no humanity left. She threw that all into me. I am her fucking *human body* after all.

"So here I am, seeing this world that I'd dreamed of since the switch. Feeling the things of this world in their real context. Tasting fruits that don't drive a person mad. Eating cream that doesn't sour on my tongue. Walking through a world where symbolism is just chance, and magic doesn't have to control everything. I wanted to see a world that's bigger than a dream, a proper *creation*, not just a concept. My desire for this world has filled up the empty half Teb left behind… I have my own purpose here now. It's my world. *My* body."

It took me a moment after that to realise that she had stopped talking; the words were still ringing in my head, over another "*Alana*," from Tanya.

"You aren't Teb," I croaked eventually, an automatic sort of denial I didn't need to think about. I didn't know how much of what it had said was right. Maybe it was true – maybe that was why the spell hadn't worked. Getting a vision of the very room I was sitting in could go completely unnoticed, I supposed. But it had hinted there was another reason. "How does this relate to me?"

"You're just as split as Teb is, but not in a way that we can all see. There aren't two Alanas sitting here arguing. Still, it's there…" she waved the letter. "You love this demon. You love Ally. It's like the Piper's big theme – dark and light, balancing between evil and good. You're wobbling back and forth, and you keep saying you've chosen, you've chosen, you've chosen… but the demon sent you the letter. He loves you and you found the hardest thing ever was giving him up, no matter how badly he treated you. And the letter got through. You know the only way you can destroy the link that lets him send these letters? To clear your mind and set yourself straight…"

"I don't think I'm going to like your suggestion for how to fix that."

"Tell her how you feel, and you'll get your magic back," the changeling said. The wicked grin was such a Teb look on her face, but Teb was never actually *evil*. I think I'd met demons who were less of a monster than this Teb/changeling.

"How do you know about Ally?" I asked, trying to stall. And also because all my anxiety kind of built up in a big sticky glob around that point.

"It's freakin' obvious," Not-Teb said, rolling her eyes in that "Oh why are you such a moron?" way I'd grown used to in Real-Teb. Out of the corner of my eye, I think I saw Tanya nod, although I'm hoping that was just my imagination being paranoid. "Probably the only reason Ally hasn't noticed – *if* she hasn't – is because she's too caught up in her little happy love bubble over the Piper. And if she *has* noticed, she's dreading you ever saying a word. She's not going to take it well, even if it does come out of the blue... But the issue is what's going on inside *your* head and *your* heart. If you want to find Teb, then you're going to need to come clean, whatever the consequences."

I glanced over to the door. Ally was outside it, probably putting off coming back in, terrified of what might be happening. She never had long phone conversations if she could help it... Was her ear pressed to the door now? Had Mom cornered her and for once actually saved me some awkwardness? Whatever she and Ally talked about couldn't hurt as much as Ally overhearing this.

"Alana..." Tanya sounded almost bored now, a kid raising her hand again and again to get the teacher's attention.

She didn't have it. "Why the fuck should I trust you?"

The changeling rolled Teb's eyes again. "Do you *really* want to keep casting that spell all night? You're *not* going to make it work."

I relit the candles and determinedly began reciting the spell again. Not-Teb sighed and sat back, watching me with amusement – infuriating enjoyment radiated from her at my suffering. Tanya leaned forward, reaching for the board. I slapped her hand away and finished the spell. It continued to do nothing, but little surprise there – I don't think I could have done *anything* in this state of mind at any time.

"*Alana*," Tanya said, exasperated.

"Alright!" I yelled at last. "Ally! Get the fuck back in here!"

The changeling smiled its smuggest smile.

The door opened, and she peered in, all confused wide eyes and chewed lip. We hadn't been shouting... Had she missed the point up until now?

"*Alana!*" Tanya said, raising her voice for maybe the first time I'd ever heard her do so.

"Shut the *fuck up!*" I yelled at her, then felt extremely ashamed for doing so when she just looked pityingly at me. I suddenly remembered earlier in the day, her hand on my arm, yanking me back before I could do anything stupid with fast-moving traffic. She was looking out for me... How could I have thought she was working with the changeling?

"What?" I asked in a more measured voice.

"You're using the wrong name," she said, leaning over to point the circle.

I reeled with embarrassment and confusion: it took ten seconds for me to even dare read the little scrap of paper I'd torn off.

"This... This all happened because she didn't put her full name? Why didn't you *say?*"

Tanya just gave me a look. I remembered how many times she'd tried and turned away, inspecting the paper. The twenty-five letters of her name all seemed to be on there — I hadn't accidentally ripped the end off or something.

Ally leaned over to look as well, resting a hand on my shoulder to bend over. "Teb Nandi... I *think* that's right? I remember it all because her first name is actually three names shoved together like that godawful baby in Twilight. We see her aunt Yazmina sometimes, and I talked to her Nan on the phone once and she's called Ayasomething but all she spoke was Punjab, so I was basically just..."

"Can't you hear yourself?" Tanya said before Ally could give us her interpretation of Teb's family tree with accompanying anecdotes. I pushed her hand off my shoulder. "What's her dad's surname?"

"Nandakishore," Ally said at once, fluently.

"What's Teb's surname?"

"Nandi. Nandi... *Nandi*... oh."

"It *was* the right name," Tanya said smugly, gesturing the notes. She sounded too fucking pleased to have worked out the puzzle.

"*Was?*"

"She changed it. She's *changing* it. Not-Teb here can say whatever she likes... You can't find her because she's sold her name."

I Did Say Not to Listen to Them

"Excuse me," I said calmly, standing up and leaving the room without looking at anyone. I went into my little bathroom and had an embarrassing minute of leaking as quietly as I could from the eyes and nose, holding back sobs with a fist shoved in my mouth. When I could finally breathe without hiccupping I splashed water on my face and glared at myself in the mirror. I wasn't really sad at anything: it was all just anger and stress overwhelming me.

My hair had gone wildly curly at some point, which happened when I skipped a single day of proper care routine, and there were bits of grass seed in it. The dye had half-washed out in the last few weeks and the effect had become much more pronounced while everything else was a shambles: the red had faded to bleached gross ginger and a solid inch of dark brown roots wound their boring way beneath the messy tangle on top. My face was blotchy, streaked with lines of dark mascara and eyeliner. I wasn't even sure if I'd applied other make-up for a few days, but it had all gone now, leaving me feeling translucent and vulnerable. I dabbed at my eyes with a cotton swab, brushed my hair and wet it, ran handfuls of product through it to stop it from frizzing up. I smoothed my shirt down and reevaluated myself. Maybe not seaworthy, but no longer a total wreck. There was enough there to salvage. I hoped the same could be said for what was inside.

I nodded to myself. "Let Tanya handle everything," I said to Mirror Alana. "She knows what she's doing."

Mirror Alana didn't reply. I hoped there was no difference between us: just light bouncing off a really shiny surface beneath the glass. No magic. Mirrors don't trap your soul or show your inside to the world. You're being silly.

I went back to my room, where everyone was silent: maybe they were just uncomfortable with talking to the changeling, maybe they had been talking about me and stopped when they heard the bathroom door open.

Ally spoke right away. "Cathy says bring both Tebs to her: she's not going into the fairy world on her own."

"And I said we can't do that," Tanya said. "We can't start telling anyone we bump into Teb has a twin they never met before."

I didn't look at any of them, but went to sit by the magic circle again. I tidied it up, relit the candles that had gone out yet again, and tried to think. They didn't say anything else, out of respect for my thinking, or out of fear. Probably that one. We'd all shouted at each other more than enough that day.

"How did you know she'd changed it?" I asked Tanya, still squinting at the scrap of paper. My eyes blurred, refusing to take in the long string of letters. *Teb Nandi* my brain told me, while I stared at a name that sprawled ten centimetres across the page in Teb's looping handwriting. Her dad's name was Nandakishore. I could make that reconcile with the word in front of me: it was basic logic. That was his name. That was the name she had used the whole time I'd known her. It was right there on the page. It was… *Nandi*. The middle syllables melted away like they'd never existed and I couldn't even see them. A trick of the brain. The most powerful magic I'd ever encountered. Someone who had completely erased two thrird of themselves from the world.

Tanya shrugged. "Something just felt really wrong when I was looking at that piece of paper with her old name on it. It seemed unfamiliar, but all your names… I know them so well. They work together almost like a spell of their own: my friends with their names beginning with…" Her voice worked silently for a moment, and she tried again. "Ally. Alana. Teb… I *know* she was like Ally. I sorted her that way. Same letter." Her eyes shone in wonder. "I can't even say it. You were out of balance because there were three of you with names beginning with the same letter and there was me with my name beginning with T, and now… There's a sort of balance that wasn't there before even though we just called her Teb anyway. I think. Teb 'n' Tanya. Ally 'n' Alana. It feels so right I can't even reconcile why I used to think so much about your names beginning with…" She gave up trying.

I nodded. Made about as much sense as anything else.

"So… Now we know what name to use, are you going to try again?"

I scribbled 'Teb Nandi' on a Post-it and rushed through the spell. The changeling didn't try to interrupt again. It had flopped back, defeated for the time being, and was watching us with sullen eyes.

I knew the spell had worked at once. I grasped for the end of my bed to support myself as my head thumped like I'd walked into bright sun after standing up too fast while drunk. I could feel myself swaying wildly, but my eyes were fixed on the gold and blue scene in front of me: the noise of hundreds of busy voices filled my eyes and the darkness of the fairy world filled the corners of my vision. But in front of me was a huge tower with a broken arch in the middle: a crumbling ruin of a church, lit up like a gold spotlight was on it. It was too big to be St Troute's, too old and bright to be anything in Bilsworth's grey modern landscape. Too damaged to be Ransley's perfectly preserved medieval village.

"Severstrong Abbey!" I gasped, and the image cleared from my eyes.

Tanya leapt up at once, dragging the changeling with her. "We have to go now! Before Teb does anything else stupid!"

"Are we going to take the train then?" Ally asked, getting up and pulling me to my feet. I swayed and grabbed her shoulder. Again. Turned out I'd not been clinging to the bed at all, but her arm. I'd not even noticed. That girl was *bony*.

"Too risky: we don't have any train fare," Tanya said, leading us down the stairs, explaining fast over her shoulder. "I'd bet that's the first thing Teb did: bought a travel pass with some syllable of her name she felt she could most part with. Which was fine back then but now she's sold seven parts of it, it's got really serious."

"What happens when she sells seven bits of her name?" Ally asked.

"That's not your regular deal. She'd have paid a price equivalent to unimaginable wealth to the fairies, and… Oh, never mind, how are we going to get to Severstrong Abbey? Can you drive yet, Alana?"

"No!"

"Well can your mom drive us? I'm assuming she can legally drive that behemoth parked out front."

"That's a classic car," I grumbled. "And we are not asking Mom to do anything. She's a psychopath!"

"Well I'd get my dad to do it, but he's in Waitington until eight tonight! Ally, when does your dad get home?"

"He's gone to London for work this week. That's why he was taking the, um, sick day before he left."

"What about the real train?" I demanded. "We might be able to get to Bilsworth station in time if there's a bus soon."

Tanya shook her head, but Ally cried, "I'll phone Mum!"

"Ally!" Tanya complained.

But Ally already had the phone to her ear as we exited the house in a hasty jumble, totally avoiding my mom, who I could hear clanking in the kitchen with the dishes. We slowed down with Ally, since she had so many problems walking and doing literally anything else.

"Hey, Mum! Can you tell me when the next train from Bilsworth to Severstrong Abbey is?"

There was a pause. "Bad idea," Tanya moaned.

"Why?" I whispered.

She nodded to Ally.

"Aw, okay," Ally was saying, disappointed. "We'd never make that… Well, we do have a bit of an emergency. We need to go rescue Teb from the fairies… No, Teb this time, not Tanya. Yeah, she's got as far as Severstrong Abbey now. Um, I suppose so? Can you drive?"

Tanya gave me a look I'd never imagined I'd see on her face: pure fear.

"Nooo," she moaned under her breath to me.

"Can't we pay for a taxi?" I asked.

"We could!" Tanya cried, seizing my arm and shaking it with delight.

"Mum says Dad took the train today and left the car," Ally said to us. "You cool?"

"No!" me and Tanya said at once. Not-Teb nodded cheerfully.

"Does she even have a license?" I asked.

"She passed a driving test," Ally said coyly. "She says just wait where we are… She'll be along to pick us up in no time!"

"Teb's corner!" I cried. Why did everyone have to know where I lived?

"Okay!" Ally chirped and hung up.

"Alana!" Tanya complained.

"Can you think of a better way? A taxi has to come from Bilsworth to pick us up, for one thing, unless we're lucky enough that they have one passing through when we call up. We save fifteen minutes right away by taking this ride. It seems inevitable, so…"

"We are all going to die in a fire," Tanya said flatly.

I wished she didn't have an uncanny knack for predictions to make me worry she was right.

Should Have Brought My Rock Haulin' Bag

It was the oddest car ride I'd taken in my life. Ally's Mum was not the most relaxed of drivers, swearing if she made the smallest mistake and reacting disproportionately to the tiniest wobbles. Fortunately, she slowed down once we got onto the main twisty road out of town – or didn't speed up any more. I think she didn't quite know any speed that wasn't forty miles an hour. Apart from that she was silent and focussed on the task of driving, and it was the least I'd ever heard her speak – she wasn't sparing any concentration on babbling about fairies.

I stayed silent too – it was Not-Teb and Tanya who took it upon themselves to have the conversation.

"So... What's it like being a pixie?" Tanya asked cheerfully, sitting next to her in the backseat and apparently completely forgetting the drama we'd had in my room not ten minutes before.

"What do you mean?" Not-Teb asked suspiciously. That tone of voice worried me: it was wising up to Tanya.

Tanya shrugged. "I dunno... Do you see in different colours from us? Are you making anthropological observations on our ways? Do you really turn milk sour just by looking at it?"

"No, because I'm technically Teb and human at the moment and she isn't colour blind, and yes, of course, and only if I'm in a bad mood."

"How can I tell if you're lying? If you're currently human you might not have to tell the truth all the time like fairies do."

"You can't."

"Awesome! Do you like shiny things?"

"Probably not as much as you, if Teb's memories are anything to go by."

I tried not to grind my teeth and looked out of the window, watching road signs tick by with the distances slowly shrinking. Severstrong Abbey was about thirty miles from Troutespond, although the first sign was after Bilsworth, so that wasn't a precise measurement. It was the sort of town we went on school trips to when they wanted to show us historic stuff without really stretching themselves to get us to London. There was a Norman-era castle that didn't charge as much as Ransley castle, presumably because admission was determined by the amount of remaining stones. A kooky little old-fashioned town clung to the side of an incredibly steep hill and of course there was the ruined abbey. The castle perched around the crown of the hill, the ruined towers giving a sort of spiky effect in my memory. I couldn't remember where the abbey that the town had eventually co-opted into its name was. Close enough, over some roundabouts and past the edge of town warehouses, to a place ringed with trees and fields, hidden from sight.

"Did you bring your English Heritage membership cards?" Ally asked as we began to draw close. I shook my head, then added a "No, we never had them," when I realised that she couldn't see me from the front seat.

"Well, that's strange," Ally said.

"Mom doesn't really care for that sort of thing... We haven't really *ever* done family things," I explained. I was making more of an effort to mention my family, I thought, which had to count for *something*.

"Wow, an American who *doesn't* love running around all our tourist sights?" Ally asked, more disbelievingly than genuinely sarcastically.

"No, that was more... Dad's... thing," I said, almost choked up by the end, as I realised there was probably a reason I never spoke about my family.

Ally hesitated for a moment before replying, "We'll show you around the abbey then. You can have your family day trip now."

"If you hadn't noticed, this is going to be the most fucked up crazy family outing ever," I pointed out.

Ally laughed, and I felt sort of warmed inside, having quickly become very fed up of the sulking, unfamiliar Ally we'd had all week.

We got back onto town streets and clung to whatever we could as Ally's Mum failed to accurately navigate the dangerous turns and narrow corners that stood between us and our destination. She slowed down when Ally pointed out a speed camera, but once she was done crawling past the painted stripes on the ground she sped right up again, until we were abruptly in a gravel car park on the other side of the town.

The changeling stretched and sighed when we got out of the car, the rest of us unclenching hands and staggering around with a newly restored joy for life.

"Well, at least the last place on Earth I'll see is really pretty," Not-Teb said as we trailed over to a little wooden hut at the side of the car park, by a path that disappeared between trees, leading off to the abbey. There were trees ringing us, and they were so tall and thick there was no way we could see the abbey yet. I felt antsy until Ally's Mum had finished paying for us to get in and we were moving again. The longer we idled around, the more I feared Not-Teb was thinking of new plots for escape.

"Doo do de do doo," Ally hummed.

"What?" I asked, distracted from my angsting by a giggle she pretty much yanked out of me.

"In computer games," Ally said.

I raised my eyebrows. She realised that I hadn't been able to read her mind up until that point, and started again from the beginning. "You know how when you're in a computer game with a load of different areas, and there's this annoying cute music that goes on and on and on in a loop so it pretty much is just playing in the back of your head for the next month? Well, we just moved to a different area. New music?"

I blinked a few times before I'd managed to process that one. "That actually... Makes sense."

"Thanks!"

"Stop saying stuff until it's important."

"Okay," she said, going back to only forcing us to listen to the tuneless scraping and flapping of her flip-flops on the gravel path we were following through the trees. The abbey was just ahead. The remains of the search spell hung with me, and after spending so long calling her name I could feel Teb close to us, but so unimaginably far away that we were probably walking right through her without knowing it.

It was about time for the epic finale of this stupid tale.

*

Severstrong Abbey had the sort of flat, square look that many places do when they've been excavated to discover their foundations, and then turf's been plastered over the landscape to make it presentable to tourists. A few random lumps of stone dotted the pristine stretch of grass between us and the looming arches of the remaining hall of the abbey. A noticeboard sunk into the ground nearby told us we were walking over the old garden and cloisters, along with a big drawing of what it should look like had it not vanished.

There was something sort of frightening about the old building – a big institution where people had locked themselves away for their religion, and I could feel in the very ground a deep unhappiness that had filled this place. It had been cold, and they'd been ill, and sick people were brought to them but the monks just wanted to rest, even when their devotion drove them to their prayers day in, day out...

"Alana, come on!" Ally said, doubling back and grabbing me, and I looked up from the ruminations the ground had handed me to see that the others had started their way along the lawn without me.

"There's no doorway," I said.

"What?"

"The monks lived an austere, dull existence – if so much as a mushroom circle had opened up near them, they'd have carefully removed it," I said. "All the ways closed long before the abbey did, and they never came back. This land is abandoned, spiritually, except a thin layer of consecration."

"What are you saying?"

"Teb's here, but unless we double back and go find another door, we're never going to get at her from in here. Also, we should come here in the case of a vampire attack in the local area. Not that vampires exist."

Tanya and Ally's Mum had joined us by now. "Are you sure?" Hester asked.

I nodded. "Can't you feel it?"

Ally's Mum nodded. "I meant about the vampires, but… If we can't get in then the only way is to make a doorway! I'm not paying eight pounds entry fee each just to have to turn back!"

"Muuum!" Ally protested. "What are you going to do?"

"The ley lines aren't so strong around here," she replied, frowning, apparently running her extensive mental map of the area through her mind. "Severstrong Abbey doesn't have any miracles or anything attached to it – it's barely a sacred site… Just a place people lived… Hmm. But if we assume it's thirty miles east of the stone circle in Troutespond, and assume there's something thirty miles west of us…"

"The sea?" I suggested.

"Other west," Ally's Mum replied blithely. "There's probably something… So that puts us at least in the middle of a line, in a vaguely-sacred site. We should be able to make something."

"We could make a cairn," Tanya suggested. "Alana knows how to do that. It'll amplify the magicness!"

I winced. "Do I have to?"

"We'll help," Ally said at once.

"Okay, get hefting rocks," I said. "I'll show you where to put them."

"Oh! So not fair!" Ally protested. "You need to do it too!"

I looked at Ally's Mum. "Where then?"

She looked around. "Middle of the garden?"

"Somewhere the English Heritage won't come beat us with sticks for ruining their nicely preserved history?"

She looked about. "Let's get into the ruins – more stones around anyway. A place will show up."

*

We found our place in a little medieval-style flower garden near the back, where there would be fewer tourists to come look at us, though the day was getting on now, and we'd been lucky we didn't have to break into the abbey. Our only worry was someone coming around for closing time and telling us to leave.

There was a corner of collapsed foundations bracketing this space and a tree grew through the middle of the crumbled rocks and cement, the trunk all chunky and twisty with age. An old oak tree, just like the one I'd built a cairn under a few days before back when my life had been simple.

"Perfect," Ally's Mum said. "I'll keep an eye out for security, you girls start piling rocks about here…" she poked the ground with a sandaled toe.

I nodded in recognition of the spot's worth. "Find large flat rocks first – as heavy as you can possibly carry. We need a good base or it'll just keep collapsing."

We scoured the nearby grounds for stones, stealing some here and there off the masonry, some larger pebbles from the gravel paths to fill up gaps, then stones taken from the side of a pond near us. Not-Teb followed us everywhere, refusing to lend a hand and making very unhelpful comments. I wanted to hand her over to Ally's Mum to give us all a break, but Hester was much more a healing, soothing sort of witch, who made teas and candles and thought hugs were the best medicine. Not the sort of offensive magic I was picking up and putting to good use on a daily basis. I didn't doubt that she could probably beat me in a fight if she put her mind to it, but she *wouldn't*, and I didn't trust her with the pixie for that reason.

It took a long time, but at least we had a pile of rocks that was beginning to pick up the energy that flowed through the earth, like a stone in a river, with the water bubbling over it and swirling around it. The power was gathering and gathering; unlike water the stones didn't just get wet, but soaked up everything the ground had to offer.

"How do we go through?" I asked Tanya, panting as I heaved around a heavy capstone I'd spent several minutes looking for. She had used the last cairn I built for that purpose, after all.

"Sing a little song," Not-Teb suggested brightly. Tanya and I glared at it.

"We should never have let the most sarcastic member of our team become possessed with a pixie," Tanya said.

"Agreed," I said.

"I don't see what's too wrong with it," Not-Teb said. "You guys are *extremely* boring."

"I suppose it would be really just a matter of shouldering your way between worlds. We're all overexposed to this sort of thing enough that we should be able to feel it. It'd probably be best to have someone stay behind and guard the stones and keep the way open," Tanya said, ignoring Not-Teb entirely. "Ally isn't too good at that sort of thing – she'll need a lot of help through a new and untested door to a bit of the world we don't even have the name for."

"Well, that's good – we can leave our most powerful and experienced witch behind to keep it open and stop any ghoulies from getting out," I said.

"Who, you?" Ally asked

"Your *mum*, you moron."

"Oh! Yeah!" she grinned. "Well, isn't that useful that she decided to come along?"

"She *drove* us here."

And so it was decided who would stay and who would go, and that, pretty much, was that – I stuck the capstone on top of the cairn, and felt the magic stabilise, settling into a pattern that would run for a million years if everything was left as it was, but in the grand scheme of things, lasted for about fourteen hours before pissed off English Heritage drones disassembled it in a grumbling way, astonished at the effort vandals would go to these days.

Come Buy, Come Buy

"You know what's really ironic?" Ally asked as we lined up near the pile of stones we'd created.

"No, what?" I asked, watching Hester start to murmur the words of a spell she was blatantly making up on the spot if the words I caught were any indication. It didn't take long for the energy around us to shift again. I hadn't sealed this cairn, and while energy had been flowing freely between worlds, now it was turning from formless, pointless magic to a carefully cut tunnel through.

"Normally pixies do everything in their power to steal humans off to their world – usually pretty girls. Well, look at us…"

The changeling had already made an attempt to run away, thinking it might be able to drag Tanya after it instead. It was still rubbing several new bruises she'd unashamedly put on Teb's real body. We'd pointed out it could get many more bruises dragging itself between dimensions, or go along nicely when we did.

"Heh," I said.

The cairn suddenly became a doorway between the worlds, invisible to one sight, but a glowing portal to the other, another flare of that magic that I couldn't see but could sense so powerfully it was like seeing. "Go!" I said, seeing Tanya step into it even without my order. The changeling kicked and struggled, but it was futile to resist the spell: like it was in a slingshot it was thrown after Tanya. Ally grabbed me as I stepped into it.

The change was instant: a breeze blew up around us, and I blinked and missed the very moment the world changed, but I suppose that was sort of the point. When I looked again the world around us has been plunged into otherworldly darkness.

"Okay, how do we find Teb?" Ally asked, looking about. She was rather more relaxed than the first time we'd taken her to the fairy world. Instead of being childishly reluctant to open her eyes she was peering around with curiosity. "Actually, you know what, all this has given me a great idea for a reality TV game show thing: 'Where's My Changeling?' You get six contestants and make changeling copies of them and then mix up the groups and make them do team-building tasks, and then at the end they —"

"Write it all down and send it to some TV people," Tanya cut in.

"Come on," I said, and started walking just to distract Ally from saying anything else.

The fairy world was shaped sort of like ours, but very different in landscape — there were usually a lot more trees, a lot more wild grasslands, and almost no evidence of boring houses or buildings. Troutespond was just the valley and stone circles it had been since forever, though with some odd concessions for the contested ground of the skate park. Severstrong Abbey was a very different sort of place.

Here everything was a sort of shadowy blue, like an endless evening, any hint of light a mere whisper to the bulky shadows that filled the world. Ancient trees, sticks lurking beneath chunky pools of dark, dotted the landscape. There were actually fewer of them than topside; most of the trees on the land had been recently planted to give the impression of woodland that actually hadn't been here before. Fairyland hadn't caught up yet and this was a flat stretch of marshy river land. The hill that the town stood on now loomed over us, taller and apparently closer than it was in the real world. The castle seamlessly merged with it, larger and spikier than ever, making a sort of sinister black crown. The abbey, in its ruined form, also filled the ground in front of us, larger than it ever had been, twisted so it looked more like the ribs of a fallen dragon with its remaining crumbling stone arches. The stone tower stretched up maybe three dozen feet higher than it did in the real world, and golden light splashed up its side, turning it into the beacon that I had seen in my vision.

The light came from within the monstrous ruins of the abbey — warm light, as if a campfire was holding the long night at bay. All around us was the darkness and misery I'd sensed as we'd walked through the ruins, but I hadn't felt this bubble of happiness nesting where the heart of the building might have been.

"What do you suppose is over there?" Tanya asked at once.

"I don't know… But Teb was there only an hour ago, so it's the best lead we have."

"Let's go then!" Ally said impatiently.

"Wait, we should…" I was talking to no one: they had all set off, the changeling pulling at the spell that bound it. Tanya let it stumble a few times before slowing a little.

Ally waited for me to catch up and fell into step. "What happens when Teb sells seven syllables of her name?" she asked me, glancing ahead at where Tanya was still determinedly leading the way, very keen on the rescue. "What if she sells the rest?"

"Tanya has a pretty clear idea that it's a serious landmark in her name-selling… Seven is a pretty big magic number. I mean hopefully now she's got that far she will stop before she has none left."

"What happens then?" Ally sounded even *more* fearful: I was terrible at cheering her up because I wasn't any more confident myself.

"I don't know what happens if you become properly nameless, but it certainly doesn't sound like a pleasant thing to be. We are supposed to worry about fairies stealing our names as well as them using them to cast bad spells on us. They *can* take the parts. I mean we're saying she's selling the bits of her name because she actually has some left, but for all we know she was tricked out of *parts* of it and is just lucky she was able to keep any of it."

"They're parts she *would* have kept, though. That's why Tanya thought it. Teb went through a phase of shortening her surname before we started using Magee instead because of her Irish heritage."

"There you go. She's doing it deliberately and we shouldn't think of her as the victim here."

Ally looked way more grim than normal, but I gave her credit for her answer, given how personal the matter was and all our earlier arguments. "Oh, I wasn't."

As we passed over the boundary of the abbey, in amongst the stones, the atmosphere changed like we'd just walked through a hot marshmallow — sticky, clingy heat suddenly enveloped us, the sweetness in the air making my teeth ache, and our progress was immediately impaired by the hundreds of goblins crammed into the same space as us, a market with dozens of tiny stalls in full swing.

"*Don't touch anything!*" I yelled as I saw the eyes of my friends go wide with excitement, taking in the barrage of colours and smells and beautiful things. The arches of the abbey loomed over the scene, creating something that felt kind of like a tent, holding the light in. In this rainless, exactly temperate land, that was about as close to indoors as you could get a pixie. The stalls were brightly coloured things that looked like wagons or fragile wooden frames surrounding tables, everything covered in swathes of cloth that would make the stereotypical medieval cloth-merchant of my imagination cry. The stalls made Not-Teb's gold dress from the station look rather plain, being just one colour, though it may have been the most sparkling. The stalls' cloths had fairy gold all over everything, but it was the richness of other colours — reds and purples and blues, deep forest greens, and pale embroidery in all the pastel colours over it, in swirling patterns — that caught the eye and wouldn't let it go until it had traced every corner of the maze sewn into the design…

I stumbled as the changeling stopped to look at something *on* the stalls, and just as soon as I was snapped from the dizzying world of cloth, I found myself in the rather more exciting realm of produce.

First, of course, was fairy fruit, because that stuff is pretty much crack on a free gold-plated phone as far as the human race is concerned – the basic reaction is to want to give pretty much everything you have for some of it, and then to eat until you're sick, and then you're trapped in the fairy world, either in your mind or *actually*, and neither of those end well. And, of course, the pixies like trying to tempt humans into eating it so they get new playmates. There were stalls and stalls of this fruit. It came in every shape and colour and size – massive peaches the size of my head, delicate bunches of apples like grapes, and weird heavy shiny fruits that looked more like they came from a cartoon than real life. Some were translucent, while some seemed to glow. Some were small and ugly but had the strongest smell, making everything in my head buzz and whir with "buy it buy it buy it!". Others didn't smell so much as looked so beautiful and soft or smooth or just plain delicious that it was a battle not to run over and grab one, just to hold it, stroke it, to feel the perfect weight, shaped just for your hand.

"We don't need anything!" Ally called to my left, fending off a pixie who was trying to pull her to a table laden with fans that sparkled and flickered open and closed like wings. I grabbed her again, and she was pulling Tanya, all of us making progress in fits and starts of powering through the crowd before stopping in awe to examine jewelled bottles or gilded instruments. We pushed past stalls laden with bubbles, or stars, or flowers plucked from dreams, caged creatures and curiosities and rarities. I wondered how much I could do if I bought my spell ingredients here, but decided I really wasn't canny enough to deal with these stall-keepers. Never mind the words the Piper would have with me if I brought anything back.

At last we made it to a space in the middle of everything, miraculously empty for a couple of square feet. We huddled into it and I did a head count. All present and correct, Not-Teb looking extremely bored.

"This place is *incredible*," Ally said.

"That's sort of the point," Tanya replied, boggling over my shoulder at some wonder.

In a moment free to breathe I tried people-watching instead. We'd been so bombarded I think none of us had managed to keep an eye out for Teb.

The pixies and goblins were shapeshifters by nature, and clearly thought it was boring being even half human at any given time when they weren't infiltrating our world. Mostly they were different combinations of animal, but I think I spotted dragons, trolls and stuff that looked more like aliens from comic book science-fiction among them. The general impression, as they were quite short, was a constant barrage of fuzz and scales at elbow or waist height, bonking into us and squealing, squawking and anything in between. Since they shrank down when they didn't have humans to intimidate, it was easy enough to see we were the only people over four foot tall in the area: there was no sign of Teb.

"Ooh, this is the old altar," Ally said, looking down at our feet. I shuffled back to see a cross gouged into the huge slab of stone we were clustered on. Consecration had no real permanent effect on pixies, but they didn't particularly want to set up stall on it.

"We should come here to do our Christmas shopping!" Tanya said, craning over her shoulder to see something else she'd had her eye on before we hauled her onto the altar.

"We do some great spiced wine," Not-Teb said. "You'd kill to drink it."

"And that is precisely why we aren't doing our shopping here," I said.

"Aww."

"Where's Teb?" Ally asked, ignoring Tanya and her new best friend of Not-Teb.

"I admit I'm kind of jumbled," I said. "I'm more worried about what she's been buying, though. Now we've seen what's on offer here... It's all trinkets and baubles and stuff no one in their right mind would waste a name like Teb's on. We need to go ask someone in charge if she's been here and what she's been buying. It may give us a clue about where she's moved onto."

"Ally should go," Tanya volunteered.

"Me? Why me?"

I pointed to her coat. In the fairy world the white patches glowed like bright sun was falling on them, the black parts swirling like the darkness in the corner of your eye when you've turned off the light at night. The whole thing oozed the power of the Piper, and though it was just a trick of the light, Ally was standing taller than normal, looking nearly as fearsome as he did. All she needed was the blank glowing eyes. "They'll respect that, if not you. Tanya's weighed down with the changeling and I..."

"Come with me!" Ally said, reaching out and taking my arm.

"Alright," I said, completely forgetting the reason I had for not wanting to go out there again. Maybe it was just cowardice talking: I felt so safe and protected standing on that old altar that it seemed nightmarishly pointless and terrifying to force the market on myself again.

Ally brushed down her coat then dived back into the press of the market, dragging me along behind her like a balloon.

Though sitting on the altar stone we were pretty much invisible to the pixies, the moment she stepped back in they all crowded around her, waving stuff her way.

"I'm just looking for my friend!" she cried, batting away a particularly enthusiastic seller who was waving what literally looked like old man's fingers at her. "She was here not long ago, selling parts of her name..."

A sort of hush fell over the goblins, and they looked shiftily at each other (as much as a particularly shifty look could be worked out of those shifty faces).

"Do you know where she went?" Ally asked. "Or what she bought?"

"We'd love to tell you," one goblin said, pushing his way to the front. He was draped in silver and gold pelts, his curly-toed shoes taking several elegant twists before ending in tassels of more gold thread. His pointed cap was golden too. This was clearly the head of the market, the greatest salesman, who sold straw for the price of gold. I wasn't going to guess his name. "But it would cost you, dear." His pointed, cunning face smiled up at her.

"Cost me what?"

"That nice coat, perhaps."

She snorted with laughter. "On you, shortie? A single sleeve would be enough!"

All the other goblins laughed too, raucous and wild. Ally smirked. I'd noticed before that she had an instinctive way of dealing with the fair folk, possibly stemming from when we had pushed her up to talk to the Green Man, though it seemed Tanya had already known about Ally's ability when she suggested it. Since she had survived that and learned all the difficult intricacies about talking to fairies, I didn't feel I would have to panic and jump in to save her at any point; she had the whole market rooting for her suddenly. They brought out a rather unusual side in her: her smile was steady, and suddenly all the fretting was gone. Relaxed, she had more of her mother's carefree attitude, but with a steely edge she only could have learned from Teb and Tanya. Her self-esteem was like spun sugar, so I wasn't going to point it out to her in case I ruined the one good thing she had going for her.

Gold-cap seemed to realise it too. "Fine! What else do you have to give?"

Ally dug in the deep pockets, and pulled out a half-drunk bottle of cola that had been in there gods know how long. "You think fairy fruit is addictive? You should try some of this." She held it out.

The crowd hushed up, all of them peering curiously at the bottle — it seemed incongruous in this world, too bright and real in its own way that made it stand out. It looked like it normally only does in the adverts. I wanted to drink it and I knew it had probably been knocking around in Ally's pockets for nigh on two months.

He took it from her, unscrewed it suspiciously, sniffed, and tasted a drop. His eyes went wide.

"How... So sweet! So... so sweet..." He screwed the lid tightly back on, his gnarly fingers deceptively strong, and with a reluctant shiver he slid the bottle somewhere inside his shining coat, hiding it from the yearning sight of all the other fairies, whose various shapes of ears had pricked up at the word 'sweet'. Many glittering eyes tracked the bottle into his pocket, while others raucously demanded to taste it too.

He hushed the crowd with a wave. "We have a deal. She went south, towards the rail line. But you don't want to chase after her. I'm warning you, pretty lady. Stay with us and we will give you any delight you ask for a song from your sweet lips. Or trade you magic for a dance."

"What did she buy?" Ally asked.

"You'll be happier if you stay here, with us."

"What did she *buy?*"

He looked down and away. "Her name was worth more than all the realms in the valley. More than everything in the market… She could have walked in and swept us clean of goods, if she was good at sales. But she did not. She was better. All the wealth you see here is not our own. She's beggared us to her whims, and I was robbed of my takings to boot. She is not the same girl who arrived on the train." It was *shame* on his face. Had Teb found the loophole on buying from fairies? *All by herself?* I knew she had occasionally wanted to be a lawyer, but this seemed to be an incredulous amount of canny.

I could feel Ally's arm shaking too, under my hand.

"Mr Trader, sir," she said, picking words very slowly and carefully. "What did our friend buy?"

His expression darkened further. "Something that was not mine to give, or my place to tell you. Leave now, to follow her, or not at all."

I got the point, and started to pull Ally away.

"Thank you, Mr Goblin sir," Ally said shrilly. "Enjoy the cola."

The trader disappeared without another word, leaving with his cohort of cronies towards a golden tent in the corner. Two larger goblins with mossy, badgerish features stayed behind to watch us go. I did not want to tangle with them.

When Ally turned around to head back to the altar the goblins actually parted for us: she waded through them and I followed, thinking hard. I was more interested in the way all the goblins looked rather unnerved about what Teb had done. I knew selling a name was a big deal, but they were *rattled* by it. Frightened. What had she done to them?

Whatever Teb did anywhere she went, She'd been Teb at them.

"Well done, you made fairy fruit more addictive," I grumbled to Ally. Ally just beamed at me.

"But having useless junk in your pockets is so useful! We didn't need to give anything up that meant anything to us!"

"I'd be more careful in future," I said. "Things have symbolic weight here. You gave him more than a bottle of syrup. That was corporations and artificial flavourings, mass-production and outsourced factories you just gave him. Imagine if the company back home started mass-producing fairy fruit."

"Ah well… If it does happen it's actually happening here, isn't it? Not our problem… Let's find Teb."

I nodded, deciding not to get into a debate about how encouraging fairies to be tricksy was a one-way ticket to making it our problem in the future.

Halfway back to the altar, in the much clearer air now the market drama had passed and most of the goblins had gone back to their regular trading, a small, weasely goblin in a formal shirt and straw hat just about tripped me.

"Move it," I snapped.

"Wait, I have to talk to you."

I rolled my eyes, but Ally halted and became an immovable object. "What?"

"Ally, don't start making friends here."

The goblin gestured to a stall of umbrellas with a sort of uncanny life to their folds, and slipped behind it. Ally followed, and I now found myself being the one dragged. I wanted to protect her. I glanced around and saw we were out of sight of the badger goblins as soon as we were behind the stall, temporarily giving them the slip.

"What did you want?" I demanded, cutting over any attempt Ally made to reason with the little goblin. It was one of the smallest here, scruffy and wild looking with its neat clothes over the top looking like someone had scrubbed up a pet ferret and put it in its Sunday best.

"You asked the wrong questions," it said simply.

"Aren't all questions the wrong ones with you people?" I snapped.

"What is the right question?" Ally asked.

"What is she?"

"You mean —" Ally gestured me in bemusement, but the light bulb went on. "Oh. What is she?"

"Ours. And we hers."

I felt a chill run-down my spine, even in this soupy rich air.

I glanced around nervously and saw the badgery goblins had worked their way around to get us back in their sights and did not look happy about us loitering, now heading towards us.

"Come on," I hissed to Ally. "The trader said where she went. Don't stand around listening to this babbling: goblins will trade riddles for your sanity if you stand still long enough. We need to get moving."

*

At the altar, we found Tanya and Not-Teb pulling on the spell that still linked them, bickering gently about going into the market. I sidled in to stand behind Tanya and scowled at the changeling. "Enough. We're leaving."

"What did you find out?" Tanya asked.

"Where she went. That's enough for now."

Tanya nodded, but she looked sharply at me, guessing there was more. I couldn't tell her with the changeling listening because I was freaked out and the last thing I wanted was it figuring out Teb had changed the game on us. Thankfully Ally was too busy looking miserably thoughtful to update Tanya — and I think resented telling her stuff anyway since March.

We pushed our way out of the goblin market, hurrying on our way towards where Tanya thought the train station was, walking in silence for a long while. There was a path of sorts through the marshland, a road marked by stones along its edge, and it seemed better than nothing to follow.

"What about Mum?" Ally asked suddenly.

"She should know where we're going," I said. "She knows stuff like that, doesn't she? In any case, if Teb's got the train there'd be no point in her keeping the portal open for us – she might as well drive back and we'll meet her wherever Teb goes."

"Teb's going home," Tanya said, unexpectedly certain, like she was coming out of a long rumination. "She got what she came for."

"What was that?" Ally asked, looking up from her phone.

"She's got the power to awaken either the fairy Queen or the Green Man."

I felt another chill, and looked straight at the changeling, hoping my distress would be obvious and stop these two talking about stuff like this out loud in front of it. The changeling was walking along pretending to mind its own business, and that made me feel sick. I should have whispered the full details of our chat with the goblin to Tanya to stop her reasoning it all out loud – should have, could have, would have, right?

"Um, why?" Ally asked. "I don't get it. I thought they had to sleep or die or whatever every summer?"

"Yeah," Tanya said. "That's how it's *supposed* to work. Teb's messing things up. At the moment, she's as strong as the most powerful things anywhere within a hundred miles. That's what she did with her name. She traded it for some sort of power. And we know what she wants… it's just whether she's going to waken the Green Man and take control of him, or go right for the Lady and…"

Ally shivered, suddenly tearful, clutching her phone to her chest. "She's leaving us again."

"And," I said, "now we have to stop Teb from completely messing up the natural order."

"Wait," Tanya said, looking at Ally. "Do you get phone reception here or did you just get your phone out to text your mum and didn't even think?"

Ally looked down at her phone. "Oh, I do. That's… weird."

Tanya pulled out her own phone. "Cool, I do too! I wish I'd known, I turned my phone off when I came here in March."

"How about," Not-Teb said, breaking its long silence, "you could take me home, pretend I'm Teb and forget all this happened." It looked directly at me. "You *know* the Piper won't like this whatever you do, but Teb's going to have that power to spare no matter what happens; you can't get her name back from the goblins, even if they think she traded it fairly. She's going to have all the consequences no matter what happens… Would it not be easier to let her do what she wants and take the win she bought, and carry on living your normal lives? I will happily act like I never was a changeling… Become your friend completely…"

"*No*," I said. "We're getting the real Teb, body and all, and things will be back to normal! You only exist in the first place so she could do her exams and not be missed so much…"

"Weeell…" Ally said, looking like she wanted to worry that thought a bit more before letting it go. "The Green Man offered the changeling and we basically just went with it because he was really hard to argue with. Teb was happy throwing away her human life completely to be with him. She wanted to leave us back then as well."

"For two months," I said. "She would have come back…" I trailed off because that thought sounded pathetic and empty coming out of my mouth. I could see that Ally nodded tearfully, not comforted at all as she sent her text and put her phone away.

I glared at Tanya. She shrugged.

"It's happening all over again," I said. "This was your whole fight back in March, when *you* ran away and that debacle left Teb as a changeling. I try to reserve judgement on Teb, I really do, but you both upset Ally in March, and she felt you abandoned her as well. And got Teb hooked on abandoning you both."

"What do you want me to say, that's fair, sorry I discovered the *magical world of fairies existed* and I wanted to go look and Ally was too boring and scared to come with me?"

"Well yeah, you can apologise for hurting someone without compromising how much you care about fairies, you know. Just say sorry for putting them above her and try and work as a team for once."

"For once?" Tanya said, eyes boggling now. "When don't I –?"

"*All the time*," Ally snapped. "Like at the station when Teb got away!"

"I –"

"Shh!" I said, a step ahead of them and first to spot a blue glow around the corner; the path had descended into the ground a little, dark grassy knolls rising above us, turning the road into a twisty maze between them.

"You think that's the station?" Ally asked.

"It is," Tanya said.

"How do you know?"

She gestured to the side, where, between two rises in the ground, we could see a white line of railroad tracks, cutting off the edge of this world. The track ended well before the horizon in both directions. Each place has its own fairy world, its own dream, with borders that ended in the oblivion of the deep sleep of the world. There was no way out except the doorways they left us. The station glowed bright blue, a beacon. It would have called to Teb as her way to escape.

"She's down there," Tanya said, sensing or knowing it about the same time I did.

(Ally, who was not psychic in any way whatsoever, looked confuddled but was at least willing to believe and follow us.)

We started sprinting, the changeling stumbling along behind us.

There was a tunnel that led into the station, and a ticket office with a barrier. A kestrel-like goblin sat hunched over a ticket machine.

"Yes?" he creaked as we clattered to a panting, pink-faced stop.

"Three and a pixie changeling thing, please," I said.

"What can you exchange for –"

"Oh, for crying out loud!" I cried out loud. I jammed my hand in my pocket, pulled out my lighter and for the first time ever flicked it and had it instantly jump into life. I focussed very carefully on the flame, and he quickly began sweating and squirming, smoke coming from the thick feathers on his neck. "Let us through or you'll be tandoori roast goblin!"

The barrier clicked. I shoved through it and gave the goblin a furious glare as he hastily fanned himself.

"Way to keep your cool," Ally commented to me.

"No, you're meant to tell *him* 'keep your cool'," I said distractedly, tugging her along after me as I hurried along the platform.

"This is why *you're* the action hero," she giggled breathlessly.

I smiled way more than was appropriate for the situation.

The train was hissing at the station amidst the glowing blue floral display that lit the platform in eerie ghost light. The same goblin conductor from before was standing at the door to the front carriage, waving our party on as we reached the doors. We leapt into the small wooden box and the door slammed shut behind us. With a long hoot and an increase in hissing and shaking, the train lurched away immediately. The schedule was definitely "when you're ready."

Over the rattling, I called, "Let's find her."

"She's in the back carriage," the conductor said.

I rounded on him with a glare. He held up his little mousy hands. "Hey, hey, just being helpful… I saw what you did to Old Sycamore Sam."

I rolled my eyes, but before I could get into an argument about how there was never a helpful pixie, Ally was dragging me through the carriage. Tanya followed, a bright smile on her face, almost oblivious to the changeling dragging after her. She was peering with interest into the compartments of the carriages, at their skeletal or ghostly inhabitants, sharing with almost-normal-looking people hunched over newspapers. Or her eyes fell out the windows hard on our left, admiring the totally blank black landscape through which the train hurtled. I wondered if she could see beyond it or into it or whatever you did to a void of nothingness.

It wasn't a long train, and we only had to hop the wobbling floor between two carriages twice before we stumbled on Teb. She was standing in the middle of the corridor between compartments as if she had been expecting us, tall and composed. Her hair was loose, not the tight ponytail she'd preferred lately, and her extra-boring clothes had been traded for an incredible purple dress made of fairy silk. Most strikingly, she'd bought a beautiful mask, a brilliant, iridescent thing, painted gold on the face, studded with swirls of dark purple gems, framed with a huge plumage of fantastic magenta and violet feathers. The shape of the face seemed to be pulled into a beak, tiny and curved over her nose. The overall impression was of a magnificent startled owl.

"Teb!" Ally cried.

Teb turned sharply, the movement reminding me of how suddenly owls could look around, and for a moment I wondered if she was already beginning to mythologize, to become a magical part of this world, filling some niche that might not even have existed before she decided to fit into it. Her eyes flashed from under her new gold brow, and then she turned in a whirl of silk and feathers and ran off, darting into one of the compartments.

"Quick – follow her!" I said, even as everyone but Not-Teb began a frantic chase. Not-Teb dug in her heels and Tanya had to drag her along. Though the spell worked in her favour under endurance, dragging ten stone of pissed off pixie is never easy.

The compartment door slammed, and Teb looked out with the same mocking sort of haughty turn of her head she'd given us on the train the last time she had made her escape. Now I could easily believe it had been her choice to swap with the changeling. I wondered if it had been right: was Teb trying to be kind by leaving us a changeling to take her place? Was that really an alternative? She couldn't have known just *how* evil it would be. If she was thinking like one of them, like it had said, then perhaps she really did see the balance in that.

Ally grabbed the handle of the compartment door and rattled it uselessly. She banged on the window, but to no effect. Teb just smiled at her from under the beak. Her brown skin looked like it had been painted over with a sheen of golden glitter. The eyes looking at us from behind the mask were a deep purple to match the dress.

"What has she done to herself?" I snarled as Ally carried on shaking the door without budging it.

"I'm pretty sure those things don't lock," Tanya said.

"Then… Why… Can't… I… Get… In?!" Ally yelled, pounding on the door.

"She doesn't want us in there with her," Tanya said. She stepped forward and took hold of Ally by the shoulders, gently pulling her back. She went limp and flopped dismally against Tanya.

Teb carried on watching us, barely seeming human with her unwavering stance despite the shaking of the train, and the keen, birdlike stare with bright eyes that never blinked.

I looked up at the changeling, in Teb's real body, with the messed up hair, standing arms folded, leaning against the window behind her, smirking. Its lip was swollen and split to match mine and there was bruising under one of its eyes, cuts and scrapes all over its knees and elbows. It looked way, way more like Teb. It could have been Teb if I hadn't put up a wall in my mind to assure me that it wasn't.

"Well, what do we do now?" Ally asked.

Tanya and I looked at each other and shrugged.

"We've lost Teb," I said. "We need to force her to swap back with the changeling. I think we're beyond asking nicely. And for that, we need the changeling." I turned to it. "How do you like the modifications Teb's made to your body?"

"Interesting," Not-Teb said. "So you think *I'll* be a goddess after the switch?"

That chill ran down my spine again, but this time with a name to it. Goddess. Teb had truly put herself on the level with the creatures she got tangled into their ritual soap opera with.

No, I didn't say. *Those powers go to the person with the name that traded them, but would I say that?*

"Worth a try, isn't it?" Tanya said.

"It is," I agreed.

"So what we do is, grab her as soon as she gets out, and you swap back with her."

"Sounds good to me," the changeling said.

We looked back at Teb. She hadn't moved, and was still watching us.

"I hope she can't hear us through the glass," Ally mumbled.

"I hope she can," I replied, and looked at her. "Teb, you selfish cow! Get out of there and let us take you home!"

The corner of her mouth turned up a little more.

I sighed.

One-Sided Coin

The train stopped twice on the way, twice bursting into a world of lights and colours outside the window, before twice more plunging back into the darkness of the space between worlds, where even the chuffing and clanking of the train seemed muted by the void.

Tanya gushed excitedly as we pulled into Ransley, the station in some sort of early twentieth-century splendour that I wasn't actually sure had ever existed, though I couldn't remember how long the train line had run this way. The two lonely platforms were bedecked in jewel-like lanterns, glittering a soft gold that seemed downright spooky between the overshadowing trees of what appeared to be an immense forest beyond.

A couple of odd, pale elf-things climbed onto the train. They clutched at the folds of woodland-coloured fabric that they wore, stopping any part of it trailing on the ground or catching on the door, and blinked their wide yellow eyes as they looked uncertainly at their tickets. They clearly did not trust this strange modern technology (I was assuming that elves didn't get out much... I had pretty much never seen anything like it).

The goblin conductor cheerfully shoved them into a compartment, sliding the door shut after them with a loud slam. He dusted off his clawed hands and caught our gaze. He tapped his hat. "Ladies. There is a compartment free just down the carriage if you want to sit down."

"Bugger off," I said.

He laughed a sharp-toothed laugh and went through to the next carriage.

Tanya pressed her face against the window and watched as the green light of that forested station vanished. Ally let go of her collar, confident that even Tanya wouldn't jump from a moving train into the void of nothingness beyond.

At Bilsworth the light was duller, the grey station bricks not at all dissimilar to the real thing. It looked like the Christmas lights were out early there: instead of mysterious and eerie floating fairy lights it really was a station lined with strings of electric fairy lights, winking on and off. Tinsel was taped up in some of the corners.

"Always knew it was a tacky place," Tanya said wisely. Ally relaxed her ready-to-pounce stance, agreeing that Tanya was even more unlikely to wander off to explore something that she found boring and below par. There was no need for her to get worked up a third time: Troutespond was our next stop.

Teb hadn't moved.

Or, I think, hadn't even blinked yet.

*

The train came to a halt, and our stand-off with Teb doubled in intensity. We were waiting for her to step out of the carriage, and she was presumably just playing with us and seeing if we'd back off or not.

"You're going to have to come out eventually," Ally said. "Unless you want to make this ride again."

The door burst open in a wave of energy that threw all of us back. When I sat up, rubbing a bumped elbow and feeling thankful that Not-Teb had cushioned me, Real Teb had vanished.

"Come on," I said, leaping to my feet. "If she's challenging the Lady she has to run all the way up to the stone circle, and if she's going to the Green Man it's still half a mile – we have plenty of time to catch up with her!"

We all struggled up, piled off the train, and ran onto the comparatively familiar platform of Troutespond station. There was a flash of purple at the barrier as Teb rushed through. We followed.

"Doesn't that barrier take us back to the real world?" Ally panted.

"Only if you want it to!" I shoved through the barrier and kept running into the sparkling yellow-green of late spring in Troutespond. It was almost normal coloured if you ignored the squishy dark sky. Having a powerful sun god give the land his blessing left our village a brighter colour than many places in the fairy world, apparently, and if you kept your gaze down you could fool yourself almost about being home. We'd been here in the past when it was blue, and I when it had been red, so I knew that it didn't always look so natural.

The path somehow felt a lot shorter when we ran it this time, and in no time the weird trees with their glowing golden crystal fruits were in sight. We passed the barrow that the rather less than spectacular ruins of the church stood on. A few paces more and we had a view downhill to where the river still ran as much more than the real world pipe under the motorway, right before the embankment of said road. That was where the Green Man slept, and there was the slightest wobble in the shape of the big motorway, which meant the construction work hadn't buried him half-alive in concrete. I was guessing that was intentional, since they hadn't worried about flattening any other landmarks along the way, and his copse of trees was hardly the most impressive.

We could see Teb haring her way down the high street, ignoring the grove to her right. She was going to turn left soon and start climbing the hill; of the two possible directions of *course* she wouldn't run downhill. This was Teb. My legs wobbled at the thought of yet another jog up the hill. I ran along, puffing and groaning whenever I had enough spare breath. Ally was behind me and wheezing, but Tanya had those deceptively long legs for her delicate frame, and was light and athletic in her build. The changeling seemed perfectly happy keeping up now it had a goal of working with us. Tanya and it streaked ahead of us, and in just a few seconds had closed the gap on Teb. With no regard for the beauty of the dress that Teb wore, Tanya collided with her and knocked her to the ground with a tackle that would have had rugby coaches crying with delight.

The rest of us struggled up to her and stopped, panting, beside Tanya as she held Teb down.

Teb struggled, but her hands were pinned behind her back.

I helped Tanya out by sitting on Teb's legs. Also: I got to sit down.

"Please, it's us," Ally said, crawling over. Teb wrenched her arms free but Ally caught them and pinned them. "Please, don't fight us... Don't run off again." Tears were dripping down her freckled cheeks now. Maybe she hadn't been making asthmatic noises after all, but had been crying as she ran. I felt a stab of guilt for not noticing, although Ally made plenty of weird noises which *weren't* crying.

"This isn't about running away!" Teb yelled, furious and probably just about ready to gnash her teeth at us. The mask had slipped a little when she'd fallen, and a corner of her jaw poked out, the eye holes askew, blinding her. Seeing more of her face made her more human – I wondered if she knew how to talk to us at all when the mask was down.

"Teb, it's *everything* about running away," I said softly.

"You don't understand! I'm the queen of this place!" Teb wailed. "This is my land – they are my people! I can have a life here!"

"You don't have a life anywhere," I said sternly, honestly forgetting for a moment that the phrase kind of had a second meaning in today's culture, but if you asked I was totally telling her to get a life. "You have a choice while you won't make up your mind, but that is all."

"I have!" she snarled. "Why the fuck do you think I'm here? I'm waiting for my King, and in the meantime I'm *making* my life here!"

"Teb! Listen to me! You haven't made up your mind, or we wouldn't *be* here. If you're as powerful as you claim, the land would have never let us past the borders. Not to mention the pixie army you have here." I sighed internally as she continued struggling – I was going to have to say more than that I wanted to win this fight.

"I know what it's like to be offered the world and more in the palm of your hand, Teb… I know what it's like to *hold* it. But we *can't*. Making really painful decisions is what makes us who we are, and it's impossible to pick the appealing option without losing all our humanity. You've already thrown away so much. Don't you think you need to cling all the harder to what you have left? I made the choice to keep mine, and it's the right choice…"

As if working with me perfectly in sync, Ally took that moment to gently pull the mask off Teb's face.

"We have to make choices we don't like all the time," I said, trying to sound soothing now, though I was still mad at her. "Maybe a compromise for what university we go to because we don't have the grades. Or compromise on who you take to the prom because you can't have who you want. But they're done because they're the best for you. And maybe something good will come of it that you never expected. For example, just the other day Chris King asked you to the prom. Have you or have you not been sighing over the fact he writes sonnets for his girlfriends since forever?" I wasn't sure myself, but Ally liked mocking his methods, so I had a hunch.

"That doesn't mean anything!" Teb complained. "Get off me! I can't talk to you this way!"

"Promise not to run away?"

"No!"

"I wasn't talking to you," I said. My gaze was up at the other Teb with us.

The changeling nodded. I pulled the restraining spell off it and wrapped it over Teb instead, miming the invisible rope like the dumbest playground game. It worked though: here in the land of fairies my magic was more than just wishful thinking. Tanya jumped off her and I retreated a couple of feet before Teb could kick me. She sat up, her hair standing up on one side, dirt all over the knees of her dress. She gave me a look of deepest loathing, furious I think because it had been me and not one of the others who had tried reasoning with her.

"Come on, Teb, you have so much more to do on Earth," I begged.

"Hey, if it doesn't work out, there's always another way back," Tanya commented. "Give us a chance?

"You're not giving me a choice," Teb said, and at the sound of relenting in her voice, I knew we'd won. Of course, there is always a choice, but sometimes you just need to pretend the other side of the coin doesn't exist and just not sound out all the benefits of being a goddess. Maybe not the Piper's philosophy there, but he wasn't allowed to make the same morality judgement calls we were. Maybe *this* was why he hadn't offered to help.

"Besides, think of all the waste of energy you put into your A Levels if you never take the exams," I said. "We're not asking you to give up this power – we can't make you. But we – well, Ally and Tanya at least – would really like to have you with us. We're not a complete group without you."

"I'm part of this land," she said, the fury mostly gone from her voice now. She'd switched to a wheedling petulance which wasn't much better. "I don't think I can go home. I don't want to. I belong here now!"

"Teb Nandi," I said. "That's all you have left now… But three is a good number… You've made a strong name of what's left. You never sold it all and I never thought you would. As long as you have those parts still, bits of your name which come from people or places or I don't know what back in the world you were born in, raised in and used that name in, you can always go back. The only things that can't cross between worlds as they please are those with no name at all. The Green Man, the Lady. Even the Piper has some scraps of his old names with him still, giving him freedom of movement. He's got the strongest presence in this village because we throw around the name St Troute like it's candy. You might never have had your name plastered on the side of a building, but there's still bits of you all over the place back there. You left your favourite shoes behind."

"Ha ha, no she didn't," Tanya said, pointing at my feet.

"Shut up!" I said.

Teb scowled at me. "Why are you wearing my shoes?"

"Blame the changeling for trashing absolutely everything about your life while you were gone. Point is, having them with me helped me find you, and if that doesn't say our world isn't dying for you back, I don't know what is. Whatever ties you have here…"

Ally butted in. "Friends can go on holiday from time to time."

I had to check Tanya's face for the look of victory I knew would be there.

"Okay," Teb said softly. "Okay. I'll go back to being me."

"Awesome," Ally said, tears appearing all over again. She let go of Teb's hands.

Teb wriggled out of her dress, revealing her old plain clothes underneath. Ally compulsively began folding the masses of purple fabric. She already had the gold stuff Not-Teb had been wearing – she was clearly collecting it. I wondered if it would show up again in one of Hester's projects.

Teb's newly deep violet eyes fell on the changeling. "Okay, now I want my body back, bitch."

"You only had to ask," Not-Teb said, with one last wicked grin. It leaned forward, elbowing me aside to get closer to Teb.

With a wide-eyed look from Real-Teb both of them collapsed, Teb-as-changeling's-body slumping forward into Tanya's arms, Teb's-body-as-changeling flopping over beside me.

For a moment neither of them were Teb or changeling.

And then Teb – our Teb in Teb's real body – opened her eyes (purple as a plum).

"I fucking hate all of you," she said, rubbing her head.

"Yay!" Ally squealed, flinging her arms around her friend even as Teb tried to take stock of her new frame, touching the bumps on her face, rubbing her elbow, wrapping an arm around her flat stomach. After a failed attempt to shrug Ally off she flopped back against her, shoulders shaking.

The changeling sat up as well, sparkly wide green eyes in a face that was already losing its Teb-ness, the colour leeching out of it to a sickly shade of off-white, if what it was off to was blue.

It was also taking stock of itself, touching its face, running scaly hands over its body.

"It didn't work," it said, seeming genuinely shocked.

"How stupid are you?" I asked it.

It looked me up and down, and I think my hand twitching towards my pocket gave it away, because it suddenly scrambled up and ran into the trees before I could reach for my lighter and put an end to this for good. It knew our names and it would have an uncomfortable connection to Teb, but she had her own power to fight it back now. Perhaps this was her problem now.

"Let's get the hell out of here," I said, deeply unsettled. I knew this was the point the Piper would want me to walk away, same as the changeling. The swap was all we'd needed to do, and that creature unsettled me enough that I didn't want to provoke it. Even here, even now, I wasn't sure I'd beat it. It knew my name and it had known all my weaknesses from the moment it had taken on full possession of Teb's life at the station.

"Agreed," Teb said, wiping her eyes and making herself sit up properly, the veneer of control and normality coming back as she settled back into being herself. "I'm starving! And days behind on my revision timetable if I'm serious about coming back to Earth…" She grabbed the folded dress and mask from Ally and tucked them under her arm as she stood as well.

"My mum's gonna be glad to hear from us," Ally said.

"Did she come with you on the train?" Teb asked, amazed.

"Drove."

"Your mum drove?"

"Yeah… It was an emergency."

"It was an emergency that could have waited another couple of days for me to consolidate power," Teb snapped.

I smiled to myself, despite how much I was just thinking of how I longed to be home and out of this. I was surprised at just how glad I was to have Teb back as she'd always been, turning a walk through the fairy world into something as mundane as a stroll to the corner shop, complete with dumb argument. A dumb argument about her becoming the supreme ruler of fairyland, but still, a dumb angle to take on such a thing. A half-jest in Teb's words to shake off the enormity of what had just happened to her.

We headed back down the road towards the station. The skate park would have been closer, but I think everyone else felt the train station's portal was a little more reliable, now we knew about it. Without a chase to distract us the walk seemed to take us forever, filled with things that could have gone wrong, moments for Teb to change her mind, or, worse, reveal it had never been changed in the first place. The trees around us were dark and strange – gnarlier than their real-world counterparts, the shadows in them bristling with watching eyes. I remembered my walk in the same area up top this morning: the fear I'd had the changeling was watching me. I felt an involuntary shudder. Having seen another face to the creature at last had not made me feel any more uncomfortable about what it had put me through. The orange glow of the station drew closer and closer, and then we were walking up the path towards its turnstile.

We were at the station. I looked around and saw nothing interesting, the trees close and almost wall-like in the way they cut off the path, and nothing behind us. The goblin in the ticket office waved to us, but I shook my head. He scowled. Okay, maybe this portal was only good for one more use before they started charging us through the teeth. Or literally for the teeth or something.

"Go through, go through!" I urged, and Tanya grabbed Teb's arm and pulled. Ally held out a hand expectantly to me, but I took her by the wrist, really not in the mood to hold hands with her (or maybe too *much* in the mood to hold hands with her, and just not interested in losing the valuable seconds that moment would cause while we were trying to make our escape).

I stepped forward as well, feeling the whooshing mass of Other World – *our* world – tugging on us, recognising us as its children and wanting us back in its bosom. I let it reach out and take me.

Ally tripped at my side with a yell as she made her way up the station steps.

I tried to keep hold of her, to pull her back up, but my grip wavered the instant when I was suddenly no longer standing in the fairy world, but was under the clear, cold, high night sky of the stars and the moon, millions or more miles from us. I looked down at my empty hand and swore.

"Ally got left behind!" I cried, shaking hard as I realised what had happened. It had to be the changeling. Oddly, apart from all the other concerns that should have been rushing through my head, the one that hit me hardest was the thought of how mad with me the Piper would be when he found out I'd lost Ally – *his* Ally.

"She can get through – she'll work it out," Tanya said confidently. "And if not, the Piper will rescue her. He won't let anything bad happen to her." At least we all seemed to know the score about his feelings even if we didn't agree. That was *really* reassuring.

"No! Have you not learnt anything from this whole ordeal?" I snapped. "The Piper does not have our back! If he even cares, if he's even watching, he is only making sure we can do this ourselves! Have you not seen what he's made us go through without helping? It's always a test and I am not asking him for help again! The changeling's attacked her… I know it! She was behind me one second, and then…"

"I've seen her fall over standing still on the spot," Teb said, unimpressed with my report.

"She was taken," I said firmly, not allowing their doubt to get to me. "I'm going back through."

"Alana, don't!" Tanya begged. "Let the Piper save her."

"*No*," I said. "He won't! And if he does… I should have been the one to do it. It's not *fair*."

I stepped backwards through the barrier as Tanya made a helpless grab for me. But she didn't follow… Perhaps she hoped I would fail, that I would call out for the Piper for a second time, and let him sweep Ally up like the damsel in distress while I sat on the side helpless and useless and all sorts of other "less".

The last thing I saw was Teb watching me curiously: she stayed brighter, clearer, even as the world faded, I could see her golden glowing aura for a second longer than everything else before the one world blinked off completely. And then the whooshy sensation of falling between worlds took me again.

"I hope I'm the right one…"

Iappeared back on the warm green path and stumbled right into Ally, who had apparently been waiting at the turnstile for me. We fell down together with the speed I'd launched myself through it in my desperation to get back. She looked up at me with pathetic relief as I blinked down at her under my arms.

"Oh wow, I was so worried you wouldn't come back for me!" she said.

I stood up, clearing my throat and blushing.

"So you did just trip?"

"Uh… No," she said awkwardly. "I'm just having a horrible nightmare." She pointed. I looked over. Another Ally was standing two feet from us, arms crossed, biting her lip, looking terrified, identical down to the scuffs on her flip-flops.

"*Fuck*," I said.

"Um," the other Ally said. "That's the changeling you just walked into… But… but you don't look convinced. Um. Please figure this out so we can go home? I'm kinda scared about staying here too long." She glanced over her shoulder into the woods.

"No pressure or anything," the other giggled in her soppy, nervous way. I quickly labelled the one who I was still helping to her feet Ally1, and the shivering one Ally2.

I took a deep breath, forcing myself to think this through before I said or did anything else. One of them was only Ally as far as the changeling – the master shapeshifter in a race of them – could work out from Teb's memories, and from what she'd observed hanging out with us. Without Ally's full name, and Ally really did not go around waving her middle name, there was no way the changeling could get into the heart and soul of what it was to be Ally. It wasn't corrupting her form in the way the changeling had perverted being Teb, but was merely mimicking.

In a way, it'd be closer than a full copy on the surface. It had to get its Ally display absolutely *perfect* to pull whatever it wanted off. I remembered how it had jokingly put on Tanya's mannerisms for just a few seconds in Teb's skin… Just a fleeting imitation, but strong enough I'd recognised it for what it was without even knowing Tanya as well as the others would after fifteen years acquaintance. Everything down to the way it controlled the most delicate muscle movements, the slightest expression that passed over our faces, could be replicated. It had clearly stopped worrying too much about looking right when it had come through the first time. To get into our world was all it wanted now, and to do that it had to be flawless. And if I took the wrong one back this time, it wouldn't be limited to the nonsense it could cause in a human body – it would have all its magic as well.

So, it would be copying Ally from what Teb knew. Unfortunately, Teb had known Ally since they were three or four. I had known Ally for two and a bit months. In two months you get to know someone surprisingly well if you click, but even so… We'd mostly gone to school and saved Tanya from fairies. There would be holes in its knowledge. Lots of them. But more in mine. If Teb or Tanya had come through with me, I could bet they'd already be leaning towards one Ally.

"I'm thinking of a number between one and ten…" I suggested, more than a little sarcastically. Both Allys said "Three!" at once, winced, and glared at each other. One Ally folded its arms, the other slumped.

I reached in my pocket and took out my lighter. I held it up – "Okay, here's the deal. I'm going to set the changeling one of you on fire, and take the other one home. That much is certain. If you'd like to identify yourself *now*, all you'd be doing is saving me a lot of time and inconvenience before the inevitable moment."

"I'm not –!" both of them started, realised or acted the realisation of a dumb comment, and stopped mid-sentence. Ally1 stuck her tongue out at the other. Ally2 pouted. Ally1 suddenly laughed nervously, slapping a hand over her mouth as giggles burst out of her. Ally2 scrunched up her face, but a moment later was laughing as well.

It was a cute and ridiculous display. Both of them were acting just like Ally would in a stupid life-threatening situation, and it was completely unhelpful. One thing was for sure: in future adventures, Ally was not on my team.

"Shut up, Ally one and Ally two," I said, closing my eyes and taking a few more calming breaths. What would Tanya do? "Okay, interview time."

Ally1 raised her hand. "Can we confer?"

"No, you moron – we're meant to be working out which one is really *you*. If you come up with an answer together I have no friggin' way of…" I stopped, mentally clutching my brain as I tried to work out what the hell *that* question was supposed to mean in terms of divining which one was really Ally. Why not

Tanya? Even she'd be easy to read in comparison to Ally... I'd even have jumped for trying to guess the Teb; I'd been preparing notes for it mentally ever since the two Tebs scenario appeared two months ago.

"Oh! Don't ask about my History essay! Teb was helping with it too!" Ally2 said. "She would know!" She pointed at Ally1.

"Yeah, but how?" the other asked, scowling. "You were made back in March! All the new stuff since then wouldn't be part of your programming!"

"Wait, so Ally two knows about the essay, so is mentioning something it hopes is out of the changeling's knowledge? And the other is just pointing out how it would know?" I pointed to Ally1. Changeling?

"Didn't it learn Teb's true name in the spell Cathy did at the station?" Ally1 mused, following up her thoughts. "She'd have had to use it, right? So theoretically it could have made a fresh download of Teb-ness and learned everything up to that point? The only thing it wouldn't know is the last two days..."

I pointed to Ally2 to see how she defended herself. Changeling? Could *anyone* phrase a sentence like Ally?

"So okay, assuming I am the changeling, *which I am not*, you're saying we get Alana to quiz us on the last two days of what the changeling was doing? Isn't that a bit... dumb? We just say we don't know because we were at home drinking tea and learning to crochet ladybugs with Mum. I never spent any time alone with Alana during that time. You're worse at logic than me... Doesn't that prove it?"

"Dear god, *stop*," I said, hands back at my side because clutching my head and weeping was not a current option. I was lost though. "This is not a time to play devil's advocate, Ally! If you are!"

"I'm just trying to work out how the changeling thinks so I can not think that way and prove that I'm Ally," Ally2 complained.

I looked at Ally1 to see how it defended itself. It would need to be *spectacularly* confusing to prove it was Ally now.

"Hmm. Logically..." Ally1 said, gnawing her lip and sliding the grip of a flip-flop in and out from between her toes in a very convincing way, "I suppose... Um, the time we spent away from Alana doesn't prove anything, since we could make up whatever and she wouldn't know it, and when I phoned up Teb Alana never heard what we said to her then. But we'd both know that anyway because I was talking to me. Um, I mean, I was talking to the changeling who was Teb but who is now me. If you get what I mean?"

She looked hopefully at me. I gave her a smile that was really a "What?" distilled into a facial expression. Ally2 was standing unnaturally still, arms crossed, as if trying hard not to give away any mannerisms. I couldn't work out if she was being wily or it was being cautious. Wily and Ally were not two words I put together.

"*Anyway*," Ally1 continued, "what we should do is get Alana to ask us about stuff that happened before this... Things we did together."

"How do I know that you didn't tell Teb about stuff? Ally's the biggest blabbermouth I've ever met."

"Only for unimportant stuff!" Ally1 defended it/herself at once.

"You can't know," Ally2 said unhappily, "considering how many secrets we have… We really don't have any secrets."

My mind was racing. There was one thing that they wouldn't have in common and I would know about for absolutely certain. (Obviously one of them knew all of Ally's secrets that she'd never shared with Teb, but I had no way of knowing those to tell if they were true or not if she'd never shared them with me). The three days between my arrival in their group and Teb's mind wipe were the brief events in question. One of them had witnessed it all first hand. The other had a fake history of the events in their head, having had no access to Teb's memories until the moment Cathy accidentally gave the game away just yesterday, and Teb's memories of the incident had been removed. The changeling would know only what had happened in the fairy world on that day, and a few details here and there that we'd told Teb in the last couple of days.

"Heh, I'm starting to get muddled about which Ally is which," Ally2 giggled. "I hope I'm the right one…"

"You, come here," I said, pointing at the other because Ally2 was clearly just trying to mess with my head now.

She tripped her way to standing right in my personal space. I looked up at her, taking in her eyes shining green in the light here. They were so vivid… I remembered the changeling's eyes and shuddered, glanced past Ally1 to the other. Its eyes sparkled just as much. Or her eyes. I couldn't find the colour that had shocked me so much: the light here was too green, so strong it rode over any subtle shades. I forced myself to look back at the Ally I had at hand.

"You… Tell me something only I would know about Ally."

"We went to the stone circle to do your Literature homework. It was about Shakespeare or something, I think. Or maybe Oscar Wilde. Someone like that." She shrugged and grinned. "There were definitely stage directions involved."

"What are you going to university to study?" I asked, deadpan.

"English Literature," she laughed.

"If you get what grades?"

"Two Bs and a C."

"And an F in Literature, I imagine," I said, rubbing an eye wearily.

"Forsooth!"

"Oh, back off, I need to ask the other you some questions."

Ally1 shuffled back. I beckoned Ally2 forward, trying to think of another question in case she'd overheard any of the first.

"The very first day we ever met… What did we do after school?"

"We went to the church, and then you came round for dinner and you blow-dried my hair," Ally2 said.

"Is that it?" I laughed. If the changeling was cheating and scraping off stuff from the top of my mind, repeating back the images in my mind, then that was the worst job it could have done.

"Well there was all the stuff with the statue holding the recorder like in a thriller except it didn't open any secret passages or anything and there were wicker turtles all over the place at home and you knocked over a big stack and the head came off one, and after I did the tarot cards I found you crying in the rain because Tanya had run off and you said you were trying to protect me and I thought you meant from the Piper and I got really scared of him and we had spinach for dinner or something like that and you ate all of it even though I thought you were going to be sick. Oh, and we watched *You've Got Mail* and then you ruined Enya for me forever by telling me she was an elf but I looked on Wikipedia and she is *not*."

I nodded.

I looked at Ally1. She smiled nervously at me. "Did we pass?"

"'It was not until they examined the rings that they recognised who it was,'" I said.

"What?" Ally1 said.

Ally2 took a step further away from Ally1. She knew a threat when she heard it.

"I always liked that line," I said. "Call me morbid..."

"That's not from *The Importance of Being Earnest*," Ally2 said helpfully.

"Nor is it from *The Tempest*," I pointed out, "But sometimes our Literature teachers are extremely unhelpful in the texts they set. If we'd studied *The Picture of Dorian Gray* instead then we'd have all this nice neat narrative stuff going on and I could have been helpfully thinking back to the essay I would have written had I actually done more than skim-read the book two years ago. I mean, okay, *The Strange Case of Dr Jekyll and Mr Hyde* might have been more useful except that the changeling brought up Shakespeare first, who is apparently the same person as Oscar Wilde..."

"I never said that!" Ally1 said, eyes going wide, waving her hands desperately. "I just meant, like, they were playwrights we both said we'd liked and we talked about how awesome they were and how Shakespeare might have been gay as well and wouldn't it be great to get a time machine and set them up with each other! You remember that?"

I hesitated. That was what we had talked about. The same sort of specific personal detail that only Ally could have produced...

"How can both of you know stuff that only Ally would know?" I asked.

"We had that conversation at the stone circle," Ally2 groaned. "The fairies were listening, weren't they? They were so interested in me at the time even before we went into their world...They all seemed to know who we were when we met them. I got mobbed by those fairies up on the hill behind my house."

"And the changeling would have been a favourite for the job if it said to the Green Man it had already been following us out of curiosity for a couple of days beforehand..." I smacked myself on the forehead. Ally2 was in the lead again:

she'd mentioned a lot of stuff that had happened all over the place, never mind coming up with a very persuasive line of logic for once to prove the other Ally wrong.

I turned on Ally1. "You're the changeling, aren't you?"

It stood there shaking and scared. Damn it, I *still* didn't dare act until it cracked! I wasn't going to attack Ally even the slightest bit accidentally. I glanced at Ally2, who was gnawing her lip.

I flicked the lighter so the little flame appeared. Come on, changeling… Break already! Of course, if I was threatening the wrong one, somehow, it would never get angry and attack me first… Just how many times could a changeling trick me?

"I'm Ally!" Ally1 moaned. "Please believe me, Alana!"

"Just kill it already," Ally2 begged.

I turned to look at her, swinging the lighter around to bear on her at the same time. "Would Ally really say something like that?"

"I don't even know what Ally would do anymore!" she cried. "This is so confusing and it makes my head hurt trying to work out what to say… I just want this over and done with!"

"I'm too nice to ever say something like that!" Ally1 cried, stumbling forwards. I waved the flame at it to keep it back before it could grab me. "Listen to it! It's heartless! A monster!"

"So would you have me destroy that one?" I gestured, waving at Ally2.

"No!" Ally2 squawked. "Alana! I thought you would work it out straight away! You're supposed to love me but you're so dense you haven't even figured out I'm me in a ten-minute conversation!"

I swung to face Ally2 so fast the lighter flame went out. I clicked it repeatedly, apparently having burnt through a great deal of its useful life in the last week. "Say that again," I croaked.

Tears had begun to leak down Ally2's face. "You're such an idiot, Alana."

I looked at Ally1. It wasn't crying yet, but then, I had come a lot closer to killing the other.

"Ally… You." I nodded to 1. "Why are you wearing that coat?"

Ally2 made a really attractive hiccoughing noise.

Ally1 didn't say anything, but looked at me with wider eyes than ever.

Changeling.

I had worn two toothed grooves into my skin from the thumbwheel on the lighter. I didn't even feel it anymore as I pushed it down with a protesting whirr. A small crack as a spark jumped out, and then the silent appearance of the flame.

Ally1… Not-Teb… The changeling turned and ran.

It got less than two paces before its plastic flip-flops melted under its feet. Flames licked up its legs, which became huge scaled talons, but crumpled under it. Its twisted, doglike body hit the ground, the flames quickly consuming it, and it screamed a horrible roar as it tried to roll. I couldn't even make out any features anymore; it became a ball of flame, then it was a streak of greasy ash on the path.

I dropped the lighter and sunk to my knees.

Ally stumbled into me, almost knocking me over as she threaded her arms around me and squeezed me from behind. I flopped back to lean on her shoulder, looking up at her.

"Oh my gods, Ally… I'm sorry," I said, my voice numb. I wondered if I was going to cry again, but I didn't.

"Well at least you realised I was me eventually," she asked shakily, her nervous laugh shaking tears off her eyelashes. One plopped on the top of my head and I straightened up, pushing her away.

"I never told you… I mean, I don't *think* I told you… Never mind. I almost *did* torch you because you said…"

"Let's get out of here," she said decisively. "And don't forget your lighter."

I nodded numbly, grabbed it and looked over at the barrier to the station. "Need a hand?"

She nodded, and I took her hand properly this time, not wanting to risk another moment of weak grip. "Don't fall over your fucking sandals this time either, okay?"

"I was grabbed," she protested, as I channelled us right back home.

✳

Teb and Tanya were still waiting for us when we came out, and neither of them had pushed the other on the train tracks or run off to some distant corner of the universe. I considered that as progress.

"What was that all about?" Teb asked. "You were gone for ages."

"My fault," I said. "I let go of Ally and so she didn't get pulled through with us. Won't happen again. I suppose time moved slower in there than it did out here."

Ally giggled, still a little snotty from crying, but pretending now that nothing had happened. She linked arms with me and gave me a little tug that almost had me tumble over myself as we set off down the footpath home.

Teb looked up at the night sky. "Urgh, home. I can't believe you made me come back here. It's such a dump. Even the stars are boring."

"And it loves you too," I said.

We walked on for a while. Teb was striding ahead, and Tanya was determined to keep up with her. I guessed she felt a lot closer to Teb — and maybe Teb felt the same way now — because they had the connection of both being sort of addicted to the fairy world and all the wonders contained therein. Ally walked a little slower, beside me. It took her a while, and a good long wait on top of that to make sure Teb was out of hearing, before she spoke to me.

"All that stuff the pixie said, and all the stuff *I* said…" she started in a low voice, before I interrupted.

"Forget it. Put it out of your mind, or at least never mention it again," I snapped, looking away.

"No, Alana… It's important. I don't want you freaking out and ignoring me because you think I hate you… Or you feel embarrassed or…"

I looked tentatively up from my shoes as they scuffed through the gravel, and saw that she was using her nervous lip-biting expression that was as close to serious as she ever got.

"I'd never freak out and ignore you unless you freaked out and ignored *me*," I assured her. "Please don't do that, by the way…"

"I wasn't going to," she said. "Do you feel bad about what you did to the changeling?"

"Not really. It was getting way too emotionally attached to us. I've stopped out of control fairies the same way before… I just never spent a couple of days learning to hate them properly before."

"I-I'm glad you did it, though. I mean, it made it sound like I was horrible for wanting to kill it…"

"Hey, if *you* feel bad because of what it said, think how I feel after I did the actual killing."

"Heh. Well, who knows what it might have done if you hadn't destroyed it?"

"If it began *really* harassing us, the Piper would really have stepped in," I reminded her.

"Still, it did all of that *without* him interfering…"

"Well, I was there, right?"

She smiled at me. "Yeah, maybe he just trusts you to look after everything. And you did! So that's all great."

I nodded, looking back down at my shoes. "Even so… I'm going to pretend like nothing happened," I told her.

Ally sighed, "Sure, I guess. Just… Don't feel uncomfortable around me, okay?"

"We've already been over this."

"For *any* reason," she said, much more emphatically.

I couldn't look at her for the rest of the walk.

He Means Me Too

We waved goodnight to Tanya when she reached her door, and then one corner later, Ally was going to leave us as well. We stood awkwardly at the side of the road, but when Teb started to move again I had to act.

"I'll talk to you when I get home," I told Ally firmly. She nodded.

"Okay." She looked away quickly, and after a moment seemed to decide there wasn't anything else to say at the moment. She turned, stumbling over her own feet. She hurried away down the dark street until all I could see of her was the white patches of her coat.

I sighed, then caught up with Teb.

"Are you stalking me?" she demanded.

"After what you did… I'll probably find that I have to. The Piper set me watching Ally for a lot less in March."

"I won't go back, if you don't think I should. I mean… Not right now, anyway."

"You'll have to. But there's a big difference between carrying on being normal and doing it as… as a sort of weekend job, than disappearing without telling your family, throwing away everything that you had in this life… I mean, there has to be *something* you like about this world."

"It's big… And the air comes from everywhere. Those little bubbles of worlds are so… stagnant. And… And I guess I was pretty excited about the fact that Chris King wanted to go to the prom with me. He doesn't – he's not like… I don't know. I had a crush on him most of my life. But how do I go back to…"

"Sometimes you just have to wade in again and try and make it your life, when you think the world has changed so much, when you don't know who you are in it anymore, you just throw yourself in and act like you belong and eventually it comes back to you, sort of like the feeling coming back when you sat on your legs too long."

"Is that what you did? With us?"

"Yeah," I admitted.

She nodded. "I suppose I want to do the exams to prove I'm as smart as everyone thinks I am. To do better than Tanya. We competed through every single year of school on every single project. And she's got a date to a prom and all her coursework sorted weeks before me… She's winning. I have to at least try, don't I?" She gave me a nervous smile.

"There you go. That's plenty to go on!"

"Yeah… We'll see what happens. Maybe I'll get bored one of these days and leave for good. I don't know. Why did you decide to stay?"

"Stay?"

"Come on, Alana. I got what you were saying when you were talking me into staying myself. You've been in exactly the same place."

"No I haven't," I said.

"Yeah?" she raised an eyebrow, not believing me. "How come you're working for the Piper then? I get the feeling someone like him doesn't always have a human companion tagging alongside him. Tanya talked to me a lot while we were waiting for you to get back with Ally, and she says that's one thing she doesn't understand. *One thing*, Alana. I'm amazed Tanya would admit it. Why are you even here?"

"I don't know why he's working with me at the moment. He doesn't have any past form for it as far as I know. I was just one dumb girl doing what hundreds of other dumb people do, but he stepped in and took me away. It was just his regular line of work stuff and then suddenly he said, 'come with me instead' and took me away from… from the proper authorities. I thought he was going to be as creepy as the last… thing. But he just took me home and sometimes called me up and gave me jobs to do. When I started your school he said I had to find someone I needed to protect, and it would all be obvious when I got there… and it was, and that's all I've been doing since then… As much as I can. If you want any more answers, take it up with him."

"I have half a mind to," Teb snorted.

"Look, you're powerful now, but not so much you can talk that way about him. Trust me on that."

She shook her head.

We reached her corner.

"Oh yeah, take your shoes," I said. I stepped out of them, leaving them neatly side by side on the pavement.

"Ew," Teb said. She glared distastefully at them, but then since they failed to spontaneously combust or spray themselves with magic Febreze or something she picked them up.

I kept on walking without looking back at her. It looked dramatic but I was mostly worried about stubbing my toe on the jagged tarmac or something. I'd brought her home, good enough. The option of 'in one piece' was very much not ticked. I couldn't stop seeing the face Teb had with the mask on. She might look human now, but there was something seriously wrong with the girl. I didn't hear her call goodnight after me, and I hadn't said anything to her.

I didn't go into my home. I wasn't sure my mum wouldn't have changed the locks and have the priest waiting to take me away, in any case. I would have this fight later, maybe: the stuff she saw with the Piper, Ally inviting herself around, the things the changeling had said… Or maybe we'd do what we did best and never talk about it again except to glare at each other over the dinner table, ticking off the days until I moved out. I couldn't deal with it yet.

The pavement was rough under my feet, the old wooden beams of the stile somehow warmer than the ground, worn smooth with use. The dirt on the other side was freezing cold but silky smooth to my bare feet after the tarmac. The grass was pricklier to my toes as I walked up to the field where I'd made the cairn.

It didn't look or feel damaged from Tanya's use of it, but maybe then the Piper had come and fixed it up while I was occupied with other things. I sat down on the dust beside it, and thought about how so short a time ago I'd been running around this tree wailing as a giant mud wolf tried to eat me. It seemed so ridiculous.

It didn't take long before I wasn't sitting alone anymore.

No one knew what the Piper really looked like, except maybe Ally, who he said the spell didn't really work on. Not sure of the details, but the general idea was that he was meant to not fit in. To me he looked just… like the Piper. Strong, absolute, slight father issues projected onto him that I'd never dare to address.

"Well?" I asked, when my patience ran out. His was pretty much infinite, but he still liked playing "who will snap first?" every damn time. "Is that how it works then? I put in all the hard work, I save the day, sort of… And I still don't even get the girl for all my troubles?"

"You did the right thing," he told me. A translucent plastic recorder, the kind you can get for 50p as a toy in a music store, stuck out of his jacket pocket. He was a joke.

"Oh, you would say that. Because you know Ally's in love with you. Tanya's trying to set you up, did you know? She was like 'oh, don't go save her, Alana! Let the Piper do it!' She's going to be recklessly endangering her friend's life because she thinks you'll crack eventually and come save her. And of course you'll just breeze in and that will be it."

"And that is why I let you handle it all," he said calmly. "I was watching," he added, when my incredulous look was beginning to make my cheeks ache from holding it so long.

"And not helping," I pointed out. "Again."

"You've grown up. I'm not worried about you doing things wrong anymore, even when it's your friends you're helping. It wasn't your fault Teb changed the Ritual, but you didn't change anything else by taking her home again. You found the correct way to bring her back."

"Are you actually going to tell me what that means?" He was a headache with a smirk, that man. Maybe he and Ally deserved each other: she said all the words which meant nothing and he said just a few words which meant everything, but either way I had no idea what either of them had intended when they opened their mouth. I did note that he had directed from talking about Ally any more though.

"Teb may not be back in this world for long, or permanently. You can't stop her returning to the fairy world again when she needs to. I know you worked hard to bring her back, but she is a part of the Ritual now. You saved her from losing her humanity and made your friends happy, which is the most you could have hoped for. But it may be that she needs to be on site every eighth of May from now on. Maybe there will be more things she has to do throughout the year, depending on just what the power was that she bought. She's part of the Ritual now; I can feel that much."

I sighed. "You keep saying that without explaining. And the Ritual is?"

He smiled mysteriously, of course. No further explanation was offered.

I looked up at the stars instead. I could guess. The Ritual had to be a shortcut word for saying "pretty much everything that's happened and is destined to happen." I think there's a big book of days somewhere, tracking the repeated twitches of the universe and all the people in it. Or a tapestry made by three mad old bats with an eye and a tooth between them, constantly being woven with the same pattern behind the irregular twists and turns of all the little threads we made. Anything that was doomed to repeat itself. And one of my friends was a minor goddess, woven with bright purple thread into the pattern as a bold, repetitive swirl.

If that was how things were meant to be, then that was the law, the natural order, the Piper enforced. He was the one who made sure each and every pattern carried on the same without unsightly wobbles and holes, extra threads or anything else that would ruin the perfect symmetry of one year to the next. You could choose to enter or leave, but you could not bounce wildly about while you were in there. There was a bigger design to maintain.

"So she's stuck."

"You did the right thing from a human point of view. I would have left Teb; she wasn't breaking any rules." I regretted not stopping while he was only complementing me on my victory, however much I knew he wasn't thinking quite as happily on it as I was.

"Well, great," I said, my mood darkening even further. He sounded so mild, almost congratulatory, and I still felt like I'd screwed up and he was rubbing it in, in his own way. That there was a more pure, less human way to do it, and ideally one day I would see that leaving people behind to let them become a part of this natural order with no human complications was a better way. Not if I could help it, but seeing through the veil at last, it made me nervous that this was where the road lead. If this wasn't my ticket off it, what would be?

"What happens to her now?" I asked, swallowing back existential dread.

"The land will continue to pull at her, and it will find a way to draw her back. Physically, she'll be fine. As long as she looks okay, humans say it's all normal..."

"She has purple eyes!" I blurted out. "And no, that's not all I fucking care about. I wouldn't even be here if I just cared about looking good. I work for you because I care about what happens to my soul. You were the one who showed me how fucked up I was, but I still had the *choice* and I took it. I had to force Teb to make the same choice today, and now you're telling me it was useless!?"

"Not useless. I –"

"I lost everything I had but I got out of it! Okay, I work for you now, and maybe that's a punishment sometimes, but I'm free, even though I was seriously messed up and did some messed up shit! She was just trying to come to terms with the world being yanked out from under her feet, and losing someone she loved and all sorts of other stupid things... None of it was her fault, but what I did – I deliberately made bad decisions every step of the way until you stopped me... I was lashing out. She was just... Just trying to rebuild her life. I shouldn't get off lightly while she's going to be punished for what she did!"

The Piper gave me this calm smile which broke my heart before he started talking because it looked so much like a comfort-before-bad-news smile. It turned out it was. "Teb is being *punished* for nothing, and she won't see anything that happens as a punishment. She hasn't shared with you how she came to sell her name, and perhaps she never will. That is her story to share, but Teb did choose to become a part of the Ritual."

"So you're saying instead that she won." I flopped onto my back, fed up to the bone. "What about Ally? I thought you cared about her. She hates when her friends abandon her again and again for magic and stuff... Ever since I met her I've had to be the dependable one who isn't going to throw my life away for a fairy... Even Teb saw it once; she told you to wipe her memory just to be normal for Ally, didn't she? But that meant you erased the important life lesson which told her not to do it again. That was why she did it. The – the pattern, the Ritual thing, it reasserts itself, doesn't it? That was why you were trying to tell her it wasn't her story, to keep her out of it... This was what was always coming for her if she went down that path."

He looked away and didn't answer, which was generally a sign I was right.

"Don't you care that now Teb has done this, I am the last friend Ally has that she can trust? And after today with the changeling... that's a barely. And I can't tell her all this deep shit we talk about either."

"This was never about looking after her," he said, and I glanced around to see him looking down the hill towards Ally's house. I wondered how far his white eyes could see.

"But you —" I stopped, halfway through struggling back to sitting, when I saw my bare toes. I didn't understand Teb much better than before... Not the new Teb. But maybe I'd finally learnt a little about the Teb I'd first met. If she was willing to give up a huge chunk of her knowledge for a friend, an *enormous* chunk of her name and the humanity that came with that for someone she didn't even remember meeting and had only dreamed of... She had to have a much deeper heart than I'd ever imagined from that surface projection. Was the Piper's reluctance to help Ally the same? Throwing away something he could have had, easily, for some reason I barely understood?

Repeatedly reminding him that he loved Ally too might not be the best route.

They might move on from each other one day, for example.

He spoke like we'd agreed to backtrack quite some way. "Your new job will be keeping Teb from using her powers against the world. *That* is where the imbalance appears. A goddess can't live amongst those who are not her people, but Teb will try. It's up to you to keep the world safe from her, should that prove to be a problem... And to protect her from the repercussions that none of us can see quite yet. She's started something new, something that no prophecy or story is ready for. One way or another it will bring trouble, and if I have an agent with her, keeping her from starting it herself..."

"So I need to jump in front of her and say 'no' to everything she wants to do?" I asked, starting to smile.

He frowned briefly, apparently *this* being what made him doubt I was the right person for the job. I know, I was petty. I couldn't help it. I was never going to be *good* again. Maybe on the good *side*, but... Pissing Teb off for the sake of keeping the world safe? Could do.

"Well, great. When do you want me to start?"

"Not yet," he said. "I believe the local ley lines are almost irrevocably messed up thanks to the antics of the last day. You have a long night ahead of you..."

"Awww, but... Hot bath! Warm bed!" I was more than ready to risk my mum again if it meant taking advantage of the creature comforts of the house.

He smirked right back at me, his knowing smile turned friendly, almost teasing despite burrowing into my deepest thoughts. "There's no rest for the wicked."